USA *TODAY* BESTSELLING AUTHOR
DALE MAYER

Dagger in the Dahlias

D1557162

Lovely Lethal Gardens 4

DAGGERS IN THE DAHLIAS: LOVELY LETHAL GARDENS,
BOOK 4
Dale Mayer
Valley Publishing

Copyright © 2019

This is a work of fiction. Names, characters, places, brands, media, and incidents are either the product of the author's imagination or are used fictitiously. Any resemblance to actual events, locales, or persons, living or dead, is entirely coincidental.

ISBN-13: 978-1-773361-43-7
Print Edition

Books in This Series:

About This Book

A new cozy mystery series from USA Today best-selling author Dale Mayer. Follow gardener and amateur sleuth Doreen Montgomery—and her amusing and mostly lovable cat, dog, and parrot—as they catch murderers and solve crimes in lovely Kelowna, British Columbia.

Riches to rags. ... Chaos quiets. ... Crime is circling. ... And cold cases never cease ...

After almost a month in picturesque Kelowna, Doreen Montgomery still can't keep her notoriety to a minimum or her nose out of other people's business. Now those suffering from the loss of a loved one seek her out, wanting her help. While the last thing Doreen wants is to have the media discover she's involved in another cold case, she is already hooked on the details ...

But even more is going on. News has gotten out that Nan's old house is brimming over with valuable antiques, antiques Nan collected and left for Doreen, and the seedier elements of their lovely town are circling like vultures. With her animals in full assistant mode, Doreen must investigate the cold case, right the wrongs of the past, and keep her home safe, all while evading the media—and Corporal Mack Moreau.

Sign up to be notified of all Dale's releases here!

http://smarturl.it/dmnewsletter

Chapter 1

In the Mission, Kelowna, BC
Wednesday Morning, One Day After Solving Her Last
Case...

D OREEN MONTGOMERY OPENED the front door to her
home, pulling away the madly barking Mugs from the
entrance. Since arriving in Kelowna to live in her Nan's
house, she'd been adapting from her old life as a wife to a
mega rich man to being a single woman living on her own –
in poverty. She and her pedigreed basset hound had been
saved from a bad marriage, where neither of them had been
loved, to her new life with Goliath, an oversized Maine
Coon cat and a talkative – sometimes too talkative – African
Gray Parrot named Thaddeus. The moment there was a
knock on her door, complete chaos ensued. Like now...

She stared at the stranger in surprise. He didn't look like
media but the vans outside, the crowd with tripods and
cameras said he most likely was. Mugs calmed slightly but he
switched to sniffing the stranger's pant legs.

Suspiciously, she asked, "Yes, may I help you?"

The man in a three-piece suit, looking extremely elegant
and way too perfect for the small town of Kelowna, particu-

larly for her neglected house, smiled and held out his hand. "I'm Scott Rosten, an appraiser from Christie's, the auction house."

"Oh my," she said in excitement. She shook his hand with a little too much enthusiasm. "I wasn't expecting you until this afternoon." At her tone, Mugs started to get excited. She shushed him and moved Mugs back so Mr. Rosten could come inside away from the media watching avidly from the edge of her property. With a satisfied shove she slammed the door to the flashing bulbs outside. She turned with a bright smile to Mr. Rosten. "Sorry about them." She waved at the media outside. "Things have been crazy here."

"No problem. My flight got in early," Mr. Rosten explained, his gaze locked on Thaddeus, her African gray parrot on her shoulder. "There didn't seem to be any reason to wait, so, if I'm not putting you out, is it possible to talk to you now?"

He motioned at Thaddeus. "Wow. Is he friendly?"

"Absolutely. This is Thaddeus."

"Welcome. Welcome," Thaddeus squawked.

"Thank you," Mr. Rosten said chuckling. "He's quite a character."

"That he is, and I'm glad you're here. The earlier the better as far as I'm concerned." She motioned to the mess around her. "Take a look around, Mr. Rosten."

"Call me Scott." He stepped further into the living room, his gaze locked on the closest piece of furniture. "Wow."

She gazed at him anxiously. "*Wow*? Is that a good wow or a bad wow?"

"It could be a very good wow." Without hesitation he

went to the first little chair, picked it up, checking the maker's mark. "You see items like these in pictures, but they aren't quite the same as seeing them in real life."

"Not to mention there's just something about the feel of real wood in your hands," she replied bending down to tug Mugs back slightly, so he wasn't in the way.

"If you're an antiques lover, there's also a reverence for the history behind each piece," he said, his fingers gently caressing the carved feet, then the edges where the cushions met. "These are absolutely stupendous."

"Do you think they're real?" She hated to ask so bluntly but didn't know any other way to say it.

The antiques appraiser looked at her in surprise. "Oh, they are definitely real."

"Right. Okay. So I know they're real wood, and I know they're real furniture, but are they real antiques?" She scrunched up her face. *Doreen, get a hold of yourself. You're acting like a fool, a greedy fool.* "I'm not explaining myself very well," she said.

He held up a hand. "You're doing just fine. What you're really asking is, are these the same rare pieces we were hoping they were. And I can tell you, for this one in my hand, the answer is yes."

"And there's that one," she said, pointing at the second one across the room. Immediately Thaddeus walked down her arm and sat on her wrist. She chuckled and walked over to place him on the mantel.

Scott walked to the matching chair, picked it up, studied it, placed it beside the first chair, then fell to his knees in front of the coffee table. "Wow. Just look at the work that went into this."

"Wow, just wow," Thaddeus cried out as he hopped

from the mantel to the back of the chair they'd been looking at.

"Don't mind him," Doreen said as Scott stared at Thaddeus in surprise. "He loves to repeat our words."

"He's amazing." Scott reached out a finger smiling as Thaddeus stroked his finger with his beak. "He's lovely."

"And he'll take all your attention if you let him," she warned.

"Good point." Scott turned his attention back to the furniture. "Can you give me a hand?"

It took the two of them to gently flip the coffee table so he could see the maker's mark and the numbers on the underside.

He nodded. "These are three pieces of the same matched set. I was so hoping the photographs didn't lie. But until I came and checked it for myself …"

"And the couch?" she asked, her voice doubtful. "It's really big." At her words, Mugs jumped up on the couch and immediately stretched out. Horrified, Doreen quickly moved him off. "Mugs get off," she cried. "Sorry, Scott."

"Don't be. The couch has been well loved. It's part of life. And the size of the couch is what makes it part of that very unique set. Montague only did two like this. It was intended for a large bedroom sitting area. He wanted it to match the bed."

Together they slowly flipped the couch, which was at least big enough to seat six. He checked it for scratches, smiled when he saw a couple, then crowed in delight when he looked at the maker's mark and said, "This is all the same set."

"Does that mean you think you can auction them off for a decent price?"

"Absolutely." He looked at her. "Are you ready to let them go?"

"Interesting that you should ask that. Before I realized this furniture belonged to my great-great-grandmother, I had zero attachment. Now that I know they've been in my family for a century, it's a little harder, but yes," she said looking around at her living room. "I can't even sit on them anymore now that I'm so petrified of damaging them."

"They have been sat on by your family for generations," Scott said. "I know you say they were in your family, and your grandmother is still alive. It's on her word that these pieces were in her grandmother's possession. Do you have any paperwork that proves provenance?"

"That's a new word I've just learned," Doreen said with a smile. "Fen Gunderson is the one who first introduced me to how important that is. My grandmother says a folder is in the house somewhere, but I'm not sure where it is. I was hoping we could move out some of these pieces, and then potentially I could find it."

"Right," he said. "I understand you have the matching bed too, correct?"

Doreen nodded, heading to the hallway. Mugs raced ahead of them.

"A bed and two night tables," she said, walking to the staircase.

Scott looked over the moon at her words.

She led him upstairs, apologizing every step, saying, "I'm sorry. I wasn't expecting you until this afternoon, so I didn't clean up yet."

"Doesn't matter. Doesn't matter at all." He chuckled as Goliath ran up the inside curve of the stairs, his movements fast and lithe.

Goliath was a huge golden Maine coon cat and had come with Nan's house as part of Doreen's gift from her grandmother. He was the size of a bobcat, but that didn't scare Scott, so the appraiser must really like animals. She knew she'd like him. And not just because he was here for her antiques.

"The animals are curious too," Scott noted.

On the heel of his words, Thaddeus cried out pathetically from the upstairs hallway, "Curious animals. Curious animals."

Scott laughed. "And a talking parrot."

"He is indeed and they are all curious." Doreen said as she scooped up Thaddeus. The large beautiful blue-gray parrot with long red tail feathers also came with Nan's house. Doreen was getting used to his constant repetitions. And definitely enjoyed his affectionate nature.

When they walked into the master bedroom, Scott stopped, delighted. Whereas she frowned. Both Goliath and Mugs had stretched out on top of the bedding. She groaned. Thankfully Scott didn't seem to care. He was standing enthralled.

"We sent pictures of the furniture in this room to Christie's," she said, placing Thaddeus on the window ledge. "I guess you've seen them already."

"And again the pictures don't do this set justice," he said with a smile. He lovingly stroked one of the large posts. "Absolutely beautiful."

"If you think so," she said. "Honestly, it's been my bed. So it doesn't seem out of the ordinary. I've been sleeping in it."

"Montague always designed a couple small drawers into the headboard. May I look?"

"Absolutely," she said, watching in surprise. "Why would he do that?"

"Because he wanted a place to put his glasses and for the pills he had to take at night. Montague built these little drawers to suit his needs. As I said, he built two complete sets. It was his way of covering his costs. One set for himself and one set for sale."

Scott sat down on the side of the bed and gently checked out the headboard. And, sure enough, it didn't take but a few minutes before she heard a light clicking noise, and a drawer popped out. Scott turned to look at her. "It's here," he said. "And now I know for sure this is his piece."

Doreen looked in the drawer, but it was empty. She hated the sense of letdown she felt when she hadn't even realized a drawer was here to begin with.

Goliath shifted on the bed beside them and rolled over, his tail flicking as he watched Scott carefully. Thaddeus hopped down to the mattress and walked closer to Scott. "Welcome, Scott. Welcome, Scott."

Scott chuckled. "He's quite something, isn't he?"

"You have no idea," Doreen muttered. Even as she watched, Thaddeus walked closer to Scott. He seemed very interested in their visitor. He didn't usually care who was here.

He got up and walked to the other side, asking, "Do you want to see how they open?"

Doreen nodded and leaned over his shoulder as he pressed a tiny little button. Sure enough, the second little secret drawer popped open. "Nan said her grandmother used to hide treats for her in a lot of the furniture, so Nan ran around and searched for stuff all the time."

"Well ..." He lifted a gold-foiled chocolate. Thaddeus

waddled closer the shiny foil attracting his attention. "That's what this is then. Maybe you should deliver it to Nan. Although it's likely decades late." Scott gently brushed Thaddeus back as he held the treat out to Doreen. "This isn't for you, big guy."

Thaddeus' crown lifted high and his head bobbed. "Treat for the big guy. Treat for the big guy."

Scott chuckled. "You'd better take this before he decides it's his."

Doreen held out her hand, completely enchanted at the thought of her grandmother as a little girl, running around the house, searching for chocolates. "This is a very special moment," she whispered. "Would you mind if we placed it back in the drawer? I want to take a picture to show her."

"If you're still willing to sell," Scott said, "I do have to arrange for proper shipping. And that'll take a couple days. Every piece has to be wrapped properly before moving them."

"Understood," she said. But she really hadn't considered what the process would be. In the back of her mind she was thinking an hour and they'd be all done. But … somehow she doubted it.

He looked at her. "But that means you don't have a bed."

She smiled up at him. "I'm also starving. I don't have a job, and I'm trying to keep the roof over my head. I can find another bed to sleep in."

He nodded in understanding. "That's good." He looked at the night tables. "To find both the sitting room set and the bedroom set is absolutely wonderful. The second set is no longer together."

"Are there other pieces that go with the set, other than

what we've found so far?"

He nodded. "Three dressers—a tallboy, a short boy, and a vanity." He looked around the room, his eyes lighting on the vanity.

She'd never seen a grown man cry. But he stood trembling in front of it, as if it was the best thing he'd ever seen in his life. She got up and asked, "Is this the vanity piece?"

He just nodded. Completely unable to talk.

"I guess that's one of the pieces then." She opened the drawers. "I haven't had a chance to go through this vanity yet."

"We should do that now," he said, "because I should check the label underneath, confirming it's part of the same set. And that mirror looks like it's very delicate."

She was afraid to move it, but they dragged it forward, with Mugs getting in the way at every step and Thaddeus insisting on riding on her shoulder. Finally Scott could slip behind and check for the mark he sought, one on the mirror and one on the vanity itself.

When he stood, such a sense of peace appeared on his face. He kept stroking the edge of the mirror. "It's definitely one of the pieces. Two hidden drawers should also be in this piece."

She looked at him in surprise. "Where?"

He chuckled. "How about I give you a few minutes to see if you can figure them out yourself?"

She didn't see any drawers like the headboard had. As Thaddeus hopped then walked the surface of the dresser, her fingers slid over the top and then the side. She shrugged and looked at him. "I haven't a clue."

"That's one of the reasons to empty the drawers. Because one of the secret drawers is behind one of the big drawers."

She grabbed empty boxes and an empty laundry hamper nearby and then opened the drawers, gently sliding the contents into the boxes. Everything from papers, notebooks, perfume, and some jewelry had been stored in the vanity. It was going to take time to sort through and this was obviously not the time.

There were seven drawers—three on each side and a big drawer across the center. With all the drawers out, sitting on the vanity stool, Scott pushed a small depression on the panel inside where the drawers sat, and a drawer popped out at the very back. He removed the drawer. Inside was a little padded velvet envelope. He picked it up and handed it to her. Thaddeus made an odd cawing sound.

"It's not yours either," Doreen said affectionately. "Regardless of what you think."

She released the catch and poured into her hand what appeared to be a locket. She opened it, and her breath caught in the back of her throat. "Oh my." Inside was an image of a woman who was maybe fifty and on the other side was a baby.

"Do you know those people?"

"I think this is my Nan," she said, tapping the woman's face. "And I'll say that's me."

"Well, there you go. Family is family." He replaced the drawer. "Is it your mother or your father who is Nan's child?"

"My father," she said, "and he died, after a wild and reckless life, of a drug overdose many, many years ago. My mom stayed friends with Nan for my sake and because Nan helped us a lot when I was growing up." Doreen carefully closed the locket and put it back in the velvet pouch. Not wanting to lose it, she slipped it into her pocket. "I'll ask

Nan about it."

"You do that. Now let's find the other drawer." It was on the right side. He popped open the other secret drawer and found yet again another gold-foiled chocolate in it. Doreen laughed in delight and took another photograph, picked up the chocolate, and put it beside the first one she had set on the windowsill. Thaddeus immediately flew to the window ledge.

"Thaddeus," she warned, "don't you dare …" With an odd snorting sound Thaddeus ruffled his feathers and shot her an injured look. She kept a wary eye on him as she turned her attention back to Scott.

He admired the vanity. "You are truly blessed."

"And I didn't even know what I had," Doreen said with a smile.

"You don't appear to have the two other dressers."

"A dresser is in the back of the closet," she said. "I can't reach it."

Scott eyed the closet, almost rubbing his hands together, and said, "It would be really good if we could see it."

She pulled open the closet doors so he could see what a nightmare it was inside. Even as the doors opened it was the push of the stuffed clothing inside being released that slammed the doors wide open. All they could see was the hangers full of garments.

Scott gasped, then chuckled. "Your grandmother is a clothes horse."

"Obviously." Doreen pushed back some of the hanging items so he could see in the back of the closet. "There's the dresser. It's short though."

He burrowed in with her. "We need to pull it out," he said in excitement.

It was very hard to do, but inch by inch, they cleared a path and moved the dresser forward. When it was finally standing free of the clutter of the closet, Doreen realized it looked to be part of the same set.

"That tells you how these pieces have been treated," she said with a shake of her head. "Instead of being prized possessions, this one was shoved in the closet for extra storage."

Scott busily examined it.

"Do we know for sure this dresser is part of the set?" she asked, waiting with bated breath to hear his answer.

He gave her a shout of joy and said, "Come look for yourself."

She bent behind him to see him gently stroking his fingers over the mark. "It really is, isn't it?"

"It is the short boy, indeed." He smiled. "This has been one of the best days of my life. Now are you sure you're ready to let all these pieces go?"

"Absolutely."

"Can we take another look around and see if you have the missing tallboy?"

"What exactly is a tallboy?" Doreen asked, when he straightened again.

He pointed to his chest. "It's about this high and is a narrow, tall chest, usually for the man."

"So this would be the woman's dresser?" She pointed at the dresser that had been pulled from the back of the closet. A dresser Thaddeus had now claimed as he paced the top. At least he was leaving the chocolates alone.

He nodded. "Yes. And it makes sense that it would be with the vanity and the bed. But I don't see any sign of the tallboy. If you did have it, it would be a huge asset. And, if you are truly ready to sell these, I will arrange for shipment."

"You'll give me receipts for them all, right?" she asked hesitantly.

He chuckled. "Absolutely. There'll be *lots* of paperwork to document this transaction."

Feeling relieved, she grabbed a couple empty boxes from the spare room and emptied the drawers of the short boy dresser from the closet.

"You don't even want to check what's in there?" he asked from behind her.

"I will go through it all," she said, "but obviously we don't have time right now." The whole top drawer looked to be scarves and accessories. The second drawer appeared to be stockings. She held up a pair.

"Those are silk," the appraiser said, "a quite beautiful silk."

She shook her head. "My grandmother had very expensive tastes apparently." She picked up several more items, placed them all in a box, and, by the time she got to the bottom drawer, out came a huge accordion file full of paperwork. At that, she got excited. "Maybe *this* is it."

Scott was at her side. "Maybe it's what?"

"The folder with the provenance," she said. "It'll take a while to go through it all. It's bursting at its seams." She motioned to the dresser. "Can you take a look and make sure absolutely nothing else is in there?"

"Let's take out every drawer," he said, "because, yes, two secret drawers should be in this dresser as well."

With all four drawers out, they could see several items had been caught in the back. With those collected, Scott pressed similar buttons as on the vanity, opening the two secret dresser drawers. One had a pair of cuff links inside.

Thaddeus stretched his neck to see them. The other two animals were stretched out on the bed ignoring the two of them.

She looked at them in amazement.

"They look valuable," he said. "I'm not an expert on gems though."

She admired the red stones. "Garnets or rubies?"

"Definitely rubies," he said with a smile.

She shook her head and put them inside the same little velvet envelope the locket was in.

In the other secret drawer was a picture. She flipped it over and back again. "Now this is Nan as a little girl." She looked at it and smiled, holding it out to him. "On the back is Nan's real name, Willa Montgomery. I am loving these little secret drawers," she said.

Scott looked around the bedroom and asked, "Is there any chance you can sleep somewhere else tonight? We've made a hell of a mess in your room."

"I can sleep in the spare bedroom," she said.

He looked at the big closet. "I'm sorry, but do you mind if I dig around to make sure more isn't there?"

"Be my guest," she said. "I do know there are shelves in the back too. I don't know why Nan would put the hanging clothes in front of the shelves."

"I think, once you get this cleared out, you'll find a space in between the two hanging portions to walk through. It's an adaptation of a walk-in closet."

"It's chaos," Doreen said, chuckling.

His grin flashed. "It is, at that."

Just then she heard the postal worker open the mail slot in her front door. Mugs barked like a madman and tore out of the room. Goliath followed and on his heels, Thaddeus flew off the dresser and soared through the hallway to land out of sight. She sighed. "I have to go downstairs and salvage the mail. My dog has decided it's something he should defend me from."

"Oh, dear," he said. "Go, go, go."

She dashed downstairs to the front door, and there was Mugs with a letter in his mouth. As he went past Goliath, the cat swatted him on the face. Mugs growled and dropped the letter. Thaddeus raced between the two, snagged the letter, and ran into the kitchen.

Doreen raised both hands in frustration. "What's gotten into you guys? Stop it." She cornered Thaddeus, who was still dragging the envelope along as he hopped onto the kitchen table. She took it from his beak and held it up high. "Stop! It's my letter, not yours."

At the commotion the appraiser had come down to see if she was okay. He entered the kitchen and smiled. "It is truly amazing that you live in this wonderfully chaotic household."

"Just not so good for the antiques," she said with an eye roll.

He chuckled.

She opened the letter-size envelope. "Interesting. There's no return address, and there's no stamp."

"Somebody dropped it into your mail slot directly then," he said.

She nodded and opened it, finding a single sheet of paper. "*Dear Bone Lady.* Uh-oh," she whispered.

I see that you're very interested in cold cases, and you have such great talent in solving them. Even ones from twenty-nine years ago. That's why I'm contacting you. I wondered if you could help me with my personal cold case. My brother-in-law disappeared twenty-nine years ago in August and has never been heard from since. I know I don't have any right to ask, but, if you're interested in a mystery, please call me. I do have some evidence, a dagger of Johnny's that I found buried at the spot where he was last seen. I found it some time ago when I went to plant a new bed of dahlias, but I don't know if it's enough to even start your investigation. I'm hopeful. Please call me.

After that plea was a phone number; the letter was signed by Penny Jordan.

Doreen stared at it in surprise. "Well, how about this? It looks like we have our next mystery to solve. Dagger in the dahlias!"

That sounded perfect.

Chapter 2

Wednesday Late Morning …

DOREEN WALKED SCOTT Rosten to her front door. As soon as she opened the door and Scott stepped out, Mugs took the opportunity to slip outside too. He headed for the grassy front lawn and started to roll. She smiled at his antics but turned her attention back to Scott.

"Don't forget now," he said. "I'll bring in the crew early next week so they can pack this up properly. I'll update you with a better time frame when I know."

She nodded but couldn't help thinking how it was a little too late to be concerned about packing up this furniture properly, when all of these pieces had been so well used for decades. "The sooner, the better. I'm afraid to use anything now," she confessed.

He smiled at her. "Obviously we don't want anything destroyed or broken in the meantime, but we also have to consider these have been gently used over the years. There will be some wear. Yes, that'll depreciate the value, but they're special pieces, and you've been very blessed to have them, so enjoy spending time with them while you can." He stopped hesitated, his gaze searching the living room. "Did you have any luck finding the tallboy?"

"Not yet, sorry," she said regretfully. "But I'll keep looking. I assume the packing will take a little time."

"Yes, possibly, but these men are professionals." He gave a shrug, almost philosophically, and a gentle laugh. "Just don't damage them in the meantime, okay?"

She gave him a bright smile. "I'll cover them in Bubble Wrap from now until then."

"It's the end of an era," he said. "And the good thing is, as an era ends with you, it opens for somebody else, so don't feel bad. The antique world will be absolutely delighted with your decision to part with these."

As soon as he left her driveway, easily maneuvering through the press, which thankfully had reduced to just one camera crew, she called Mugs back into the house and closed the door. Her fingers instinctively went to her pocket to the strange letter she'd received. She'd been so busy that she hadn't read it a second time, and it worried away in the back of her mind.

Her life had gone off the rails but in a good way. All yesterday afternoon and today, she had been smiling a happy smile. She'd survived an ugly attack from Cecily, found the little boy who had been missing for almost three decades. And Doreen had cleared the handyman's name of all kinds of accusations that must have hurt everybody who had loved him. However, his wife had passed away before that mystery had been solved, but at least the rest of his family now knew that he hadn't been trying to hurt the little boy nor had he attempted to start a whole new life with him. Instead they'd both drowned due to the record flooding that particular year. Definitely an unfortunate and sad event, but an accident nonetheless.

Yesterday, as Doreen had walked home, the Kelowna Detachment Police Commander had seen her on the streets. He'd pulled over, hopped out, and came to shake her hand. She'd been touched.

"We need people like you," he'd said with an expansive smile.

She'd chuckled. "I'm not sure Mack agrees with you."

The commander's eyes had twinkled like Christmas bells in the sunlight; then his voice had deepened as he said, "Oh, I'm pretty sure Mack is happy with the scenario too."

All in all, it had been a very special event and apparently had touched a nerve for someone else, if the letter in her pocket was anything to go by. No return address was on the envelope, no stamp on it, just a plea for help inside. Doreen wanted to help. She would absolutely love to help, but beginner's luck wouldn't hold her in good stead all the time.

She took out the letter once again to reread the details. They were sketchy, but that plea for help tore at her heart. And the woman said she'd found a dagger at the root of the dahlias in the same garden where she'd last seen her brother-in-law.

The problem was, the dagger had been out in the weather for so long before being found. Doreen highly doubted any forensic evidence remained on it at this point. Yet, as she already knew, DNA *could* last forever, and maybe some would be in the joints where the knife handle met the steel? But that didn't mean she could convince anybody to test the dagger. Particularly Mack.

She had to admit she was getting cold-case fever. How sad was that? But the puzzles fascinated her.

Who would have known Kelowna was such a den of evildoings? It almost made her smile, but, of course, there was nothing funny about that. Still, she *was* closing cases rapidly. She loved what she was doing. But how long could her winning streak go?

"This has turned into a full-time hobby," she muttered.

She folded the letter again and shoved it deep into her pocket. She wandered into the kitchen, where Goliath was stretched out on top of the kitchen table.

"Goliath, what are you doing?" she asked. "Get off the table. We've had this discussion before."

He looked at her, flicked his tail, and slid, as if boneless, to the nearest chair at this table, where he curled up. But he made it so slow and so of his own prerogative that she knew it was a case of *I'm doing this because I want to and not because you told me to.*

"Who knew looking after a cat would be so much trouble?" she asked out loud. "Who knew looking after a cat ..." She stopped, smiled, and added, "... would be such a heartwarming experience?" She leaned over and scratched Goliath behind his ears, loving the soft silkiness to his fur.

As soon as she pulled away her hand, he swatted her, his claws lightly digging in to pull her hand back down.

She chuckled, squatted in front of him, and said, "You're totally okay with your new life, aren't you, buddy?"

He didn't have to answer. As he rolled onto his back, giving her his belly, and then stretched forward and backward, making him look even more monstrous in size, it was obvious he was a happy cat. If she'd done nothing else, she'd given him and Thaddeus a good life.

And speaking of Thaddeus, where was he? Because, wherever he was, trouble was sure to follow. There was just something about that bird.

She walked back into the living room. "Thaddeus?

Where are you, buddy?"

But she got no answer.

She walked through the lower part of the house, then headed up the stairs.

"I know you were here earlier because, when the auction house guy was here, you were all over him. Now where are you? … Oh, that's right. I last saw Thaddeus stealing off with the letter …"

When she saw no sign of him here in her bedroom, she went back down the stairs and, on a hunch, opened the front door. *Maybe he followed Scott outside.* "Thaddeus," she yelled. "Thaddeus?"

And, sure enough, he hopped out from underneath the bushes and looked up at her.

"What are you doing out there?" she said, walking to him and bending down to scoop him into her arms. "You have to stay close."

"Stay close. Stay close."

"Yes, Thaddeus, stay close. Now repeat after me, *Thaddeus, stay close. Stay close.*"

He stared up at her and never said a word.

She groaned. "I don't get it. You say what you want, when you want, but you won't be trained to say what I want you to say."

"Stay close. Stay close," he muttered. He reached up as tall as he could and brushed his head against her cheek.

Her heart melted yet again. "Okay. You guys have so enriched my family," she muttered, closing her eyes and cuddling him close. She walked back into the kitchen, carrying Thaddeus. "But honestly, it's time for a cup of tea."

"Thaddeus likes tea. Thaddeus likes tea."

"I know," Doreen said. Sadly she did know because he

had a habit of drinking from her teacup. "Maybe I'll make you a little bit in a bowl. How's that?" Although she should probably look up on the internet if tea was good for him. And then she laughed. "Of course it's not good for him. He already flies around the place like he's loopy. It'll probably just make him fly faster. Or crash into things more often."

Then Thaddeus didn't fly well to begin with.

She sat him on the kitchen table, only to have Goliath shoot her a dirty look. Right. Different rules for different animals. "Look, Goliath. You're too big for the table. Thaddeus is just the right size."

Just then Mugs reached up with his front paws, looked at Goliath on the chair, and she realized Mugs wasn't allowed on the chairs.

"See?" she told Goliath, pointing at Mugs. "Everybody has their own rules," she confirmed, hoping that would end the discussion.

Instead Thaddeus looked at her and said, "Thaddeus is hungry. Thaddeus is hungry."

She groaned, picked up a bowl she kept with a lid on it, like a sugar bowl, pulled out a pinch of sesame seeds and put them down in front of the bird. He went to work.

Goliath jumped up, stuck his nose into the seeds, and sniffed, sending seeds flying, then backed away, shooting Doreen another look, followed by a plaintive meow.

She groaned, picked up the cat treat bag, and gave him two. "Remember how you're on a diet?"

Mugs woofed at her feet.

With no other option but to make it fair, she picked up the dog treats and gave him some. "You're on a diet too," she admonished.

With all three of her animals happy with their midmorning snack, she plugged in the teakettle and waited for it to boil. In the meantime, she looked at the letter again. "You know what? To go down this path, Doreen, you're likely to end up a failure. If the police haven't solved it in all this time ... But then that doesn't really mean anything either, does it?" she said, immediately countering her argument. "Because they do their best. But they have a lot of active cases, and they're short on man-hours. They don't get to sit here with a cup of tea and meander through the cold-case files, one at a time."

With that thought, she took a chair beside Goliath and opened her laptop. The name on the bottom of the letter was Penny Jordan. She typed in *Penny Jordan in Kelowna*, and several articles about a church's Christmas bazaars came up. Penny was apparently some major volunteer. But the dates of those articles were from at least eight years ago. Doreen continued to read through articles that mentioned the Jordan family name, but they were few and far between.

Doreen groaned, closed the laptop, got up, and made her tea as she thought about that tidbit of information. "The only way to learn more is to contact her directly and ask. The letter did have a phone number. But nothing else." *Hmm.* "So are we doing this?" she asked her trio.

They all stared back at her.

Then Thaddeus bobbed his head; Mugs, probably because of Thaddeus's head-bobbing, woofed. Goliath swung a paw and smacked Mugs on the head.

She'd take all that as a joint yes.

"Okay, good enough," she said. "We'll give Penny a call and see what it's all about. But no guarantees. Just because we've had a run of good luck doesn't mean this case will end the same way," she warned.

Chapter 3

Wednesday Noon ...

"HI. THIS IS Doreen," she started the phone conversation, a notepad and pen in front of her. The animals relaxed, surrounding her. "I'm looking for Penny Jordan."

"This is Penny," a woman said. "*Doreen? Doreen.* Oh, my goodness. You're the bone lady."

"Well, that's what some people call me," she said. "I certainly appear to have made the reputation for myself since I arrived."

"Everybody also knows you as Nan's granddaughter," Penny said with a chuckle. "Not sure what you prefer."

"How about just Doreen?" Doreen said with a smile. "Although my grandmother is definitely a sweetheart and has a reputation all her own."

"That she does," Penny said smoothly. "You got my letter then?"

"Yes. Yes, I did. But you didn't give me a lot of information. So your brother-in-law went missing?"

"Yes, my husband's younger brother. He was twenty-one at the time. The thing is, the police thought he chose to leave without telling us. Heading west, doing what all young men do. I will admit, you know, that he had some bad friends who were into drugs, but I think it involved the lighter stuff, like marijuana," Penny said anxiously. "I don't want you to get the idea Johnny was some cokehead and became homeless."

"Which happens," Doreen said quietly.

"I know," Penny said. "And honestly, for years, my husband drove around this and neighboring towns, looking to see if Johnny was just sitting on the streets, homeless, but we never heard any more from him."

"Is your husband okay with you contacting me?"

There was silence over the phone, and then Penny said sadly, "He died of a heart attack last year, and his dying wish was that I find answers before I passed away too. I keep his urn on the mantel as a reminder of his last wish."

"I'm sorry," Doreen said, wincing. "How old did you say his brother was when he went missing?"

"Twenty-one," she repeated. "We have accepted the fact he's probably dead because he and his brother were very, very close, and no way he wouldn't have called him all this time. So I have absolutely no doubt something bad happened to him. But it would be nice to have a body that I could bury and to have a memorial for my husband's sake. It mattered to him."

Doreen nodded, even though Penny couldn't see her doing that. "Your brother-in-law's name was Johnny?"

"Yes. There were just the two brothers, Johnny and George Jordan," she said. "Johnny went missing twenty-nine years ago, about the same time frame you've been dealing with. That's why I contacted you."

"Interesting," Doreen said, considering the time lines of

the other cold cases she had helped solve. "Are you thinking this had anything to do with the other missing person cases from back then?"

"No, no, no, no," Penny said. "I don't think so at all. I think Johnny got in with a bad crowd, and a lot of those people have since passed. So it's a really onerous job I've asked you to look into, but, for my husband's sake and for the sake of closure, it would be lovely to get to the bottom of this."

"And what's this about a dagger?" Doreen laid down her pen and picked up her tea, taking a sip.

Penny sighed. "The last time we saw Johnny, he was sitting on an alcove bench in the backyard. I was looking out the window, talking to my husband, and we were laughing and smiling at Johnny. He had a beer in his hand and a big grin. He lifted it up, as in a cheer, took a big swig. I went to the kitchen to clean it up a bit before I made dinner. My husband went back to the home office. We never saw Johnny again. We searched. The police came. They searched. About ten years later we decided to move that bench because, every time we saw it, it caused us pain. So we moved it to a far corner of the yard. I decided to plant dahlias where the bench had been, to change the atmosphere of the spot."

"Right," Doreen said. "Well, dahlias are beautiful, and they would certainly give you a lovely memorial for him."

"Exactly," Penny said. "We brought up this dagger when we dug up that area. The ground there wasn't very good, having been under the bench the whole time. We added soil, enriched slightly with some of the topsoil we brought in to top-dress the front yard."

"Okay, so the dagger wasn't in the dahlia tubers," Doreen said, switching her cell phone from one ear to the other. "It was buried in the dahlia bed or what became a dahlia bed afterward. Is that correct?"

"Yes, and, up until then, it was nothing but an empty space under the bench because obviously nothing would grow there."

"No, it's hard to grow anything without sunshine. I bet you had plenty of moss though."

"Oh, yes." Penny laughed. "The moss really liked that corner."

"So what did you do with the dagger?"

"I called the police and told them. They were sympathetic but said, chances were, nothing would come of it. But I couldn't let it go. I bagged up the dagger and took it to them. I asked them if they could test it, and they said the budget was so tight that they were only testing items with a viable chance for finding DNA. Of course, a knife found many years after my brother-in-law went missing, with no blood evidence to say it was from the scene of the crime, made no sense to them."

"Ah," Doreen said. "That is the exact issue right there. It made no sense because absolutely no forensic evidence was found at the spot where he went missing. So you haven't had the knife tested, correct?"

"No, and I have it still, sitting here."

Doreen added that tidbit to her notepad. "Had you ever seen that dagger before?"

"That's one of the funny things. It's Johnny's," Penny said. "That's another reason the police weren't too bothered because I told them how Johnny used to sit on that bench and have a beer, and he would flip it back and forth between his hands, like a lot of young men did back then. It was just this cool movement they were trying to do, and, at times, he would stab it into the ground, almost like he was playing darts, but with imaginary targets on the lawn."

"So the police assumed Johnny had stabbed it into the ground beside him one time when he was having a couple beers and forgot about it. Then, over time, it just worked itself into the ground. Or somebody unknowingly stepped on it, didn't recognize it, leaves piled in, the mulch, etc." She made another notation regarding this.

"It's of zero help, but, at the same time, it's a connection I can't mentally let go of."

"I don't mind taking a look at the dagger, unless you have photos of it."

"If you would take the dagger, I would be very happy," Penny said. "I know it probably has absolutely nothing to do with the case, but, every time I see it, it sends chills down my back."

"Okay, will do," Doreen said. "Where do you live?"

"I'm about a mile away from you. Up the creek."

"That's not a lot of help though," Doreen said with a laugh. "I haven't had a chance to explore much around town."

"Look. I'm planning to go shopping later," Penny said. "Do you want me to stop by and drop it off?"

"That would lovely," Doreen said. "If you wouldn't mind. And drop off any information you have—any police reports you might have a copy of, any interviews, anybody who was a witness. Just anything you have would be helpful."

"I have a folder of information we've collected over the years, but it's mighty thin."

"That's fine," Doreen said. "It'll help me get my mind wrapped around what happened."

"I'll make a copy for myself and bring you the originals. How about in a couple hours or so, about three o'clock? Is that okay?"

Doreen checked her watch. "About three o'clock then. That's fine." She hung up the phone and stared at the animals, though not really seeing them. Her mind was locked on a twenty-one-year-old, strong, young, healthy male going missing from one moment to the next.

"How awful, Mugs. You see a family member sitting on a bench outside in your backyard, and then you never see him again."

She was glad the young man, Johnny, had lifted his beer in a half salute of "Hey, it's a good moment" because at least it was a good memory of the last time Penny and her husband had communicated with Johnny. So many people had a fight before going off to work and getting killed in a car accident. The survivor's last memory for the loved one was of the fight. Not the way anybody wanted to be remembered.

Pondering, she went around the house, dusting off the furniture Scott would be collecting shortly. She was so afraid something would happen to these pieces. She'd joked about protecting it all with Bubble Wrap, but, then again, she was half serious. She just needed nothing to happen to these pricey antiques over the next few days.

She went upstairs to her bedroom, reminded of the ton of clothing she still had to go through. Plus that her bed would be moved next week. She hadn't asked Scott about the mattress. Maybe the mattress could stay, and she could sleep on it on the floor. That would be an easy solution as to where she would sleep tonight. Maybe not as regal an answer to her dilemma but definitely a workable one.

She had Scott's contact information and texted him as to the mattresses. His response came back quickly. As they were newer mattresses, they were hers. So that was good, but there wasn't much room to put the mattresses on the floor beside the big four-poster bed frame. There could be though, if she managed to clean out that corner. If she rearranged some things in here and then moved a lot of stuff into the spare bedroom, she could make it work. Or she could move into the spare bedroom until the bed was gone; then she could decide what to do with the mattress and box spring.

On that note, she walked into the spare room for a look. Mugs followed walking around the room, sniffing the old floor. The room had just a single bed but an old one that squeaked like crazy, even more noisily than the big bed in the master bedroom. She knew trying to sleep on this spare room bed would drive her nuts. Every time one of the animals rolled or shifted she'd wake up too. So what was the answer? She had to clear a spot on the floor in her bedroom. Before bedtime tonight.

She stepped back into her bedroom. Doreen had a lot of Nan's clothing due at Wendy's shop. With that thought in mind, Doreen bagged up the stacks designated for Wendy's consignment store and took them downstairs to the entry hallway. The next time Doreen went to town, she could drop them off and see what Wendy would like to keep.

Doreen had decided to keep an awful lot of Nan's clothing. She picked up an armful of those, still on their hangers, and walked them into the spare room, hanging them in that closet. At least it helped her to separate the old from the new, the keep from the don't keep, what she'd sorted from what she hadn't.

It took several trips to hang up all the clothes to keep.

But it felt like a bit of space had opened up in her bedroom. Considering the bed frame wouldn't be taken for a few days, she figured there was really no point in taking the mattresses off right now. Yet part of her said she should tear it all apart and inspect the pieces before she lost the opportunity. What if something else had been hidden in the bed? Besides, she also needed to change the bedding.

Except ... all the animals had given up on her, passing out on the bedding. And yes, they'd twisted and woven into weird contortions around the mess of stuff they'd placed on the bed earlier. Gently rousing them one at a time, she stripped off the duvet, tossed it to the side, and then went after the sheets. A big thick mattress cover was under the sheets as well. She took that off to be washed too, something she hadn't done since she had moved in. And she could see that the mattress, although older, was still in excellent shape. It had a big cushion top with no rips or stains or tears. All of which was good.

She went to the other side of the bed, lifted up the mattress awkwardly. She stood on the box spring so she could scoot the mattress completely off the box spring, ensuring nothing was underneath it.

Then she lifted the box spring from the big wooden bed frame and checked underneath it. Satisfied no envelopes were taped underneath and no hauls of cash were otherwise stuffed under the bed, she stepped inside the bed frame and slid the box spring over the side of the bed onto the floor. Now she was really making a mess.

It was her first chance to take a look at the four-poster bed without the mattresses. It was amazing. Absolutely amazing. The box spring was at an awkward angle, leaning against one of the four-poster corners, teetering, but it gave her a chance to check with her hands under the bed frame itself, all around the sides, though she couldn't see the back of the headboard.

She'd torn everything apart, so she might as well keep going. And she still had that accordion file to go through. She winced. Scott had specifically asked her to do that, and she'd promised she'd get to it. And here she was, off in a whole different direction.

She'd go through that paperwork as soon as she could because it might make a huge difference in terms of the value of the pieces. She slid her hands under and around the bed frame, checking, but absolutely nothing was here. The newel posts didn't even come off the four posts.

She slid the whole bed toward her enough so she could see nothing was behind the headboard either. "Good enough," she said. She pushed the four-poster toward the door, and the box spring collapsed onto the floor. She looked at it, frowned, and then shrugged. "Well, you were ending up there anyway," she said. "So, what the hell. Might as well stay there."

She quickly rearranged this corner of the room and, with a little effort, moved the big heavy mattress and box spring into place beside the big bed frame.

Mugs immediately jumped inside the slats of the big bed and barked, sniffing, his nose going steadily underneath. When he wouldn't stop, Doreen looked at him. "Seriously, Mugs?"

He barked again, his nose touching the center slat. She hadn't checked under all the slats, so she reached down to do so now. As she got to the slat where Mugs was, she could feel something taped to the underside. Excited, she didn't want to just rip it off—she didn't dare rip up whatever was here.

Someone had to have a reason for doing this, but how could she lift up the massive bed frame?

When her doorbell rang, she groaned and said, "Well, this will have to wait a moment, Mugs."

Only Mugs was already downstairs barking himself hoarse.

Chapter 4

Wednesday Afternoon ...

DOREEN RAN DOWN the stairs lightly, making her way past all the bags of clothing. She pulled open the door to see a lovely older woman standing outside, nervously holding a big brown 9"x12" envelope in her hand. Mugs dashed out and circled around their visitor. At least he was quiet now.

The woman looked up at her and smiled. "It is you! You've been all over the media." She smiled down at Mugs. "And of course, your trio of animals."

At that Mugs barked once as if to say, *'of course.'*

Doreen just rolled her eyes. "And you must be Penny. Come on inside. Let's see what you've got." As the woman stepped in, Doreen said, "Sorry. Please excuse the mess. I'm sorting through all of Nan's stuff and getting a lot of this cleaned out."

"I wouldn't doubt it," Penny said. "Nan has always been a collector of antiques. My husband was too."

That stopped Doreen right in the middle of the living room. "Really?"

Penny nodded. "He and Nan had all kinds of discussions. He loved this set, but Nan would never sell it. She said it was her retirement fund."

"And now that she's retired," Doreen said, "she doesn't need it."

"That's the best thing ever," Penny said with a smile, making a Vanna White arm sweep to the room. "Think about it. Nan doesn't need the money she set aside. I think that's a success in itself."

Doreen laughed. "May I see your file?"

"Oh. I'm sorry." Penny handed over the envelope. "The knife is in there too. And I did keep a digital copy of everything. I should have done that a long time ago. Then I could have just emailed them to you."

"If you could do that too, that would be great," Doreen said, "because I might do more searching that way."

"Sure. It's already digital anyway. Need your email address," she said, "and I can send it to you when I get home."

Doreen gave her the email address. "Now you understand that … I can't guarantee this will go anywhere, right?"

"I know," Penny said, inputting Doreen's contact info into her phone. "I feel almost guilty asking you. It's just the police don't have anything to go on. Nobody I've talked to over the years has any idea what happened to Johnny. It's so very frustrating. I guess I'm hoping another pair of eyes will turn up something different." She grinned at Doreen. "You do appear to have a very different pair of eyes."

Doreen smiled. "Apparently I have a different perspective that's shaking things up a little. You're still in the same house you lived in when Johnny went missing?"

Penny nodded. "Yes, but not for much longer. I guess that's another reason why I'm feeling the time pressure to solve this. I'm listing the house for sale soon and hoping to move into a condo closer to my older daughter's as soon as I get my house sold."

"So that could be within two weeks, or it could be two months," Doreen said.

"Or two years. Depending on the market. But it's a lovely family home."

"Okay," Doreen said. "Would you mind if I come and take a look myself, to see the backyard and to get a feel for the location he disappeared from?"

"Sure," Penny said. "I'll give you my address when I send you the digital file."

"I'm sorry," Doreen said. "Would you like to sit down?"

"No, but thank you anyway. I don't want to bother you any more than I have, and I should be going. Whenever you're out that way, just pop on by. The thing to remember is, I don't know where the crime scene is, if there was one— whether he went for a walk or met his buddies over the back fence because a park abuts our property there or where he might have gone from our home."

"The park is behind your property?"

"Yes, and, to make matters worse, he used that gate all the time. I think he came and went most of the time that way."

"So, if somebody called to him from the park or sent him a text, he would have gone to meet him, using that gate, correct?"

"Except for the fact we couldn't afford to buy a cell phone back then, and texting didn't exist," Penny said with a smile.

"Right, of course not," Doreen said with a shake of her head. "But that doesn't mean he didn't have somebody who stuck his head over the gate and called out to him."

"We saw his friends do that often. At one point we had to stop him from buying drugs that way."

At that, Doreen's eyebrows shot up.

Penny nodded. "But what can you do? He had just George in his life. Their parents had died a couple years earlier. Johnny had been a teenager then, and George had given him a home, helping him to grow up. But Johnny was fighting that. He had a job at the hardware store. He had a girlfriend, but that relationship wasn't stable. As a matter of fact, the girlfriend said, at that time, they hadn't had anything to do with each other for a couple months before he went missing. She didn't mention any reason behind their breakup. Just that she'd found somebody else soon afterward."

"Is her name and other pertinent personal information in the file?"

Penny frowned. "I think so. Her name was Susan Robinson. She died of breast cancer about a year ago."

"Oh, wow," Doreen said. "So is everybody from his circle no longer around?"

"Yes. Johnny's two buddies and his girlfriend. They were together all the time. They didn't really hang out with any others to the same extent. At least not that I knew of. And, yes, they are all dead now. All you have are the witness statements in most cases. And I don't have copies of all those." She hesitated, then looked sideways at Doreen. "I know this is very inappropriate and pushy," she said, "but I was hoping you would have connections with Mack, and maybe you could get the other information I don't have."

"I'm not sure he can do that," Doreen said. Just then Mugs slumped to the floor half on and half off her foot. Squatting to scratch Mugs behind the ear. "I don't know what their rules and regulations are, but I can ask him."

"Right. I'm sure all kinds of red tape stop him from giving you too much information," Penny said with a sigh. "And how frustrating is that? All I want to know is what happened to Johnny."

"You've had no contact since, and he was a healthy young man?"

Penny nodded. "He was healthy. He was footloose and fancy-free. He was a young man, but he didn't have a whole lot of purpose. He didn't really know what he wanted to do. He didn't like working at the hardware store. He had visions of a much bigger, more grandiose lifestyle, but honestly he hadn't reached the point where he wanted to put in the work to make it happen."

"Oh. So a typical young man," Doreen said with a smirk.

"Exactly," Penny agreed. "George got really frustrated with him, and that was hard because I always heard about it. But, at the same time, I couldn't do or say anything to make it any better."

"No. Young men have to be young men, and they grow up in their own time frame," Doreen said.

"Do you have any children?" Penny asked.

"No," Doreen said. "Not yet. At my age, probably not likely to happen."

"We have two daughters," Penny said. "And I have to admit that it was much easier to have daughters than to always look at a son and wonder if the same thing would happen to him. We kept a very close eye on the girls growing up, but I think they understood just how devastating losing their uncle had been for us. Yet, of course, young people know it all and have all the answers." Penny laughed a little.

"Only as they get older do they realize they never had any wisdom to begin with." She gave a wry smile.

Doreen nodded. "Okay, I'll go through this. Please don't have any expectations that I will find anything."

"No," Penny said. "Of course not." She reached out a hand and squeezed Doreen's. "I'm just happy to know somebody will look into it and that Johnny won't be forgotten forever."

"I can understand that," Doreen said slowly. "I think that's one of the reasons why I pursue these cases. Because families are waiting for answers. People need closure. Some folks' whole lives are lost in worrying and wondering what happened. I can't imagine anything worse."

Mugs got up and walked over to sniff Penny's leg. He rubbed his head against her calf.

She bent to pet him. "Well, he's a new addition."

"He is, indeed," Doreen said. "Mugs came with me. Goliath is still here. So is Thaddeus."

Penny nodded, as if the names didn't mean anything to her, and it occurred to Doreen that she didn't know how long Nan had had Thaddeus and Goliath, a name Doreen had given the cat. So there was a good chance Penny hadn't met either of them.

Penny turned and walked back to the front door, smiling at the bags of clothing. "You have a lot of stuff to go to Goodwill."

"I do," Doreen said. "Honestly I'll probably take a bunch of this to the consignment store. Nan had some very good-quality clothing."

"Oh, that's a lovely idea," Penny said. "I shop there quite a bit. Wendy has a lovely store."

Interestingly she didn't look ashamed or in any way put

out by telling somebody she shopped at a secondhand store. "I'll have to check it out," Doreen said. "I dropped off some clothes already, but I've been so busy that I haven't had a chance to look for anything for myself."

"Wendy has a great selection," Penny said. "Check it out while you're there." With a wave of her hand, she walked onto the front porch and down the steps.

Once again Doreen stood on the front porch, waiting for somebody to drive away. She didn't know why she needed to make sure people left. It probably had to do with the fact she was still hoarding all these expensive antiques in the house.

As soon as Penny had driven down the cul-de-sac, Doreen stepped back inside, brining Mugs with her, set the alarm again because now it was almost four o'clock, and headed into the kitchen. "Now to check the back alarm, then go upstairs to check that bed out," she said.

Her phone rang then. She groaned as she looked down at Mack's identification. "How do you always know when I'm getting ready to get into something?"

"What are you up to?" he asked as soon as she answered.

She rolled her eyes. "I'm trying to figure out what is taped underneath the bed frame in my bedroom," she said. "The packers will come early next week. Hopefully on Monday. I need to know about anything hidden in the furniture before they take it. And we found something, but I can't lift the massive bed frame."

"With your mind-set," he said, "I can certainly understand that. What's underneath it?"

"I don't know, that's what I'm trying to figure out. I've moved the box spring and the mattress to the floor, because the movers are not taking those. But the bed frame itself is very heavy. Mugs won't leave it alone. He kept barking at one of the slats, so I checked, and, sure enough, something is taped under it."

"Mugs, huh?"

"Right. That's why I'm trying to figure it out. For all I know, it's nothing. But the bed is heavy. How do I lift it and check out the slat?" She paused. "Are you on your way home?"

"Yeah. I'm leaving the office in five. Why?"

"Well, you could swing by," she said in a cheerful voice, adding, "and you could lift the bed, and I could look underneath."

"*Umm ...*"

She could almost see him give a mental shrug.

"Yeah, I can. I'll be there soon." And he hung up.

"Now that is perfect," she said to Mugs.

He just stared at her. She chuckled and headed the way back to her bedroom.

As soon as Mugs returned to the bedroom, he'd hopped inside the slats, which she found amazing because he was pretty rotund. He'd parked right where that piece of paper, or whatever it may be, was. It felt more like plastic than paper. She didn't know what that meant.

She continued to move stuff out of the master bedroom into the spare bedroom closet. She rearranged some of the furniture in her room so the movers could easily dismantle the bed when they arrived. Then she put new bedding on the mattress. By the time she'd fluffed up the pillows and put them on her makeshift bed, it looked mostly normal on the floor. Then she heard Mack drive up.

Mugs barked and turned around with his belly flat on the floor. He crawled underneath the edge of the bed frame and headed down the stairs. He knew it was Mack. How could he not?

She followed him to shut off the alarm at the front door and got it just in time.

Chapter 5

Wednesday Late Afternoon ...

MACK EYED HER as she opened the door. "Why are you so flustered?" He bent to pet Mugs and Goliath at his feet.

"I had the alarms on," she said. "I had to run downstairs and shut it off before you opened the door."

His eyebrows shot up. "Are you keeping them on, even when you're home?" He seemed a bit worried.

"I will until the antiques are picked up," she said. "I can't take the chance of something happening to those pieces."

He nodded. "I guess I can understand that."

She led the way back up to the bedrooms, the animals dashing ahead of them.

When he stepped into the master bedroom, he whistled. "Wow. That bed is even bigger than I remembered it."

"Right? I moved the mattresses to the floor and now it looks even more crowded. Look at the size of that bed frame."

"It's huge." He shook his head. "I'm not even sure how they'll take it apart."

"Well, someone got it in here somehow," she said. "Although I may have to ask Nan about that."

"I'd say so. She might have a trick or two," he said. "What is it you want lifted?"

She pointed to the bed. Just then Mugs wiggled underneath the frame again to the same slat, sat, and growled. Goliath hopped on top and swatted him. Thaddeus was on top of the bedpost staring down at them.

Doreen pointed. "Something is underneath the bed right there by Mugs."

Mack groaned, reached down with one hand, then bent his knees, lifting the bed frame.

Doreen dove underneath beside Mugs who shoved his snout right at her. She checked all the other slats first. "Nothing else is here, but, whatever this is, I don't know if I'll get it off."

He lifted the frame a bit higher. "Why don't you come out and grab those two chairs or the boxes you've got here, and we'll put the edge of this frame on them. The ceiling and the four posters to this bed won't allow me to lift this any higher."

Following his instructions, she propped up the frame on the boxes she was collecting for Goodwill and the consignment shop.

He tested the weight. "It's not supremely safe, but it'll be fine for a few minutes." Then he crouched under the bed and took a look. "It looks like a letter's been taped to the slat inside some plastic. Likely to protect the paper over the years."

He pulled out a pocketknife from his pants pocket and very carefully slid it in the top layer of plastic, just enough so he could pull out the letter. Once it was free, he handed it to her. At that point Mugs laid down under the propped up bed, Goliath had dug his claws into wood and had slid until he was stretched out fully.

She opened it and gasped. "It's from my great-great-grandmother. It's a letter to Nan's mother. I think. Nan was named after her mom, so they both share the name Willa. Another thing I'll have to clarify with Nan."

"*My dearest granddaughter Willa,*" Doreen read aloud. "*I'm hoping you'll have my passion for antiques. I'm not sure why so many have absolutely no love of things old and well-loved. This entire set is for you. I know what it's worth, and so do you. I also know it doesn't matter to you. Enjoy it in the spirit it was intended and know that it's listed in my will. But, should there ever be any contention, keep this letter with the bed so all will know it's yours. With all my love and the hope that you have an absolutely wonderful and fulfilling life, Nan.*"

Tears were in Doreen's eyes when she stopped reading. She held her hand over her mouth and looked up at Mack.

"So does that mean you don't want to sell it now?" he asked drily.

She gave a shake of her head. "No, that's not what I mean. Obviously I'm not in a position to argue about the need for the sale, and the furniture is really not my style. But to think a piece of my own personal history is here, that's so important."

He pointed to the date. "And look at that."

"Wow, 1909," she read. "Nan wasn't even alive then," she said.

He shrugged. "Makes sense to me."

"Wow," she repeated. "And she passed it on to my Nan. Just wow." She shook her head. "I want photos of this letter."

"Take photographs, and, if you can scan it, then do that too."

Doreen went downstairs to her printer and scanned the letter, then took a photograph of it with her phone too. She walked back upstairs smiling.

"This is really great. It's also huge for proving provenance," Mack said.

"Yes," Doreen said with a smile. "Nan is seventy-five-ish, and her mother would have been at least twenty or thirty years older."

"I don't know if you've had a chance to find the paperwork for any of this, but this gives you a specific date to go by." Mack turned to look at the bed frame. "Are you ready for me to put the letter back in?"

She nodded.

He carefully reinserted it into the plastic sleeve, where it had been kept safe all these years. "Now you can tell your auction house guy that you have that letter. Maybe send him a copy by email."

She nodded and immediately sent a text. Then, through her email function on her phone, she attached a copy of the letter and sent it off. She sniffled back her tears. "I can't wait to show this to Nan."

"Sounds like *Nan* has always been used as the name for the grandmothers in your family, hasn't it?"

Doreen nodded.

With his help, she removed the boxes tilting up the bed frame and helped him lower the massive bed frame to the floor. She moved the boxes back to where they had been.

Mack looked at her. "What are in all those boxes?"

She motioned toward the closet, both of its doors open, revealing the mess inside. "I'm slowly sorting through all of

Nan's clothes. The boxed-up stuff here will go to Goodwill. I have all the bags of clothing downstairs that will go to the consignment store. Items I'm keeping currently are in the spare bedroom closet."

He nodded. "That sounds like a good system with all the sorting to do here. And I'm glad to hear you're keeping some of Nan's clothing too. You might as well wear them, since it's expensive to replace it all." He motioned at the over-stuffed closet. "Still a ton is in this closet alone."

"Speaking of which," she said, suddenly remembering what else she'd caught sight of in the back of the closet. "An old bookshelf is in the closet. It's jammed in the back. Who knew a closet could be this deep?"

He looked at her in surprise.

She pushed all the hangers to one side and pointed it out to him.

He shook his head. "Do you want me to pull that out for you?"

She looked at him in delight. "Absolutely I do."

"You should send pictures to your appraiser. Didn't you show him this piece?"

"No, it's not one of the pieces he was looking for." She removed more hanging clothes to give him access. Then stepped in and quickly dumped the contents of the shelf onto the floor under the hangers. A temporary solution at best. "I will send Scott photos though. And he can check it out when he returns to pack up this stuff."

It took a bit of maneuvering, but finally Mack dragged the bookshelf along the carpeted floor out to where Doreen could access to it. It didn't resemble the other pieces in any way. It was also scratched and beaten-up some.

"Can you imagine," she said, "that it's been in there for

probably fifty years?"

"Probably since Nan moved in." He nodded. "And with the passage of time and too many possessions, it got buried in the back. Still, it's quite useable, lots of life in it yet."

"It's pretty amazing," she said. "Nan seems to think nothing of leaving all this stuff behind."

"I think she left it behind for a very specific reason, and she was more than happy to share this with you," he said.

She smiled. "Maybe. I just hadn't expected it."

"No," he said, "but it's all good. I think you're doing the right thing."

She appreciated that. "I have to admit that it does wake me up in the night. I feel like I'm letting my family down."

"Not at all," he said. "I think the worst thing you can do is hang on to things out of guilt or because you think it's the right thing to do. I think it's time for you to do what's right for you."

She beamed at him. "You know what? Honestly it's been a pretty good week so far."

"No kidding," he said. "Yesterday certainly made it a great week. That was a very good thing you did."

"But it wasn't necessarily what I did." She hated to feel guilty about it. "I mean, really anybody could have sorted that out."

"The difference is," he said, "at the time, we didn't have most of the technology we do now. And that cold case hadn't been reopened because nothing new had been added in the way of facts or evidence or witness statements. We would have eventually reviewed it before boxing it up and putting it aside, but that's just the facts of life. You came at it from a very different angle, and you solved it."

"It was the license plate," she said.

He nodded. "That makes sense. And that's when we got that needed pop on the case. However, we didn't have time to take another look because you'd solved the case already."

She beamed at him. "Praise from you is high praise, indeed."

"Have you made another omelet yet?"

She shook her head. "I haven't had time," she confessed. "And I'm scared to. I figured that was beginner's luck."

He chuckled. "I haven't had dinner. If you haven't touched the ingredients, there's probably enough for another one. I suggest you try again, and we'll split it again."

She looked at him in surprise, then the nearby clock. It really was dinnertime. "I haven't touched anything. Do you think it's all still good?" She looked at him anxiously. "That's another thing I don't know anything about. How long does food keep?"

"Four to five days for sure," he said. "Come on. Let's take a look."

Downstairs again, they walked into the kitchen, and Mack opened the fridge. He pulled out the bacon first. "See here? A Best Before Date is printed on the packaging, and that's still another four days away. And the spinach, it's okay. It's wilting a little, but it'd make a good spinach omelet. And the eggs ..." He brought out the carton, checking the Best Before Date on the end of it, nodding, putting everything on the counter. Then he leaned against the counter and crossed his arms over his chest. "Go for it."

She looked at him nervously. "I haven't prepped."

"No prep required. No videos to watch. Just go by memory."

She wrinkled her nose at him as she stepped forward. "Are you trying to put me on the spot?"

"No," he said. "I'm trying to get food. It's been a very long day."

She laughed and got started. Since he had stopped by to lift her bed frame—and ended up moving that bookshelf as well—it was the least she could do.

Chapter 6

Wednesday Dinnertime ...

AS THEY SAT down to eat—and, boy, was she proud of the fact that her second attempt was damn near as perfect as the first—Mack looked at the big business-size envelope beside their plates.

"Johnny Jordan?" He frowned. "Why does that name sound familiar?"

Shoot. "I don't know," she mumbled. "Do you know that name?"

He glanced at her sideways as he took a bite of the omelet. "First, the omelet is divine. You did a great job."

She beamed at him. "It's not as hard as I thought."

"Nothing is," he said. "You just have to learn how."

She hoped so. But she didn't have the confidence yet to make that discernment.

Then he said, "And, second, you're up to something."

She sat back with a sigh. "How do you know?"

He snickered. "Because you get this weird little glare in your eyes and a wrinkle in your forehead as you bring your brows together. And it's almost always directed at me, as if to say, *I don't know what you're talking about.*"

She glared at him but could feel the wrinkles forming between her eyebrows. She reached up and eased them back.

His grin just widened.

She glared at him once more. "I'm not up to anything."

"Well, you just admitted you were," he said.

"Not really," she said. "But I do have an odd request." She patted her pocket and pulled out the letter and handed it to him.

As he popped another bite into his mouth, he picked it up and read it. His eyebrows rose toward his hairline. "Wow. Now they're bypassing the police and coming straight to you?" He shook his head. "What the hell will you do with this? Do you realize how dangerous this could be for you?" He looked at the letter again, then at the envelope. "Did she mail you that too?"

She groaned and sat back. "No, I didn't know what to do," she said, "so I called her. The end result is, she was here this afternoon and dropped off that envelope. I did warn her that I could probably tell her nothing because not only was it a long time ago but no crime scene was found. And no further word came from the young man in all these years. ... For all we know, it was possible he drowned, but he went missing *after* the heavy flooding that year. So it was doubtful he ended up in the lake." She let Mack ponder that for a moment, then added, "The dagger Penny was concerned about is in the bigger envelope she left with me earlier today." She tapped the big business envelope on the kitchen table.

"Yeah, for a while there," he said, "they were doing these 'stabbing it into the ground as hard as they could' kinds of things. Like darts, but downward with knives. It was a cool move but wasn't very good for the blades." He looked at the envelope. "You haven't opened it yet?"

She shook her head. "Mugs had just found whatever was under the bed when she arrived. I had to run downstairs, and, after she left, I set the alarm and came back upstairs. Then you came."

"You know what? For somebody who has nothing going on," he said, slightly sarcastically, "you're sure busy."

She nodded. "Almost too busy," she admitted. "But that's all right because it's pretty hard to not love life right now. The trick is, is there any way to figure out what happened to this poor Johnny guy?"

"I didn't know the family well. I can't recall much about the cold case. I remember opening it at some point, but there was nothing new to move forward with."

"No," she said, "and I'm not sure there is now either. It's a hard case. I'm also not sure what clues might be found in the witness statements either. So many witnesses have died." She hesitated. "I can't read the statements in the police file, can I?"

He shook his head.

She nodded. "That's what I expected. His girlfriend from around that time died of breast cancer last year. And his brother is gone now too."

"That is sad because then his brother never got closure, and even the girlfriend must have always wondered right up to the end."

"She certainly didn't leave any confession saying she'd murdered him," Doreen said drily.

"To date, we have no reason or no evidence to think Johnny was murdered," Mack said. "That was an excellent omelet." He slid the last bite in his mouth, put down his fork, and pushed back his plate. "The young man could have just gotten up and walked away."

"I get that," Doreen said. "But what would make a young man do that? What makes somebody, who is close to his brother—and we only have his brother's wife's word on that—but supposedly close to his brother and his sister-in-law, yet who gets up and walks away forever?"

"I think at the time they leave, they plan on returning, riding high on some future big successful wave. When that doesn't happen, they don't want the family to know they are a failure. A lot of people, after too much time has gone by, don't know what to say anymore, so they never say anything. Meaning they don't return either."

"That's very sad," Doreen said. "Somebody has to know what happened to Johnny."

"There's always another option," he said quietly. "You have to consider that, even though we have much higher statistics today, still an awful lot of suicides of young men happened back then."

"Wouldn't his body have shown up though?"

Mack frowned. Thinking about that, he pushed back his chair and looked at her. "Do you mind if I put on a pot of coffee?"

"Please," she said. She collected the dishes and walked to the sink. "I mean, surely if he'd shot himself, jumped off the bridge, or I don't know—I guess one of the favorite ways is a drug overdose or even driving into a semi coming down the highway or something—there would be a body. Obviously I don't know anything about committing suicide, but there's always a body left behind."

"There's *almost* always a body," Mack corrected. "But we don't always find everybody who is lost at sea, like we don't always find everybody who's been lost in the lake."

"Right," she said.

"And, if you think about all the country backroads we have here, all kinds of places exist where Johnny may have gone for a joyride and driven off into a ravine."

She stopped what she was doing, turned around, and looked at him. "Do you think, even after twenty-nine years, that would still hold true?"

"Of course it would," he said. "Think about the miles and miles of roads around here. And what would have been seen back then wouldn't necessarily be seen now, considering all the natural growth since then. Maturing trees and bushes can hide a lot."

"But we have satellite now," she argued. "People have drones traveling all over the place."

"Sure. That doesn't necessarily mean they know what they're looking at because a piece of shiny metal doesn't mean a vehicle is stuck underneath there. Besides, did Johnny have his own vehicle?"

"I forgot to ask Penny," she said. "She's sending all the digital files to my email too."

"Forward them to me as well," he said. "I'll take a look at what's in the police files again. I'm not promising anything, but, if something pops, maybe it's due to a communication error. Unfortunately we've seen that happen with cold cases too."

"What do you mean by *communication error?*"

"Different departments don't share info. Particularly back then. What if Johnny headed to Vancouver and got absorbed into the big-city life? He could be homeless. He could have been a John Doe in the morgue. We didn't any automatic way to check across multiple jurisdictions. It had to be done manually."

"What if we got something of George's? Could we run DNA and check through some database to see if his brother has shown up elsewhere?"

"We could, except there's no budget money for things like that," Mack said. "In a perfect world we'd have lots of money, and we could run DNA for every missing family member. And, even if something still exists of the brother's DNA to check, sometimes it's not a close-enough match to ID a sibling."

Doreen sighed. "I know Penny is hoping to put her house on the market, but she hasn't done a heavy clean out yet. Maybe, if she kept a locket with strands of her husband's hair, we should ask her to preserve it, just in case."

"Back then DNA had to be directly collected from the missing person. So some evidence of Johnny's DNA might be hanging around related to his missing person file."

"That would be evidence, wouldn't it?"

"Obviously," he said. "But unfortunately stuff goes missing. So, when I return to the office tomorrow, I'll take a look and see if we have anything on file. And you might want to send Penny an email, asking her if she has anything of her husband's. A hairbrush would be ideal."

"Right. How much do you need?"

"Not too much," he said. "But we do need something. Hair, nails, skin, blood, tissue, bone. Things like that."

She wrinkled her nose at him. "What if he was cremated? I doubt there'd be much left in that case."

"Possibly not," he said. "It depends if she kept the ashes."

"She did. The urn is on her mantel. Can you get DNA from the ashes?"

He shrugged. "I'm not sure. I hear bone fragments remain, even with cremations at high heat. Bones retain DNA. However, in most cases, those remaining fragments are ground to ash before being handed over. I don't know that the ashes can be tested for DNA. It seems like DNA testing is moving forward in leaps and bounds, and nobody knows what we can get from whatever until the test is done. Now they're doing ancestry DNA, and that's making huge changes in cold cases."

"But, in this case, we don't have any foul play suspected. So we have no suspects to go after, like a killer."

"If you mean that we don't have any DNA of a killer at a crime scene, you're quite right. We don't even have a crime scene. All we have is that this young man got up one day and walked away."

"Supposedly. What about the dagger?"

"Same problem," he said. "Found years later, buried in the ground. When we opened the missing person's case, no DNA testing was really done back then. Great advances have been made, so who knows what it'll tell us now? It's a knife that Johnny owned, that he played with all the time. Of course he cut himself on it. Everybody would have at least once."

She sighed. "I get that, but it just seems like, if somebody had murdered him with the dagger, there would be skin cells of whoever killed him."

"Maybe," he said. "But I doubt it after all that time."

"Right, but can they test for other tissue?"

"Lab tests can certainly separate different people's DNA, plus what kind of tissue was found for each person," he said, "as in semen versus epithelial versus hair, for example."

She nodded. "I just don't know enough about it, but at least I have the knife, and, no, I know it won't be of much value. I think what Penny is really hoping for is that her brother-in-law won't be forgotten."

"That's the hardest thing for any cold-case file. It's a cold case to the public. But it's never cold to the family. It just sits there forever."

"That's why she hung on to the dagger. It's a reminder. Not just of Johnny but of his life and probably his death. Of all that's hanging over her life all this time."

He stared at her. "And seriously? A dagger in the dahlias?"

"They had a bench in the backyard, where Johnny was last seen. It became something they found very difficult to look at. So they moved it and were digging a new bed and putting in dahlias when they found his dagger."

"Which makes sense, if he always sat there."

"I agree," she said with a shrug. "I don't have any angle to go on. And there was another thing," Doreen said with a sigh. "Penny was hoping that because of my association with you—and how the heck does everybody know about that?—she was hoping I might have access to Johnny's cold-case file. But ..."

"Which you know I can't give you," he said firmly.

"I told her that. I did explain that I couldn't do much," she said. "She seems to think I can do more than I can."

"But knowing you," he said, "you'll do your best anyway."

Chapter 7

Thursday Early Morning...

A S SOON AS Doreen had breakfast the next morning, she cleared off the kitchen table, except for her coffee cup, took out the large envelope from Penny, opened it up, and carefully spread out everything from inside. The dagger was small but had a lethal-looking blade with a very fine tip to it. She laid that off to the side.

She then read the collection of papers. There wasn't much—a couple newspaper articles about Johnny having gone missing, a poster asking for anybody to come forward who knew anything about Johnny's whereabouts, and a couple statements with a time line the family had given to the police. They all offered nothing new.

She frowned. "There isn't anything to go on. I'm sorry, Penny, but I have no clue what I'm supposed to do with this."

As she sat here pondering, an email came through from the appraiser about the letter she'd found under Nan's bed.

This is lovely, he wrote, *and definitely proof of provenance.*

She smiled at that. As she read further, she realized he still wanted her to go through the accordion folder of documents for any more paperwork related to the antiques. She didn't know why she was hesitating, but she needed to sort through it.

Putting everything back into the envelope Penny had given her, Doreen worried that she could do nothing for Penny. All Doreen could hope for was that Mack would send her something of interest from the police file when he had time.

After a trip to her bedroom, she walked into the living room with the accordion folder she'd found in the bottom dresser drawer. She sat on the couch and pulled out the envelopes stuffed inside, each with a handwritten generic label of its contents. Everything was in here from Last Wills and Testaments and personal certifications to medical records. They were important documents, but nothing to do with the antiques.

The very last envelope she brought out was only half the size of the others. She slowly set out its contents on the coffee table. The receipts were old; some were handwritten and hard to read. She could not make out very much of any of it. Maybe it would make sense to the appraiser, but she had no reason to believe these receipts had anything to do with what she and Scott were particularly looking for.

She put everything back in that envelope, then decided the only way through this was to ignore the envelope designation and sort out all the contents themselves. She took everything out of the accordion folder and laid it all one at a time on the coffee table.

She didn't find what she'd hoped for—provenance confirming a gold mine of million-dollar antiques—but still Doreen unearthed a gold mine of family information.

She pulled out the medical file and opened it, found a

copy of her own birth certificate, which was not surprising, until she saw a DNA certificate and froze. Nan had had Doreen's DNA tested against her son's to make sure Doreen was Nan's blood granddaughter. Doreen winced at that. But she couldn't really blame her grandmother because her mother had been much less than a one-man kind of woman.

Doreen laid that down along with her birth certificate and slowly went through everything she had from the first envelope. It was a hodgepodge file of everything her mom had sent over time to Nan. It brought back memories, but it was also sad.

Doreen put everything back in the appropriate envelope, reminiscing about a childhood she barely remembered. Obviously Nan had kept mementos of it all. And at least the DNA had confirmed she was truly Nan's granddaughter. She wasn't sure what Nan would have done if she'd found out that Doreen wasn't her blood relative. That would have been hard too. Particularly with her father gone, it would have been devastating for Nan to learn otherwise. And to think that Nan had some reason to get Doreen tested was just sad.

She went back through the other stuff, only to find nothing of the further provenance she searched for. A copy of Nan's Last Will was here, but it was sealed. Then the paperwork on the house, which was great because now Doreen had a place to file the new deeds when they came. Nan had saved copies of receipts for work done on the house years ago, like how the roof was fifteen years old. Also good to know that she'd at least get another five or ten years out of it hopefully.

Other receipts went even farther back but nothing regarding the antiques in questions. Another envelope was full of correspondence. Doreen pulled it out and looked at all the cards and letters; some of them were on very thin tissue paper. She went through them carefully, smiling at some that appeared to be from lovers who Nan had walked away from. Nan had led a wild and colorful life.

Doreen picked up a piece of paper, recognizing the handwriting. Checking the signature on the bottom, she saw it was to Penny from Nan. Doreen read it quickly—Nan sending condolences on the missing state of Johnny and hoping for a quick resolution to the problem. *How very like Nan*, Doreen thought. The letter was dated twenty-nine years ago. So then why was it in Nan's possession and not Penny's? Maybe Nan had written it but hadn't sent it? Doreen would ask Nan about it. She set it off to one side to deal with later, but … she needed to know *now*.

She phoned Nan. When her grandmother answered, she said, "Hi, Nan. How are you doing today?"

"I'd be doing much better," Nan said in a testy voice, "if you came down and gave me all the facts clearly."

It was unusual for Nan to be in a difficult mood. Doreen wasn't sure what was going on. "What facts?"

"The bodies you found in the lake," she said.

"Oh," Doreen said, frowning. "You mean about finding Paul Shore?"

"We know what the news reported and how you're the one who put it all together." Her voice warmed as she added, "And of course it was you. You're the biggest sweetheart."

"And yet, you sound kind of cranky," Doreen said humorously.

"Well, everybody here was mad at me because I didn't have all the information from you."

"Oh my," Doreen said. "I never even thought to fill you in on the rest. Yesterday was fairly trying and very emotional.

I came home, and I didn't want to deal with people. Although Mack did come over for dinner." Then she remembered what she'd found earlier. "Oddly enough, I just found a letter from you to Penny Jordan, but it doesn't look like you ever sent it."

"*Hmm,*" Nan said thoughtfully. "That doesn't make sense."

"It's about Johnny, her brother-in-law who went missing."

"Oh, yes, yes, yes," Nan said. "I was writing the letter, giving her my condolences, then realized it sounded like Johnny was dead. I didn't want her to think Johnny was dead. We all hoped the young man had just gone away to make his fortune and would come riding back into town as the 'big I am' he thought he was."

A tone in her voice made it sound like she knew Johnny better than Doreen had suspected. "Did you know Johnny?"

"He used to rake my yard every once in a while, but, like so many kids, he thought he should get paid way more for the little bit of work he did," Nan said with a sniff. "But he was pleasant enough. He was running around town with the wrong gang, and that made things difficult when he went missing."

"When you say, *the wrong gang?* Who?"

"Well, Freddy Black was bad news at the time. And Thomas Burgess. I can't remember who else. But they were always getting into trouble with the law. You know, like throwing rocks at cars and just generally being a nuisance. Vandalism. Then they got into the drug scene. But I don't think it was all that bad. At least I didn't hear too much about it."

"So you knew Johnny fairly well then?"

"Enough that, when he went missing, I felt sorry for the family. To think of it being almost thirty years ago now, that's so sad."

"It is, isn't it?" Doreen said sympathetically. "Penny asked me if I'd look into the case."

At first nothing but silence came over the phone; then Nan laughed. "Oh my," she said. "That is fantastic."

"No, it's not," Doreen grumbled. "I have absolutely nothing to go on. All of the cases I've worked on so far have had connections and trails, things I could follow up on. What am I supposed to do with a young man who walked away from his family's backyard twenty-nine years ago, for heaven's sake?"

"Well, you can't speak to the two people I mentioned because they're both dead. They were killed in a car accident not long after Johnny disappeared."

"Oh." Doreen walked into the kitchen and wrote that down on a notepad. "I wonder if it had anything to do with Johnny going missing?"

"Meaning, they might have committed suicide because of what they did to Johnny?" Nan's voice dropped. "You know what? I never even thought of that. You have a different perspective than most people. I'm glad you're looking into this. Now it's a big mystery I really want you to solve."

"I will try to solve it for Penny's sake," Doreen said, "but there isn't anything here for me to work with. Otherwise I'm sure the police would have done something with it."

"Cold cases from before the widespread usage of the internet and cell phones and DNA," Nan said, "just weren't the same types of investigations. We have so many more tools available now."

"Sure, but there was no body, no crime scene," she said. "We don't even know if he is dead or not. There were so many runaway kids back then that no one even tracked them. I swear it's in the thousands every year now."

"I think it's probably more than that," Nan said. "But, back then, we didn't have any way to maintain communication or to share databases between provinces. For all we know, Johnny went to Ontario and built a life for himself there."

"Did he have a vehicle, do you know?" Doreen asked.

"Yes," Nan said. "It was an old car. I don't know what kind it was, but I do remember it was the car the two guys killed themselves in."

Doreen straightened. "His friends were driving *his* car?"

"Yeah. We were all wondering what that was about, but the police didn't seem to think anything of it. When Johnny first disappeared his car did too, so we just thought he'd drive home any time. Only he didn't and the boys died while driving it."

"I suspect they did think *something* of it," she said, "but, if the car didn't reveal any evidence, then I'm not sure they had anything to go on."

"True," Nan said. "But you might want to cross-reference their case to Johnny's."

"Sure. What were their names again?"

"Burgess and Black."

"Okay. Got it." She wrote them down, then said, "I'll send Mack an email, asking if they're mentioned in the case files."

"Ha! He's a great source of information for you."

"I don't know about that," Doreen said with a smile. "He's not allowed to tell me much. But, in an unusual twist, the police commander stopped me yesterday on my way home after we found the two bodies in the lake. He shook my hand and thanked me."

"Oh, my goodness. Isn't that lovely? Peter Cochran is a nice guy," Nan said. "He was a little young for me, but, for a weekend or so, he was great fun."

Doreen's eyes popped wide open. "Are you saying you had an affair with the commander?"

"A very long time ago," Nan said with a delightful laugh. "He wanted more, but I wasn't the right person for him. He needed a wife, three kids, two dogs, one cat, and that perfect house with a white picket fence." She chuckled. "But that doesn't change the fact he is good at his job, and I'm very happy he did well by you."

Doreen was still struck by the admission that Nan had had an affair with a police commander. "If you know anybody at the old folks' home who has any information on Johnny's disappearance, let me know, will you?"

"Why don't you come down and have tea?" Nan said. "I'll get more details from you on yesterday too."

Just then Doreen remembered the letter she'd found underneath the bed. "Nan, that's an excellent idea. I have something to show you anyway."

"I'll put on the teakettle. You get the animals and come on down." Nan sighed. "I have to admit, I could use a hug today." And she hung up.

Chapter 8

Thursday Late Morning …

IT TOOK A few minutes to round up the animals. Mugs was well-mannered, until he heard the leash rattle; then he barked all over the place, chasing Goliath, who appeared to take deep offense and cornered Mugs in the kitchen, swatting at him twice. Trying to separate the two was not fun.

Finally she got them all calmed down with a treat or two and had another pocketful of treats handy. With Thaddeus on her shoulder, she opened the kitchen door, and all four of them headed out to Nan's place, via the creek. There was just no other path for her. Any chance she had, she chose to walk by the water. Besides, she wanted to avoid her front yard and anybody wanting to talk to her.

So many things had changed since she had moved here. The animals were just one part of it. She used to deal well with people, mostly because she had a polished glossy tone, not giving offense, not taking offense, kinda like being dead inside. And now here she did everything she could to avoid people, at least certain people.

She was happy to see the sun shining. She loved the way

the long shadows of the sun's arms touched on the green leaves as they gently waved in the wind. This was a nice thing about her house being on the creek; it was in a bit of a valley, and the wind whistled down with such gentleness that it always made her smile. Listening to the water, listening to the wind and the birds, it was incredibly peaceful.

She wasn't sure when, if ever in all of her marriage, she'd had an opportunity to enjoy Mother Nature as much as she did here. And who knew it was something she would fall in love with, without actual gardening involved. Here she could listen to the birds for hours, just sitting beside the creek, dipping her toes in the icy water, even though she knew what had come out of it in the last couple weeks. The creek remained special. It made her feel connected.

She was thoroughly jealous of all those people who lived in the countryside. Not that she wanted to milk cows or to raise chickens for their eggs or anything, but she yearned to have some real space to wander without being hemmed in by houses or people. Yet what she had here was a great first step in that direction. She loved to dip her fingers in the creek, to feel that connection, that sense of peace, that oneness. How fanciful of her. Still, if she had learned one thing with all the recent chaos, it was that life was short, too short. What she really needed to do was find a way to make the most of what time she did have. She'd lost so much with her pending divorce, and yet, she'd already gained so much more. If she'd had any idea a life like this existed for her outside of her marriage, she'd have left a long time ago.

Of course she hadn't really left of her own choice. She'd been replaced. She'd fought it kicking and screaming; that had been because of fear—fear of what was happening, fear of what would happen to her afterward, fear of where she'd live, fear of the future. Those thoughts were so bad, so detrimental to her. Because of how absolutely stunningly wonderful her future was, even this early version of it.

Smiling, she opened her arms wide and did a jig, dancing and twirling on the path. "I know, Mugs. I'm acting crazy," she stated gaily. "But life is good. How can anybody not appreciate this?"

Mugs barked, jumping around with her. She chuckled and resumed walking, her footsteps light, her heart even lighter. "Let's go visit Nan," she said. "Unlike us, she hasn't had a good day."

In fact, her grandmother worried Doreen. Nan alternated between being "all there" in mind and in body and not even close. Now that Doreen finally had Nan back in her life again, Doreen didn't want to lose her grandmother. She'd do anything to give that special woman another twenty years on earth with her.

As it was, it was hard to know how to help her. Nan had friends and a busy life. She seemed to enjoy her current lifestyle too.

Doreen had the photocopy of the letter she had taken from underneath the bed. She wasn't sure if that would add to Nan's despondency or if it would make her feel better. Doreen wanted it to make her grandmother feel better obviously.

She was bringing back a lot of powerful memories. She didn't want to upset Nan any more than she had to. She was the sweetest old lady. Okay, so she had this gambling habit. But it really wasn't so much *her* gambling right now; it was Nan getting other people to gamble.

At that, she laughed out loud. "Nan, you keep Mack hopping. That can't be a bad thing."

She went around the corner, watching the traffic as they crossed the road. They weren't very far from the old folks' home. As she approached, she saw the gardener standing out front, talking to somebody. As soon as he saw her, he put his hands on his hips and pointed his finger at her. She stopped and asked, "And what is it you want me to do? I can't take the animals in the building. So, if I don't cut across the lawn, how do I get to Nan's place?"

"You come without the animals." His voice was gruff. "It's bad enough you walk on the grass, but now you get all the animals on it too." He crossed his arms, not budging an inch.

Not to be deterred, Doreen walked around the corner to where Nan sat with her teapot on a little bistro set. When she looked up and caught sight of Doreen, Nan waved gaily.

"Oh, there you are," she said.

Doreen nodded, pointing at the gardener. "He won't let me cross the lawn."

"Of course he will," Nan said. And then she held up her finger. "Oh, right. I forgot all about those."

Curious as to what she was up to, Doreen watched as Nan bent, then stood, holding something heavy in her hand. At least it looked heavy because her grandmother's arms were straining. She watched her grandmother study the patio, then the grass leading to the sidewalk, then very carefully placed one stepping stone on the grass. Then she repeated this until five were in the grass, leading from the sidewalk to her patio.

The gardener roared and raced toward her. But it was too late. Doreen skipped easily from one to the other until she was in Nan's little garden. Mugs and Goliath walked on the grass. The cat stopped short of the patio, lay down, and twitched his tail.

"That's perfect." Doreen leaned down to give Nan a hug.

"That's perfect. That's perfect," Thaddeus said.

But the gardener was having nothing to do with it, picking up one of the stepping stones.

Nan stopped him, crying out, "Leave those there. You won't let her cross that lawn because it'll hurt your grass. So now we fixed it. Put that back."

"I can't," he roared.

Thaddeus squawked loudly.

"The lawnmower will get caught on them every time."

"So dig them into the lawn," Doreen said. "Just take a cutting knife, draw into the sod all the way around each of the stones, lift up the sod, and place the stones down." She gave him a shrug. "That's hardly a big deal for a *gardener*."

He glared at her. "We'll see about that," he snapped. He picked up the first stepping stone and carried it inside the old folks' home.

Nan sighed and sat down, reaching out to calm Thaddeus, whose feathers were ruffled from the raised voices. "Now he'll complain to the manager."

"And what's the manager likely to do?" Doreen asked curiously.

"It depends if it's a good day or a bad day," Nan said with a smirk. "If he had fun with his girlfriend the night before, I'd probably get away with it. But, if they're fighting, as they usually are, then he'll get mad."

Doreen shook her head, sat down on the bistro chair, and smiled at her grandmother. "You look like you've had a tough day today, Nan."

Nan nodded. "I did. I had a bit of a tiff with an old

friend." She gave Doreen a wide smile. "We'll get over it. We always do. But it's a reminder that life is short, and, for those of us who have been around for a long time, we should know better, but we're still human," she said sadly.

"I'm so sorry." Doreen reached across the table and squeezed her grandmother's hand gently. Her translucent skin worried Doreen. "Are you eating enough?" she asked. "Have you had lunch?"

Nan gave her a lusty laugh. "I definitely am eating and had lunch. More to the point, are you eating? Did you have lunch already?"

"I am, and I'm not hungry yet, but thanks," Doreen reassured her.

"Just let me know when you are ready for a sandwich. I have some wonderful ham and homemade sourdough bread."

Doreen nodded, her smile grim. "I'm sorry about your friend. It's difficult when you are on the outs."

"And you know all about that too, don't you?" Nan said. "I'm so sorry your friends walked away from you when you left your husband."

"Just meant that they weren't friends, at least not mine," Doreen said with a smile. "And that's really what I have to remember. Just because I wanted them to be friends and thought that's what they were, you don't really understand what a friend is until you hit the rocks and need somebody to be there for you. And that's just called life." She shrugged. "I wouldn't give up what I currently have for anything in the world." She gently stroked the back of Nan's hand. "I'm so sorry I missed all those years with you."

"Not to worry," Nan said. "Just think about how good everything is now for us. Sometimes you have to wait for what you can really appreciate. If I can have all my remaining years with you close by, I'll be absolutely in heaven."

Doreen chuckled. "On that note, let me tell you what I found underneath the big bed." She reached into her pocket, pulled out and unfolded the photocopy of the letter. She handed it to Nan.

When Nan read it, tears came to her eyes.

Doreen immediately regretted bringing it to her, but Nan smiled through her tears.

"I'd forgotten this was there," she said. "A few times in your life you will find real turning points, and, with the death of *my* Nan, my life definitely changed too."

"Are you still okay if I sell that bed though?" Doreen asked. "I'm afraid you'll hate me for it."

"Of course I don't mind," Nan said, lifting her head from the letter. "I know the house is full of things, but honestly *things* are not what I care about. And the older I get, the more I realize it. For a long time I valued my independence. Now I value family, and that's you. The bed has a lifetime of memories for me, but it only represents them—it isn't the memory itself. And, when you sell the bed and move it out of there, it doesn't take the memories with it."

Doreen was delighted to hear that. "Well, I did separate the mattresses from the frame today. I'm waiting for a phone call as to when they'll pack up everything. I found some paperwork in a folder thing in the bottom dresser drawer."

Nan frowned, then poured their tea into the two cups. "I think that's all of the paperwork," she said, puzzled. "You didn't find anything about the pieces?"

"No. Oh, wait, we did find something ..." She pulled out the two foil-wrapped chocolates and held out her palm. "Do you remember these? We found them in the secret drawers."

Nan's face lit up with joy. "Oh my," she whispered, staring at the chocolates. "I remember those. My nan used to hide them all the time for me to find." She looked up at Doreen. "I'm so delighted you brought these. Such wonderful memories are stored in that furniture."

Guilt seared through Doreen.

And it must have shown on her face as Nan reached a thin arm across the table and squeezed Doreen's wrist. "And, no, that doesn't mean you shouldn't sell it. Those are my memories, not yours," she said in such a firm voice that Doreen relaxed.

"If I hadn't found that letter," Doreen said quietly, "there wouldn't be any proof of how long we've had it." She then brought out the locket and cuffs. "We found these too."

"Oh my," Nan held it carefully, then clicked it open. A warm smile blossomed on her face. "Lovely to find this again."

"It is indeed." Doreen accepted it from her grandmother and pocketed it. "I still haven't found the paperwork on the antiques though."

Nan tapped her fingers on the table. "*Hmm*, I'm pretty sure more paperwork is somewhere. As you clear out the place, you'll find more and more pieces."

Doreen frowned. "Are you talking about the antiques or the paperwork?"

Nan blinked. "Both?"

"I know you inherited the bedroom suite, but did you invest in all the other pieces with your money?" Doreen asked half in delight and half in outrage. "Why would you do that?" She was generally curious because, if *things* didn't matter to Nan, why bother putting money into valuable antiques?

"It's not that the things mattered," she said. "It was the history of a piece that mattered. Once I realized who might have been the previous owners and why they had it, that's what I was fascinated by. But it was at the time when I was lonely. And what are you supposed to do when you're lonely? Well, you find things to fill your time with. You find things to be happy with. I was always very taken by everybody else's stories. And that's what antiques are. They are wood that has absorbed the stories of all the people who have owned them. So you'll find an eclectic mix of pieces in the house. And, no, I don't mind if you sell all of them."

"I worry you don't have enough money," Doreen said quietly. "It would bother me to think you had invested all your money in all these things. Then I sell them, and I get the money, and yet, you're suffering."

Nan's gaze opened wide. She patted her granddaughter's hand. "You really are a sweetheart, but I am *not* suffering," she said firmly. "I have lots of money, money in my accounts. I'm hoping you'll do something with the antiques, so you have some income, and so you won't be starving."

"And speaking of starving," Doreen said, straightening in the chair, "I made omelets the other day."

Nan clapped her hands together and chuckled. "Wow! I am so happy to hear that. Is that what you and Mack were eating?"

Doreen frowned at her. "As a matter of fact, it was, but I don't want you to make too much out of it."

"Not at all," Nan said. "And, if Mack is teaching you how to cook, then I am doubly delighted. If I was still there, I'd be helping you myself." She leaned forward and in a loaded whisper said, "But this gives Mack a really good reason to stop by all the time, doesn't it?"

"I don't think he needs any reason right now," Doreen admitted. "We have so much going on in our lives that keep intersecting. I don't think it's much of an issue."

"I'm glad you came over today," Nan said. "You've really put a sparkle back into my mood."

Doreen chuckled. "Ditto. I do love that it's just a short walk to visit you." She lifted her teacup, took a sip, and, when she put it down, she said, "Do you have any of your favorite recipes written down?"

Nan nodded. "They're still at the house. I don't do much cooking now. If I do, it's nothing I don't already know by heart."

"That would be lovely," Doreen said. "I can't wait until I can do things without recipes."

"You do lots of things," Nan said. "What you did for Paul's family was tremendous. Not to mention for the poor handyman who was accused of stealing that poor little boy."

"I guess everybody is talking about that now too, aren't they?" Doreen asked.

"Of course they are," Nan said. "Just think about it. Look at how much you've done for the families."

Doreen nodded. "Much less so for the Family Planning Center though."

"That Cecily was a problem to begin with," Nan said. "I warned my neighbors about her a long time ago. She was just trouble. Very strict, very opinionated, that woman," Nan said with an admonishing finger. "I'm sorry the other two were killed, but I really could see her life ending in a bad way."

"Well, she'll be in jail for a long time," Doreen said.

"So tell me more. I need all the details on how you

found Paul and the handyman. Don't leave anything out. The residents here are immensely curious." Nan smiled and waited.

Doreen sighed. She couldn't talk Nan out of this. For all Doreen knew, Nan was acting as bookie for many related bets among the old folks here on this particular cold case. Sighing again, Doreen began her tale. Nan had many questions. Doreen figured each one had to do with Nan's particular gambling matters. Shaking her head, Doreen answered each one. An hour later, Doreen was hungry. "You know what? That ham sandwich sounds pretty good right now. I'll make one, unless you want to share one with me?"

Nan shook her head, jumping up. "I've got this. You sit here and rest." Nan returned shortly with a sandwich and some baby carrots. "So what are you working on now?" Nan asked, easily sliding in that question.

Doreen caught herself from telling her grandmother everything she knew and settled on the basic truth. "Just the case of Johnny Jordan, who went missing."

"I think it's fascinating that Penny contacted you. And I do love that you came here to talk to me about it. It's like we're coconspirators or something," Nan said with a chuckle.

"Potentially we are," Doreen said, laughing. "Because everybody here is such a huge source of information that it would be absolutely amazing if I could find out more stuff on what Johnny was like, what his friends were like. Just think about it. I mean, there's a whole world I can't access because I didn't live here back then, but those of you who did, that's massive. You all have huge memory banks I can't even imagine."

"That's true enough," Nan said. "And we definitely have an awful lot of people here who would have been around back then." She pursed her lips as she thought. "I'll have to talk to some people here. I know Penny's neighbor. I think her name is Ginger. She lived there at the same time Johnny went missing. She might remember something about it."

"It would help if it wasn't a family member," Doreen said, "because family members always tend to remember the deceased with a kind eye but not necessarily an honest eye. Nobody wants to think of their family members as being anything other than delightful. But the truth is, as you and I both know, not everyone is always as delightful as the family members want to remember them."

Nan chuckled. "Well, Ginger is here, and she wasn't family, so I'll talk to her. If I can pin her down that is. She's gone lots."

"If you could, that would be awesome. I really have absolutely nothing to go on. A big strapping young man gets up one day and walks away. The end."

"Not necessarily," Nan said. "We know his vehicle was involved in an accident not long after he went missing that killed two of his buddies. We always wondered if they'd had something to do with Johnny's disappearance. Plus, how did they end up with his vehicle?"

"I'll ask Penny about that," Doreen said. "I plan to walk around her property to get an idea on the last-known location for Johnny and where his dagger was found."

"If you walk home on the other side of the creek," Nan said, "you'll get there in half the time. It's probably only a ten- or fifteen-minute walk." She glanced at her watch. "You could probably walk by her place after our tea."

Doreen loved that idea. She finished her tea and the last baby carrot, and said, "In that case, maybe I'll go now." Giving Nan a big hug and leaving her the copy of the letter, she turned and headed back out with the animals.

She stopped for a moment to orient herself, and, using the stepping stones, though of course one was missing, skipped across to the sidewalk, went down and around, then behind the old folks' home. She could cross the creek on this side and walk over and probably hit Penny's within a few minutes. At least according to Nan.

As Doreen rounded the corner, Mugs sniffed all over the grass, as if it was a common walkway for dogs. She was forced to tug him forward quite a bit because the last thing she wanted was the gardener to think that Mugs would pee on his perfect grass. She couldn't even imagine if Mugs left a turd somewhere close by. The gardener would probably have a heart attack. Smirking, she led her menagerie toward the sidewalk.

Chapter 9

Thursday Late Afternoon ...

DOREEN CROSSED THE bridge and walked happily, enjoying the late afternoon sun. She hadn't been very long at Nan's, although the hours had disappeared quickly. Still, she had time to check out Penny's home and to figure out where the missing young man had possibly gone to from there.

It wasn't long before she came to the row of houses described by Nan. Doreen wanted to check out the park behind them.

She took the access path to the large open green space. Goliath alternated from being distracted to running ahead. Mugs, well, he just moseyed along, sniffing with his big nose, and Thaddeus hummed at her shoulder. She noted a couple goalposts, as if for casual games of football. A pitcher's mound sat on the other side of the park. The nearby houses were all fenced with gates to the park—all chain-link construction per the park's guidelines for a consistent and symmetrical look. So, if Johnny had wanted to, he could certainly have opened the gate and stepped into the park, where anything could have happened.

Thaddeus flew to the ground and walked along the fence.

She wandered up and down it with him, considering what the growth of the trees and the shrubs would have been like some twenty-nine years ago. Many of the bordering properties had cedar hedges; some were very thick. Back then they would have been smaller, and anybody on the other side of the fence would be visible.

Somebody might have called out to Johnny. He would have willingly gone to them. It wasn't likely that somebody would have gone into the backyard, knocked him over the head, tossed him over their shoulder, and carried maybe a 180-pound male through the park without being seen. It was late afternoon on a sunny day at the time of his disappearance. Surely someone would have seen such an altercation.

His friends could also have asked him to pick up booze or to go to a party. The fact was, she didn't know what happened to him or, for that matter, to his car from the time Johnny went missing twenty-nine years ago to his friends dying in it just a few weeks after Johnny's disappearance. Anything was supposition at this point. And she knew what Mack thought of those …

As she stood, she heard her name called. She turned to see Penny peering over the gate.

"It *is* you," Penny stated happily.

Doreen walked toward her. "I wanted to see what the area was like," she confessed.

Penny opened the gate. "I'm so glad you're taking this seriously. I know George is smiling in heaven right now."

Doreen hoped so. It was kind of creepy though to think of all those faces up there, smiling down at the other poor sods who lived their life on earth. She walked around the backyard, studying where the kitchen window was and what the view would be like. "Well, I doubt someone would have come onto your property and knocked him out, picked him up, and carried him away," she said, "particularly with you watching."

"Although we weren't necessarily watching the whole time," Penny admitted. "We often wondered what we missed."

"Makes more sense to call him into the park, although any number of people could have seen him there too."

"Sure, but no one reported having seen him at that time on that day."

"What happened to his vehicle? I understand he had a car?"

"Yes. He had George's old car. The two worked on it constantly."

With Penny's assistance, they went through the motions of where the bench had been and where the knife was found. With her cell phone, Doreen took several photographs, including one of the gated entrance into the park.

She also noted that, if Johnny had wanted to, he could have gone around either side of the house into the front yard. "Do you know how his friends got the keys?"

She shook her head. "I assumed they stole them. Johnny may very well have had the keys on him, or he may have just left the vehicle unlocked. For all I know they were out for a joyride, they killed him and then took off in his car. I don't know. I understood that, for a while, they were all laughing at being able to hot-wire cars. They might very well have thought to pull that prank with his vehicle. But Johnny and George had done a lot to soup it up. Johnny was pretty happy with the aftermarket stuff they were doing to it. He really wanted to get himself a muscle car. But George cautioned Johnny about getting rid of this car too early. Though Johnny wanted to sell it, George didn't want him to."

"It's quite possible that one of his friends decided he should sell it regardless, and, if he didn't sell it, he should just give it to them, whether he liked it or not. So, when he went missing, they might have taken it as their due."

"That's a possibility," Penny said. "I know we tossed around an awful lot of theories back then. I don't know if that one in particular was ever brought up, but, in a way, it does make sense. I know he wouldn't have sold it cheap though. The aftermarket upgrades cost thousands even back them."

They talked a bit longer. When she felt she could learn nothing else, she started to leave but turned back. "Do you remember anything about the vehicle? License plate, model?"

Penny shook her head. "No, but I'm sure Mack can get it from the files."

Doreen nodded. "I'm sure he can. It doesn't mean he will share it with me though." She gave a slight wave, and, with the animals, headed back the way she'd come.

Penny called behind her. "If you go along the creek, you'll come up on the north side of your place."

Doreen looked at her in surprise, then tried to reorient herself from where she was. "Thanks. I'll try that." She headed off to the right.

The sun was setting and getting to that half-dusky light outside. That was a bit of a concern. It was also getting cooler. It was spring, but a breeze had picked up. Trusting in Penny, Doreen kept marching forward until she came to the creek.

She stopped, studying it, then realized Penny was right. Doreen was farther up from where her property was. Now if she could find a way to get to her familiar path on the creek, she could walk across the little bridge to her home.

Mugs barked and kept up a snuffling sound as he went through the bushes toward the path. Thaddeus took several steps closer to her, and she wasn't sure if that meant he was nervous or if he thought they were going into the water. Goliath appeared to have absolutely no issues either way as he raced ahead of Mugs, who wanted to run after the cat.

Pulled along by the basset hound, Doreen ran onto the path and took a right. "Well, this is definitely a different way to go home." She looked back but saw no sign of Thaddeus, so she tugged on Mugs's leash to slow him down while calling for the bird. Thaddeus came around the corner, then flew up, missing her shoulder and smacking into her head. She cried out and caught him before he fell. "Okay, you're staying with me, big guy. So no more freak-outs. Okay?"

"Okay, okay," Thaddeus shrieked, then snuggled in against her chest.

She continued homeward, marveling at the shadows lengthening around her. The moon was rising, but still enough sunlight remained to see. She wasn't scared in the dark, but it was hard to see the path. Definitely rockier than she was used to on her side—as if not many people ever walked here, which also made sense because she'd not seen many people come down the creek past her place either.

Finally she came to her little bridge, maybe twenty feet long, and her house was easily visible on the other side. She had left lights on inside, and something about it was almost fairy-tale-ish. "No, maybe more gingerbread-house-y," she said, chuckling.

And then she froze, sure she saw a shadow cross the window. *Inside.*

Her heart raced as she had forgotten to set the alarms before she'd come out with the animals.

With her companions in tow, she ran across the bridge, sneaked up the side of her fence, around to the front, and froze again. Mack's car was in her driveway. She groaned, picked up the phone, and called him.

His voice was irate when he answered. "Where are you?" he snapped.

"Maybe the question should be, where are you?" she said drily as she opened the front door. She could see him in the kitchen. Mugs barked, racing ahead to greet him.

He spun and put away his phone, bending to pet Mugs. "I was trying to get you on the phone for the last hour, and you wouldn't answer. I came over here to make sure you were okay and found the place empty and the alarms *not* set," he said accusingly. "You didn't even lock the front *or* the back doors."

She transferred Thaddeus to the kitchen table. He squawked in protest, then tilted his head and said, "Mack is here. Mack is here."

"Yes, he is," she said. She checked her phone, and, sure enough, the ringer was turned off.

She groaned. "I came down the creek and saw a shadow inside. I thought you were somebody after my antiques." She waggled her phone. "And the sound was off."

"I could have been an intruder," he said in a stern tone. "What's the point of setting up a security system if you don't use it?"

She raised both hands in frustration. "Okay, okay, okay. It was a foolish thing to do. Nan sounded pretty lonely, so I grabbed the animals and went to visit her."

He frowned. "So then why did you come from the far end of the creek?"

She wrinkled her nose at him. "You saw me, did you?"

"No," he said, but then he shrugged. "Well, I might have caught you coming around the corner."

She glared at him. "You saw me coming into the backyard anyway, and you still had to ask where I was, huh?"

He gave her a sheepish grin. "I wondered if you'd tell me the truth."

She rolled her eyes at him. "Of course I told you the truth. What's the point in lying?"

"I'll give you that." He chuckled. "In your case, you're not a great liar anyway."

"No, I'm not. But I'm not a terrible one either," she snapped. She walked in and checked the clock. "I didn't realize it was so late. I was hoping for a cup of tea before bed, but the caffeine might keep me up."

"So have something herbal," he suggested. "Particularly if you have something to help you fall asleep."

"Such as?" She walked to the drawer of teas. "Look at them all here. I have no clue what any of them do."

"If it says *Sleepytime*," he said drily, "I'm pretty sure it's not meant to give you energy during the day."

"Ha, ha." She picked up several more. "Chamomile, yarrow root, and dandelion. Are we seriously thinking dandelion leaves are crushed up in these packets?" She opened one of the little yellow boxes that had a picture of dandelions all over it, pulling out the little tea bags.

"Yes," he said. "I wouldn't be at all surprised."

She shook her head. "The only one I would count on as safe to drink in the evening is *Sleepytime*."

"Which wouldn't be a bad idea," he suggested. "You will be sleeping on the floor tonight, and that'll feel very different. You might need something extra to help you."

"That's a good idea," she admitted. She walked to the sink, filled the teakettle, and turned it on. Then she leaned against the counter. "Do you want a cup?"

"No," he said. "Now that I know you're safe, I'll go home." He walked toward the front door.

"Wait." She stopped him. "What were you calling me about earlier?"

He hesitated a moment. "It's really nothing." He continued to walk toward the front door.

"Well, if it was enough to call me," she said, trailing behind him, "it's enough to tell me now."

"It's the cold case you're working on," he said. "Two friends of his were killed in a car accident driving his car."

"Yes," she said. "I know that. What we don't know is how they got his car."

He looked at her. "According to one of the kids' fathers, his son bought it off of Johnny."

"Did that make sense at the time?" she asked. "Did he have money to do something like that twenty-nine years ago?"

"The dad said he paid a couple hundred bucks. He'd been saving up for it."

She shook her head. "Well, he might have been saving up for it, but no way Johnny would have accepted that money."

At the doorway Mack turned to her. "How do you know that?"

"Because Penny was just saying how George and Johnny spent hours working on that thing. Sure Johnny wanted another rig. He wanted a muscle car, whatever the hell that is," she said with a wave of her hand. "But the thing, the two brothers souped up that car, and it was worth a lot more."

"This was twenty-nine years ago," Mack reminded her. "A couple hundred dollars bought a lot more back then."

"But they had put serious money into it," she argued. "According to Penny, they did an awful lot of aftermarket upgrades. I mean, like a hot rod for the kid."

Mack crossed his arms over his chest and leaned against the door. "And that can cost a bundle," he admitted. "How badly did Johnny want another vehicle?"

"Pretty badly. But what he wanted was out of his price range," she said, "and I doubt that a couple hundred bucks for his car would have done the job. Plus it didn't begin to pay George back for the money he put into the car either. Plus he didn't want Johnny to sell the car. Feel free to contact Penny and ask her yourself."

"No," he said. "But, if you want to ask her what the vehicle might have been worth back then, it wouldn't hurt to find out. Although I doubt it's value had a financial aspect for the two men who worked on it so much."

"Good point." She looked up at the clock. "I'll think about asking her but I'm too tired to do that now though. She did say thousands of dollars in those upgrades so a couple hundred bucks doesn't make sense. I'll feed the animals, then maybe have a hot bath before I settle in for an early night."

He nodded. "Exactly. Get to bed and get some rest."

"Right. Tomorrow is a whole new day," she said with yet another heavy groan.

"What's wrong with tomorrow?" he asked.

"Tomorrow is Friday," she said. "I'm still waiting for

that phone call from Christie's, but I will head to your mother's and spend a few hours weeding, as planned."

"Right, a phone call about the antiques. I keep forgetting." He looked around the living room, shook his head, and said, "I can't imagine what this place will look like when those huge pieces are gone."

"I know," she said. "But I'm still looking for paperwork that Nan says she had. Apparently what I found wasn't it."

"I'm not sure what you're looking for," he said, "but it's hard to find anything in here."

"I know," she said with a sigh. "And one of these days I'll venture into the garage. I did open the inside door to the laundry room finally, but then I had a hell of a time closing it. The garage is stuffed." She just shook her head. "I don't know what Nan was thinking."

"I would guess that, like a lot of older people," he said quietly, "she found it hard to let go of things."

Doreen smiled. "That could very well be. It was really nice to see her today. I would hate to lose her anytime soon."

"I'd hate that too," Mack said. He opened the door and stepped out on the front step. "And what are you doing as soon as I leave?"

She frowned at him. "Taking a cup of tea upstairs."

He banged his head lightly on the doorframe. "No. You'll lock this door and set the alarms."

"Well, I meant that too." She shooed him away. "Go, go, go, go. The sooner you leave, the sooner I can go to bed."

He snorted. "Now, if you had somebody you were going with, that would make sense. Otherwise, I don't know." With that cryptic remark, he turned and walked to his car.

She closed the door lightly behind him, reset the alarm, and checked the back door. She fed the animals, while snacking on cheese and crackers. With the animals in tow, she picked up her tea, shut off all the lights, and walked up the stairs.

She could only hope everything went well with this antique stuff. She wanted it all gone, safe and sound, as soon as possible.

She walked into her bedroom and turned on the light. Everything looked the same, except for her bed on the floor. That was just a shame. She set down her tea and walked into the bathroom. It still amazed her that such a lovely bathroom was the only thing Nan had renovated in the house. She'd yet to mention it. Every time Doreen was with Nan, Doreen also forgot to bring it up. She needed a list for all the things she wanted to ask her grandmother.

Deciding a hot shower would be better than a bath, she got in under the spray. While stepping out, drying herself, she heard a commotion in the bedroom. She grabbed her robe, threw it on, and stepped out of the bathroom. And glared. "What are you doing, Mugs?"

Mugs was at the closet doors, barking like a crazy man. She frowned and thought about it. Mack had been here, but who was to say somebody hadn't come inside ahead of Mack?

Both doors to the closet were closed, but she tested them just the same, then tied the doorknobs together with a pair of nylon stockings, and stepped back into her bathroom. She pulled out her phone and called Mack. As soon as he answered, she said, "Was anybody in the house when you arrived?"

"Of course not," he said. "You were out."

"Would you mind coming back then?" she asked in the hushed whisper. "And fast."

Chapter 10

Thursday Evening ...

DOREEN QUICKLY REDRESSED in the same clothes she'd worn earlier, pulled her hair into a ponytail, making sure it was out of the way. She had no weapons, nothing that would do the job against a possible intruder. And since Mugs had entered the bedroom, he hadn't stopped barking. She knew she would have to make her way downstairs in order to let Mack in and to disengage the security system, but she didn't want to do it too soon. She had no idea if anybody was in the closet, but no way would she open it without Mack here to take a look with her.

She waited ten minutes. When she heard a vehicle, she crept to the hallway. Mugs still barked away at the closet. She ran down the stairs, entered her security code, and unlocked the front door. "Upstairs. I need you upstairs." And she bolted up the staircase, Mack behind her.

He grabbed her by the shoulders. "What's the matter?" he whispered.

She tried to explain, but it was garbled, as she was afraid the scenario had changed while she'd been gone. Thankfully Mugs still stood at the closet doors, barking like a crazy dog.

Goliath sat right beside him. Not to be outdone, Thaddeus perched on a newel post of the bed, overseeing the pair on the floor.

Mack strode toward the closet door, raised an eyebrow at her over the nylons.

She shrugged. "I didn't know what else to do."

He untied the nylons and opened both doors. He saw nothing at first. But Mugs dove under the clothes and growled.

Yelps sounded from inside, and somebody yelled, "Get him off me. Get him off me."

Mack dove into the closet, bringing out her intruder and tossing him to the floor, where Mack pinned him down.

"Well, well, well," she said, recognizing the intruder she had caught in her house just last week, taking her fireplace poker after him until Mack arrived and took him to jail, only to run into the same damn intruder on the loose again in the grocery store parking lot soon afterward. Sometimes the judicial system sucked. "So you *are* a Peeping Tom, just like I told you before, stealing into women's bedrooms at night too."

The man turned away, his astonished expression taking over his face. "No way," he argued. "You're not putting that on me. I'm only here because"—he waved at Mack—"he was coming inside, so I ran up here to hide. I'm not a Peeping Tom. No way."

"His name is Darth McLeod. And he's supposed to be locked up. I'll have fun finding out why you are loose once more." Mack pulled him to his feet. "You won't be getting out on bail this time. No matter how good a lawyer you have." He proceeded to march her intruder down the stairs.

Darth McLeod. Well, that was a name to commit to

memory. Hopefully she'd seen the last of him now. She followed them down and blocked the front door. "Check his pockets first," she said. "For all I know, while you and I weren't here, he made five trips out of the house with my stuff."

Darth sneered. "You don't even know what you've got here," he snapped. "There's a bloody fortune for the taking."

"No, there isn't. It's mine. You're not taking anything. And I might not know everything yet," she said, "but I'm learning."

Mack searched his pockets and pulled out a list. He held it up to her and said, "Does this make any sense to you?"

She frowned. "Snow globe, blue china vase, silver tea set." There were a few other items. She pulled out her phone and took a picture of the list, then returned it to Mack. "Thanks very much for letting me know what might be worth something," she told Darth.

He just glared at her. Nothing else was in the other pocket, so Mack led him outside. She shut the door keeping the animals inside.

"Should you drive him to the station on your own?" she asked.

Mack shook his head. "I sent a text for backup."

And, sure enough, an RCMP vehicle came around the cul-de-sac and up to her driveway. Two men got out.

"Hi, Chester," she said, recognizing one of the men.

Chester gave her a sheepish grin. "I see you can't stay out of trouble, can you?"

"Not my fault you guys let this jerk out of jail. You should add Peeping Tom and stealing underwear to his list of crimes."

"I didn't steal any underwear from you," the intruder

bellowed. "That's gross."

"You were in my closet and looking in my underwear drawer," she said, pointing to the open dresser drawer. "So, as far as I'm concerned, you're after women's lingerie too." She gave him a fat smile. "Let's see what the other prisoners think of that."

The two uniformed men roughly grabbed her intruder and forced him into the back of their car. With a wave to her and Mack, they took off with the prisoner.

She smirked at Darth as she waved goodbye; then she turned to Mack. "Now please don't let him out again."

"No," Mack said. "I'll talk to the prosecutor about him staying in jail until his court date."

"Good idea," she said. "We also need to figure out where his vehicle is and make sure he hasn't been hauling stuff out of my house."

Mack pulled out his phone. "I'll get a run on his vehicle in the meantime." He looked around the cul-de-sac. "Do you recognize all these vehicles?"

She looked around. "All but that truck down there."

Together they walked in the dark to the truck. It was an older model. Mack took a picture of the license plate. Then he bent down, brushed off some of the mud on the plate, took more pictures, and called it in. "Looks like it's his," he said, after ending his call.

"Can we search his vehicle?"

"He was caught in the act of a felony," Mack said, "so, yes, I can." With his phone flashlight turned on, he found several bags in the back of the truck bed as well as a box. He opened the box and pulled out a large snow globe.

"Wow! That's beautiful." The bottom of the snow globe had Nan's name written on it. "That dirty, rotten little thief," she said, stamping her foot. "Can I take this back up to the house?"

"No, I'm afraid not yet," he said. "We'll have to keep all this as evidence."

"How will I know what's mine?" she asked.

They went through the rest of the box and found a blue china vase with a lot of Bubble Wrap around it.

"That was on the front room mantel," Doreen said in a daze. "I have the pictures at home to prove it."

He nodded. "I can see that too. We'll have to move these to my car. But I want the entire vehicle gone over. Apparently Darth has a good eye for what he can pawn. The trouble is, I don't know what else he might have taken, and we'll need to give this truck a good once-over."

She hopped into the bed of the truck with her cell phone out. There was one more box. She opened it up and frowned. "I don't recognize this," she said. It was a carving of a dolphin's head.

"No," he said, "but I do. It's from another reported break-in."

"Well, now you know who your burglar is," she said with a snort of disgust. "Geez, as if we don't work hard enough to get where we are, and then to have somebody like him stealing all this stuff."

"Sure," he said. "But remember where you came from, and remember how you got your stuff."

At his dry tone, she stopped, considered his words, and winced. "I'm sorry. That was incredibly arrogant of me. I came from money, lost it all, and am eternally grateful to now have all Nan's stuff."

"Yes, it was arrogant," he said cheerfully. "But one thing I like about you is how you always admit to your mistakes."

She hopped out of the vehicle and opened the front passenger door. "Looks like a notebook's in here."

He opened the driver's side and reached across to get it. He laughed. "You see? The smartest thieves often have the dumbest systems."

"Are you telling me that he wrote down everything he stole?" she asked in amazement.

"Looks like it," Mack said. "So we'll definitely impound this truck and everything in it. We'll move the valuables in the back of the truck into my vehicle, and I'll get Darth's towed to the police lot."

"Good. I hope he never gets it back."

The bulk of the inside of the truck, outside of fast-food packages and a travel mug, appeared to be stolen goods. She searched behind the seat; it was empty but for more garbage, as best as she could see. She opened the glove box and whistled.

Immediately Mack was at her side. He moved her out of the way and took a look. "Now that's an interesting item to find in his glove box." He removed a handkerchief from his pocket and using it, he pulled out the small handgun and said, "I wonder if he has a license for this thing."

"Even if he does, he still must have a special one to keep it in the vehicle, and isn't that only good for a couple days?"

Mack shot her a look. "Interesting you would know that."

"My husband had guns," she said. "When we moved from one house to the next, he had to get a permit to move them."

"I'm surprised he cared enough to get a permit to move them," Mack said.

"He got the permit for the weapons the cops knew

about. And then just did what he wanted with the ones the cops didn't know about."

Mack stared at her.

She shrugged. "Come on. You know how many people have guns around here."

"A lot more than I would like," he admitted. He went through the rest of the glove box while she watched but couldn't find anything else of significance. He made a few phone calls, then, with the gun in his pocket, moved everything from the truck bed to his car.

"Are you leaving now?" she asked.

"Not until the truck is picked up," he said. "We have to consider Darth McLeod might be working with someone."

"That's a good point." She looked back at her house, the door wide open. The animals were milling around them at the intruder's truck, getting in their way. "Maybe I should go back inside. I hate to think somebody else has gone in there—or is still in there," she said with a wince.

"Come on," he said. "Let's get you back inside. I'll make sure everything's good. Then you set the alarms again."

"Yes, yes, yes," she said. "It was a little distressing to realize the intruder was *inside* the house. Not much good having an alarm system—"

"—if you don't set it," he snapped.

They walked into the living room to Mugs barking in excitement. Mack shut the front door and checked every room in the house, including closets and underneath the bed in the spare bedroom. Mugs followed his every step sniffing into every corner to.

Doreen laughed, "We'll make a watchdog out of you yet."

Finally he walked back downstairs. "Looks like you're

good to go."

Just then they saw the lights of a tow truck. "Perfect timing," Mack said. "If I can get that thing moved, then maybe I can go home to bed."

"Yeah, and you'll probably sleep," Doreen said without hesitation. "I'm not sure I will."

He looked at her in understanding. "It's been a trying time for you, hasn't it?"

"Particularly since I found out something valuable was in the house," she said sadly. "It's like a loss of innocence that I hadn't really expected to feel personally."

"Finding you had expensive possessions? Or the intruder?"

"Both," she said. "Realizing my husband had taken everything I owned before, I was feeling extremely possessive about everything here. One intruder was one thing, but to know he came back after more and was pilfering stuff from my house made me really angry. But now I'm just sad. It's an ugly world we live in."

"It might be an ugly world, but you don't have to let that ugliness touch you. Remember that. This is all about you. Your perspective. How you want to live your life."

"What am I supposed to do about people like Darth?"

"You learn a lesson," he said. "Some people are thieves, and all you can do is guard against them. But you can't judge the rest of the world by the actions of a few."

She smiled, knowing he was talking about more than just intruders. More likely he was talking about her husband. "I don't judge all men the same as my husband. I'm working on forgiving him. But he didn't have to be so mean as to take everything from me."

"Right. I need to check in with my brother about that."

And, with a honk from the tow truck driver, Mack raised a hand and said, "Now remember to lock that door again and to set the alarms."

And then he was gone.

Chapter 11

Friday Morning...

SURPRISINGLY, THE NEXT morning Doreen woke up feeling rested. She rolled over and stared at the massive bed frame beside her. She wanted to laugh out loud, but, at the same time, she was also sad because she was letting go of part of her heritage. She knew it was important in order to make her future easier, but something was just so very comforting about the thought of all the nights her grandmother had slept in that bed. Not to mention all the nights her great- and great-great-grandmothers had slept in the same bed.

Doreen's past was part of that piece of furniture, and she didn't want to minimize the effect selling it had on her. She closed her eyes and sent out a moment of thanks to the women who had gone before her. They were strong; they had been through so much, and yet, they had survived. Not only survived, they had thrived. Doreen wanted to do the same. She wanted to do well for herself. She knew the challenges she faced were different from what the women in her family before her had faced, but that didn't make it any less important that Doreen also do her best at every turn.

She got up slowly to find Mugs had approved of their new mattress-on-the-floor situation. He slept at her feet. Goliath lay on the pillow beside her head. Thaddeus had retained his spot atop the closest newel post on the four-poster bed.

She'd forgotten to put newspaper under him, so she found one bird dropping. She walked into the bathroom, grabbed some toilet paper, cleaned it up, and used a spray bottle she kept close by to wipe up the last little bit.

With that done, she dressed. Casting another look at the antique bedroom set, she meandered downstairs, looking at the bright early morning sunshine outside. "One thing about being here in Kelowna," she said to herself, "the weather is divine." Unlike Vancouver, as a coastal city, which had constant rain. While living there with her soon-to-be ex-husband, Doreen had had lots of places outside where she could walk under cover. Yet it wasn't the same as seeing and feeling the sunshine. Kelowna did get winter here, but it was mild. At least she hoped it was.

She put on coffee and looked out at the yard, remembering last night's events—the intruder and the items he'd stolen from her. The outrage ...

She walked from the back door to the front door, releasing the alarms at each entryway. That done, she poured herself a cup of coffee. With the animals in tow, she stepped onto the rear veranda and down the few steps to walk along the backyard, just wearing a pair of pink flip-flops on her feet as she meandered through the garden. It was a lovely sunny morning. The backyard looked so much bigger with the rear fence down, but she still had a lot of work to do on the garden beds. And yet, she didn't want to just dive in. She needed to make a plan and to see what all was here first. By now she should know, but so much of it was overgrown. And she'd been a little busy ...

And, since today was Friday, that meant she needed to return to Mack's mother's house and do some more gardening there, which also meant more money tomorrow. She grinned at that. It hadn't been quite a week since she'd last been there, but there was no end of work to do on Millicent's lawn.

Doreen chuckled. "Hey, thanks, Mack. You're doing a good job keeping me in food," she said out loud. She also needed to pack up more of those clothes she'd set aside to take to Wendy's. Not to mention all the Goodwill boxes. She'd left it all sitting around the house to move out to her car, but she had yet to do so. And that was foolish. It was a relatively easy job, and it would relieve some of the household clutter. That would certainly make it easier when the men came to pack up the furniture.

With that thought uppermost in her mind, she checked her watch and found she had overslept. She went back inside, poured herself a second cup, then moved all the bags for Wendy's store out to her car. She had hoped to take a load to Goodwill at the same time, but it didn't look like that was possible. She'd have to make a second trip. She could do Wendy's first, as Wendy opened early.

With Mugs at her side, locking the other two animals in the house, she soon drove to Wendy's store. The proprietor of the consignment store, Second Time Round, was just unlocking the door when Doreen arrived.

"Aren't you out bright and early?" Wendy said with a smile. She motioned at the bags. "Are those for me?"

"They are, if you think you can sell them," Doreen said hopefully.

"Come on in. Let's take the bags right to the back room, and we'll start sorting."

"Sounds good."

Mugs stayed close on her heels as Doreen grabbed the bags one at a time, parking them on the sidewalk. By the time she had all the bags out, Wendy had come back out for two more, carrying them to the back room.

Inside the store, she turned on the lights and escorted Doreen to the rear section where she had large tables set up. "Do you want to wait or check in with me later?" she asked. "I do have to open the store before I begin. I can give you a call later, and you can come back and pick up what I don't think I can sell."

Doreen hesitated. "If you don't mind, I will come back when you give me a call. I have a busy morning planned."

"No problem." Wendy waved her off. "I might not get through it all today though. You brought me a lot."

Doreen chuckled. "And there's still more to come."

Wendy's eyebrows popped up. "Wow! Who knew Nan had so many clothes?"

"Right. And some of these are pretty stylish. I've kept quite a few for myself."

Wendy chuckled. "Why not? All the styles in fashion way back when are coming around. There's really nothing new in life. It's just patterns and cycles."

"I agree." Doreen gave a wave and walked with Mugs out to her car.

Back home, not giving herself a chance to slow down, she loaded up all the stuff for Goodwill and drove in the opposite direction. They were also just opening, but they had a drive-through section, and employees unloaded the stuff from her car. Doreen liked that system.

When the car was empty, she gave a bright cheerful toot of the car horn and pulled away. "Mugs, now it's time for breakfast."

He woofed beside her. He hadn't eaten either.

Back home she fed the animals, then studied the stove and wondered if she dared. She was a little lacking in the ingredients she needed—only eggs and cheese remained in her fridge—but it would be lovely to have an omelet again.

Very carefully, using the stove on a low heat setting, she proceeded to do the same thing she'd done twice before, and, lo and behold, she ended up with a beautiful-looking cheese omelet.

She sat down and chuckled. Then she took a picture of it, cut it in half, arranged the pieces a little more picturesquely on the plate, and took a second picture. She sent it to Mack. He should be happy to know she did it on her own.

While she ate her omelet, she thought about everything else she had to do that day. Finishing up her breakfast, Doreen got a call from the antiques appraiser.

"The men will be there at noon on Monday," Scott Rosten announced.

Her heart sank. "Okay." She tried not to let anything show in her voice. "I was hoping you'd come today. I'm nervous about having all these pieces here. There's been several break-ins already."

"Oh dear. I'm so sorry to hear that. I'm coming as soon as I possibly can. Maybe ask the police for some assistance?" he said. "I'll be there Monday."

She smiled as the call ended, placed the phone beside her, and it rang yet again. She recognized Mack's number. She hated to admit it, but something lightened inside her. "Good morning, Mack," she said cheerfully.

"Well, you're awfully happy for a Friday morning," he said. "Is it because you slept well?"

"Sure," she said. "Why not? And I made my first omelet, all on my own."

"I saw the photo you sent. Good for you."

"And the antiques appraiser just called and said the guys are coming Monday at noon to pack up."

"Not until Monday then," he said. "That's too bad. I was hoping, for your sake, it would be today or tomorrow."

"Me too," she said. "But it is what it is. Please tell me that you haven't let that thief out of jail again."

"No, he shouldn't be getting out anytime soon. But I have yet to talk to the judge."

"Do you *have* to talk to the judge?"

"No, that was just a phrase. I have to talk to the prosecutors. They will ask the judge to make sure McLeod doesn't get bail."

"Well, he's obviously not had a change of ways," she said. "And he remains a danger to society still."

"Sure enough," Mack said. "We have tagged and photographed the pieces he stole from you, but we'll have to keep them for a while yet. I'll let you know when you can get them back."

"Okay," she said. "As much as I'd like those pieces sold and moved into somebody else's hands for safekeeping, at least if they're in your hands, if you break them, you get to replace them."

"Ouch," he said with a laugh. After a moment's hesitation he asked, "What are you up to today?"

"I just made two trips, one to the consignment store and one to Goodwill. I'll probably go back upstairs and do some more cleaning out of my bedroom before the movers arrive.

But it's also Friday, so I'll work on your mom's garden for a couple hours."

"Right," he said. "I'll stop by tomorrow with some cash for you."

"Good," she said. "Then I can buy more omelet ingredients."

That brought a startled chuckle from him. "So what do you want to learn to make next?"

She hesitated. "What do you mean?"

"What else do you like to eat?" he asked.

"Well, what I used to like to eat, and what I like to eat now, are very different things," she said with a chuckle. "But, the fact of the matter is, it doesn't really matter what I used to like because I can't afford it."

"True enough," he said. "So, along with your change in budget, you've had a change in taste. What do you like now?"

"I used to love pasta," she said. "I had it with scampi and all kinds of mussels and fresh seafood." She warmed to the subject. "But I was wondering if pasta itself, without all the expensive toppings, would be cheap and possible to cook."

"Absolutely," he said. "Pasta is very easy to cook."

She brightened. "Are you serious? Or are you teasing me again?"

"Look it up on YouTube," he urged. "It's very easy. Just boiling water, a little bit of salt, a little bit of oil, pop in the pasta, and you've got plain cooked noodles. It's what you do with those noodles afterward that makes a difference."

Images of all the lovely pasta dishes she used to eat filled her mind. "I wasn't allowed to eat very much," she said in a low tone. "My husband used to tell me how it would make me fat, so he would cut my portions."

"Your husband was an asshole," Mack said. "Remember? We've already determined that."

"True enough," she said. "So what do you put on the pasta?"

"If you're broke," he said, "you put butter on it. If you can afford a little more, you put cheese with it. If you can afford even more, you can do a spaghetti sauce. You can also add steamed vegetables. You can do chicken and a white sauce. That's a chicken Alfredo. You can do amazing things with different ingredients. You know what? I think that's a really good place to start."

He sounded like he was warming up to the subject. She wasn't sure if she should ask or not, and then she decided there was really no point in *not* asking. She knew that he didn't mind helping her because he'd taught her how to make the omelet.

"So does that mean you're up for teaching me how to make some pasta dishes?" she asked. When she heard the hesitation on the other end of the phone, she tried to backtrack. "But that's asking too much. Just forget it."

"Not only will I remember that you asked," he said, "but I was figuring out where to start."

"You said with a pot of water, salt, oil, and pasta," she said drily. "And I'm broke. So, if we have just butter with it, that sounds pretty good to me."

"Maybe," he said. "But I'm not that broke. Although I like plain buttered noodles, I can also make sauces."

"Can you?" she asked eagerly. "Like a tomato sauce with ground beef?"

"Only if it comes with mushrooms, green peppers, and red wine."

"That sounds divine," she said excitedly. "After you

bring by my gardening payment, I have to go out shopping tomorrow. Maybe I can pick up a few of those things." But she could hear the doubt in her own voice. "I honestly don't know what to buy, how much to buy, or how expensive everything will be."

"We'll do the same as last time," he said. "I'll pick up the items and come to your house, and we'll cook."

"Okay," she said slowly. "Repeating it on Sunday too?"

"I'm not sure it'll work that way with the spaghetti sauce," he said. "Let me think about it. And stay out of trouble today, will you?"

"Of course I will. Easy peasey," she said. She hung up the phone, made a cup of tea, and said to her animal family, "I think we should get the gardening done while we can."

She poured her tea into a travel mug. With all the animals, she set the alarms and walked to Mack's mom's place. There Doreen set to work, weeding and pruning, like she'd done last week. Millicent's yard really did need more than two hours of Doreen's time a week, but, as long as she could do that much, it would keep it all mostly under control.

She had just begun work when Mack's mom appeared on the back steps and called out to her. Doreen lifted her hand. "Good morning." All her animals took off to greet Millicent too.

"You're here early," Millicent said, chuckling as she scratched Mugs's ears. Then she stroked Goliath's back as he rubbed against her. Thaddeus squawked and hopped up to the top of the porch railing, looking for attention too. "I figured, with all the excitement this week, you might not come today."

"Oh, I'm here," Doreen said with a smile, resting on her heels. "How are you?"

"I'm fine," the old woman said. "And you must be doing much better too. Everybody is just buzzing with the news about little Paul."

"Did you know him?"

"I didn't know the little boy," she said, grinning as Thaddeus nudged her hand, "but the handyman was a family guy. We all knew him."

"Well," Doreen said, "somebody asked me to look into another cold case, but I don't have any feelers." She stared at Millicent, guessing this woman was probably in her eighties, would have been in her fifties back when Johnny disappeared. "Do you remember when a Johnny Jordan went missing?" She walked toward the woman on the porch.

"*Johnny Jordan.*" Millicent sat down on her rocking chair. "I don't think I remember that case. Can you tell me any more details about it? Jog this old memory of mine?"

"He was sitting in the backyard of his brother George's place," she said, stopping short of the porch steps. "Then they never saw him again. Nobody knows what happened." Doreen shared a few of the details about George and Penny.

"Oh, poor Penny," Millicent murmured. "I remember something about that now. Everybody thought Johnny had just run away. Then two of his friends were killed soon afterward. For a while rumors were flying that maybe he'd killed them and taken off."

"Wait … what?" Doreen asked. "Why would anybody think Johnny had killed his two friends? I thought they died in a car accident not too long after Johnny's disappearance."

Millicent nodded, pointing her finger at Doreen. "They did, but they died in his car."

"According to the father of one of the young men who died," she said, "his son had bought the car off Johnny."

"Oh, I don't think so," Millicent said, shaking her head rapidly. "No, no, no. That car was his baby."

"So you *do* remember him?" Doreen asked to be certain.

"I knew George," she said. "If you had told me that Johnny was George's brother who had gone missing, I would have remembered. George used to talk all the time about how he and his kid brother were working on that car."

"But maybe George cared more about the car than his baby brother did."

Millicent gave Doreen an assessing look. "That's possible too. Often we do things, thinking the other person we're doing them with or for is enjoying it as much as we are. But maybe Johnny didn't."

"What I don't understand," Doreen said, "is, if Johnny *accidentally* hit his friends, running them off the road, why would he take off? It was an accident. Nobody was at fault, as far as I know."

"No, and I don't think the police found any evidence of that either," Millicent said, "because the car went over one of the cliffs. The fire finished the vehicle afterward. They had a hard time identifying the bodies."

Doreen straightened. "So how did they know it was Johnny's friends?"

"I don't know," Millicent said, shaking her head, watching Thaddeus strut up and down the porch railing, flapping his wings to some unnamed rhythm. "But it was definitely a sad day in town here. We didn't have the same size population back then." She lowered her tone, as if nobody was allowed to know that tidbit. "With a lot less people living here, we knew each other better. And honestly, if they said it was those two boys, I trust it was those two boys."

Doreen nodded, but, in the back of her head, she wondered. She returned to a nearby garden bed, bent down, reached for more chickweed, pulling up several strands. "Do you remember anything else from back then?"

Millicent pondered that question for a long moment.

Doreen went back to weeding, staying close to the porch so they could still talk.

"You know? I don't think so," Millicent said. "I know George was terribly devastated."

"And he passed away last year," Doreen said, "so he never did get answers to the mystery."

"No, and that's very sad too. I just wonder if it had something to do with the families of those two boys. There had definitely been talk about those boys being involved in something they shouldn't have been. Although that's almost a normal state for young men."

"In what way?" Doreen asked.

"I can't quite remember. I know there were definitely some ill feelings among the parents, as if blaming each other's child for having led their son down the wrong road."

Doreen snorted. "Now that sounds familiar too."

Millicent gave her a wise look. "Nothing's so perfect as your own child," she said with a smile. "Just ask me."

At that, Doreen laughed. "Mack is a lot of things," she said, still chuckling, "but *perfect* he is not."

"Of course he is," Millicent said with a teasing smile. "He's my son. Therefore, he's perfect. Although ..." she added, "he was too young to have worked the original missing person's case. But then he never wanted to talk to me about his investigations, even when I expressed an interest in them. Said the details would give me nightmares. Plus he thought what I knew was based purely on gossip."

"Well, that explains why he treats me the way he does

with his cold cases. But you know what? Sometimes a kernel of truth can be found in gossip. So both sets of parents would have thought their children were perfect too, right?"

"Yes," Millicent said. "They would have blamed the other child. In this case, there were three boys who hung out together."

"One disappeared, and two were killed."

"Yes. So interesting circumstances but nobody ever heard from Johnny again."

"At least I'm not tripping over any bodies this time," Doreen said with a chuckle.

"Ah, that's because you've been looking in the wrong place. Those three were forever hanging out at the old park."

"What old park? And does Mack know about it?" She pulled out her phone and quickly asked him in reference to Johnny's disappearance.

The response came back almost immediate in the affirmative. Sighing she put the phone back in her pocket and refocused on the conversation.

"Of course he does. I'm talking about the one by the Central City area. It was pretty rough down there. A lot of junkies hung out in that park. If Johnny was killed anywhere, I'd have said that was the most likely spot," Millicent said. "There used to be lots of ravines on that edge of town. I always wondered if Johnny didn't go down there, and somebody maybe pulled the bank over on top of him."

Doreen winced at that. "That doesn't sound good. By the way," she said, straightening up, "was it only the three boys who hung out together?"

"Those three boys were really tight. There was another guy, and I think a couple girls. That one girlfriend was a little dodgy."

"If you're talking about Susan, she died a year ago from breast cancer," Doreen said. "So it'll be hard to get answers from her."

"Oh, not her. Another girl hung around with them a lot. Although she went from one boy to the next. It seemed like she was just moving through the four of them."

"Most likely all the relationships shifted constantly. Males and females alike, particularly at that age," Doreen said. "Do you know who that fourth boy was?"

"I don't remember. … I mean, after all, when one goes missing and two die, there's not really a gang left. So the fourth guy must have hung out with a new group." Millicent spoke once again in that wise tone.

"True enough," Doreen said. "Do you remember what his name was though?"

"Alan," she said suddenly. "I think. Ask Penny. She'll know."

"I can do that," Doreen said. "I wonder what happened to him."

"If he were smart, he moved away. It seemed like that whole gang had a black mark against them," she said. "And that would be a tough way to live in this town."

"But it wasn't really a black mark, right? They weren't charged with anything serious, were they?"

"No idea," Millicent said. "Maybe ask Mack. He might know."

"But, as you also know," she said gently, "your son won't tell me much."

"Not in so many words, but he could certainly let you know little bits and pieces, and, if those boys were charged with anything, that's public record. Alan was his first name. I can't remember his last name. I want to say Hornby, but my old memory box isn't quite what it was."

Doreen chuckled. "I think your memory is just fine." She kept working and talking to Millicent, losing track of time. Finally she sat back on her heels once more and said, "I think I'm done for this week."

"Good," Millicent said, standing up, giving each of the animals a goodbye cuddle. "Then I'm going in and taking a nap."

"That's a good idea," Doreen said. "And, if you don't mind, I'm heading home."

"Perfect. It's nice to see you like this." Then she stopped. "Oh my," she said. "I meant to give you some zucchini bread. Hang on." She went inside and came back a moment later with what looked like one-half of a loaf of zucchini bread, sliced and wrapped up. She handed it to Doreen, who met her on the porch, and said, "Thank you so much for coming, dear."

With a finger wave, Doreen and the animals started back. As soon as she was out of sight, she had her phone out, looking up Alan Hornby. It turned out the Hornby family used to live in the same cul-de-sac where Penny lived. Doreen frowned and said aloud, "How about we walk the long way around, guys?"

And, with that, she turned in the direction of Penny's house, fully intending to see where the Hornby house was. Maybe Penny had a few more answers to help tie up some of this mystery because, if four men were originally involved, Doreen needed to hear about the last guy still living. To learn that two girls and another guy were hanging around the three boys, she had a lot more questions she needed to ask. And one of the biggest was, who identified the two boys who died in the vehicle?

Chapter 12

Friday Afternoon …

A S DOREEN WALKED toward Penny's house, she knew a phone call would be faster, yet she found she preferred to do hands-on sleuthing. Not to mention the animals loved the fieldwork.

She chuckled out loud. "Hey, Mugs, listen to me. *Sleuthing. Fieldwork.* Doesn't that sound all professional?"

For a fleeting moment she wondered if she could get a private eye license, but that would mean sleuthing full-time. Would she still enjoy it like now? This was fun. This was intriguing. This kept her mind occupied and let her dwell on somebody else's troubles. She figured, by the time she got a private eye license, it would become drudgery and *work*. She'd be stuck in people's divorces, a thought to make her cringe. And the police certainly weren't hiring any private eyes. As a matter of fact, they probably hated them. Of course she was basing all this on the TV shows she watched occasionally.

She nudged her trio along. They were more into meandering than walking today. Thaddeus, well, he seemed to be singing.

As they neared Penny's house, Doreen stopped and reoriented herself, looking for the Hornby house. It was across the cul-de-sac at the corner. So the kids really had lived close together. As she walked up to Penny's door, Penny opened it and stepped out.

"I could hope," she said, "that you have good news."

Doreen shook her head. "No, just more questions."

Penny leaned against the doorjamb, crossing her arms over her chest. "Well, let them fly. What do you want to know?"

"Alan Hornby," Doreen said.

Penny glared across the cul-de-sac. "Yes, another one of Johnny's friends. Five or six of them used to hang around in a group. Another very unpleasant man."

"I think we only discussed the three guys," Doreen said, worrying slightly at the number that continued to grow.

"Alan and his family lived over there," Penny said, motioning across the way. "They used to be a family. Then his father lived alone in the house. Then Alan returned—not even sure where he went to begin with—and now his father is in the retirement home." She turned to look at the other houses. "It's hard to keep track of everyone."

"What happened to Alan and his mother?"

"A divorce," Penny said simply. "Let's clarify that. An ugly divorce." She gave a half smile.

Doreen winced. "I understand about those." Penny's eyes lit with interest, but Doreen quickly moved past the topic. "Did you see much of Alan after Johnny went missing?"

Penny frowned. "You know what? I'm not sure. It was so long ago. But I should remember, shouldn't I? It's probably important."

"Anything to do with anybody back then," Doreen said, "is important. It could be the slightest thing that helps this case. Somebody lying even a little bit can unravel a whole pile of new information."

"I hear you. It's just really hard to go back to that time and to remember the details." Penny shook her head. "You know? I remember Alan's mother coming over in tears, telling me that she was so sorry. At the time I didn't think much of it because everybody was telling me that they might have seen Johnny or that he'd come home soon, how he was just a wayward boy and not to worry."

"I know," Doreen said. "Everybody gives you their condolences, but it's only afterward you wonder if they really meant it or not."

"So you do know what I mean," Penny said. "I hope you didn't lose somebody too."

Doreen shook her head. "No, thankfully not. But I became very distrustful and leery of people's behavior for a while."

"And Alan's mom was very emotional. It seemed over-the-top. I wasn't sure what was going on," she said. "And because I didn't have any answers, I was just trying to move people along."

"Where was this conversation?"

"It was here," Penny said. "I was talking to the pastor at the front door. He'd come to talk to me too. And then, after he left, Alan's mother came over."

"Do you think she misunderstood? Maybe if she saw you talking to the pastor, she thought Johnny was dead?"

Penny rolled her eyes. "Honestly, with her, it's hard to say. She was not the smartest book on the shelf."

Doreen almost chuckled at that. But it was totally inappropriate to laugh, especially when they were talking about a missing person. She smiled and nodded instead. "Another question. … Who identified Johnny's friends' bodies?"

"George and one of the boys' fathers did," she said. "The other father wasn't capable of doing the job. And he had asked George to see if it was his son. The two men went in separately, but you have to understand the remains were in bad shape."

Doreen didn't push any further. "It was nice of George to do that."

"Honestly, I think he was secretly wondering if it was Johnny," Penny said. "And it would be so like George to step in and do something like that. Just to make sure."

"Of course. But it wasn't Johnny though, right?"

Penny shook her head. "No, it definitely wasn't. Unfortunately, no." Then she caught herself. "Oh, that sounds terrible. I didn't mean it that way. But, at least, if it had been Johnny, George would have known what had happened to him. He would have had a body. He would have had something to grieve over, and he would have had answers to the big questions."

"I think that's always the worst, isn't it?" Doreen said slowly. "Always wondering what happened and why."

"How true," Penny said. "George suffered terribly without the closure he needed so badly."

Doreen backed away. "That's the only thing on my mind."

"Is that all?" Penny asked. "You could have phoned."

Doreen nodded. "But I love to walk, and it's good for the animals." She looked around but saw no sign of Goliath. "The trouble is, Goliath has a mind of his own."

"You should get a leash for him," Penny said. "I see

more and more people walking their cats."

"I think Goliath would be walking me."

Penny chuckled. "Well, he is a cat." As if that explained everything.

"That would be an explanation for everything to do with Goliath." With Thaddeus snoozing gently on her shoulder, tucked up in the crook of her neck, Doreen waved goodbye and headed back down to the sidewalk. "Goliath," she called out. "Goliath." But she got no answer. Heard no meow. She stopped, turned around, and looked. "Goliath, come on." She was getting a little worried. "Where are you?"

Just then he popped his head out of a huge dahlia bush in the front yard.

"Oh, thank heavens," Penny said. "I was afraid you'd lost him."

"Yeah," Doreen said. "I couldn't imagine." She called him, but Goliath wouldn't come toward her. "Come on, buddy. Come on."

But the cat was digging. Mugs barked and chased Goliath out of the bush. And then Mugs started to dig.

"Uh-oh," Doreen said a sinking feeling in her stomach.

"Did he find something there?" Penny asked, a note of excitement entering her voice.

"I don't know. With these animals, you can never really tell. I swear to God, they think they're some kind of amateur sleuths." She unconsciously echoed what she had said about herself earlier.

She yanked on Mugs's leash, but he wasn't having any of it. Instead the basset hound leaned in his shoulders and put all his weight behind him to stop Doreen's efforts in dragging him back. Not wanting to hurt him, she walked closer and grabbed his harness, trying to lift him. He growled, and finally she let him go.

"What's gotten into you?" But inside she knew it was something important, and he wouldn't let her stop him from finding out whatever this was. When she looked up, Penny came toward her with a shovel. Doreen laughed. "It's almost like you think my dog's found something."

"I've heard stories about these animals of yours," she said.

Just then Thaddeus, waking up from his nap, flew off her shoulder, landing on the big dahlia bushes. The stalks were thick, promising to be big with huge blooms.

"These are beautiful bushes," Doreen said.

Penny nodded. "Dinner plate Dahlias. They are huge blooms. I moved some of the same plants from the back garden, where Johnny used to sit. They multiplied so much that I needed to divide them up."

"Oh, really?" Doreen looked at her, wondering how Mugs knew. "Do you mind if I grab that shovel then?"

A pall settled over the two women as Doreen deliberately stepped in front of Mugs to push him away. And then, switching out the zucchini bread with the shovel, she gently wiggled the dirt in and around the base of the dahlias. When she thought she heard a metallic clink, she went down on her hands and knees, using her hands to dig deeper into the soil. When her fingers closed around something small, she pulled it up, brushed off the dirt, and revealed a medallion. She held it up, and the color drained from Penny's face. "Do you know what it is?"

"It's a medallion Johnny got from their father," she said in a shocked whisper, reaching out to touch the object. "Johnny would never have left it behind."

"Meaning that, if he ran away or walked away from you

guys," she corrected quietly, "he would have taken it with him?"

"I mean, he *always* wore it. It was *always* around his neck."

"So then how did it get here?"

"It must have happened when I divided up the bulbs and transplanted this group here."

"But I want to know how it came off his neck." Doreen had a theory, but she didn't know if she should say it out loud. When Penny stared at her, dread in her eyes, Doreen nodded. "It likely came off in a struggle." She picked up the chain that hung from the medallion. She held it so Penny could see it. "It's broken."

Chapter 13

Friday Midafternoon ...

WITH THE MEDALLION and the chain wrapped up in newspaper from Penny's recycle bin and in a plastic ziplock bag, and with her zucchini bread, Doreen walked back home. Lost in her thoughts, when her phone buzzed in her pocket, it startled her. She pulled it out to see it was Mack. "Hey," she said.

"What's wrong?" he asked.

"I don't know if something is wrong or not," she said, "but it's definitely something that makes me think."

"Explain," he said, as if unsure what she was saying.

"I went to Penny's to ask a few more questions, but, instead of getting answers, we found more questions. Mugs and Goliath were both digging in her dahlia bushes. Dahlia bushes she had moved from the garden in the backyard years ago because the tubers had multiplied and became these massive plants."

"Stop," he said. "I don't need a gardening lesson. I need an explanation."

She sighed and checked that the road was empty before she crossed it, so she could hook back onto the path along the creek. "Well, when I dug around the plants, we found a medallion on a broken chain. Apparently Johnny's, and he never went anywhere without it around his neck. I think he died the same evening he went missing."

Silence followed before Mack finally spoke. "Well, we don't know that for sure," he said. "Because you didn't find a body … right?" His tone sharpened.

"Nope, no body—at least not yet," she said. "Just remnants of the life of a person who's gone missing."

"I guess I can see how that would be upsetting, but that doesn't mean Johnny is dead."

"No," she said, "but it doesn't mean he's alive either. However … your mother told me that Johnny and his friends used to hang out in the Central City park, among the drug sellers and buyers. At first I thought that would be a viable lead, but, now, finding this medallion at his home, I don't think so anymore."

Mack gave a huge sigh, which carried clearly over the phone. "Have you got the medallion with you?"

"Yes," she said. "I figured he must have been involved in a struggle and lost it."

"That would indicate maybe somebody saw him in the backyard. And yet, you say George and Penny didn't see what happened to him."

"Apparently," she said. "And, yes, Johnny was in the backyard, but Penny was cooking dinner and was busy. She didn't see him leave."

"Right," Mack said. "So good timing on her part that she saw him when she did. That narrows down the timing somewhat."

"Which hasn't helped yet."

"I'll take a look at it when you get home," he said.

"I'm almost there. I'm walking along the creek, coming down the back again."

"I wish you wouldn't walk there alone," he said with an unhappy sigh.

"What difference does it make?" she asked. "It's still sunny out. Besides, I am not alone. I've got my dog and Thaddeus on my shoulder and Goliath walking beside us, quite put out that I wouldn't allow him to keep digging."

"Of course Goliath found it."

"Well, he did." She chuckled. "Then Mugs jumped him in the bush, chasing him away, and the dog started to dig. Then I took over." She shrugged. "I'm at my little bridge now." She walked across and headed to her house.

"Is the alarm still on?"

"I'll find out in a second," she said.

"I'm glad your antiques guy is coming soon," he said quietly. "I won't stop worrying until those pieces are gone."

"Me too," she said. "At least this case gives me something else to focus on."

"That's nice," he said. "I sure wish it wasn't another murder you're trying to sort out."

"I didn't say it was a murder," she objected. "I just said we found a medallion and its chain, and Johnny was adamant about keeping it close. It was from his father, who was dead."

"Ah," Mack said.

She walked up and hit the alarm code to undo the security and let herself in. Immediately she could feel herself settling, almost like a sigh.

Chapter 14

Friday Late Afternoon ...

ONCE INSIDE THE house, Doreen reset the alarms, put a tea bag in a cup, and put water on to boil in the electric teakettle. She still had Mack on the phone. "I'm inside, safe and sound. The alarm was set, and I've reset it."

"Good. You take care."

"Yeah, I will," she said. "When are you coming for the medallion?"

"I'm heading into the office right now." His voice was distracted. "Depends on how late it is when I'm done."

"Well, it's not late right now," she said, "although, with that cloudy sky moving in now, it seems like it is."

"If I'm only about an hour longer at work, I'll swing by afterward and grab it." He hung up without saying goodbye.

She wasn't sure what was on his docket that he would go by the office at this hour, but he juggled a lot of cases.

As she let her tea steep, she carefully laid the medallion on the kitchen table and studied it. Thaddeus immediately walked over for a closer look. Although it was dirty, the motif on the metal was clearly visible. She thought about a young man who had hung on to probably the only possession he had left of his father's, and she thought about what circumstances it would take for Johnny to let that memento go. She kept coming back to the fact that Johnny wouldn't have given up the medallion willingly. So potentially an argument at the bench where he'd been sitting.

"It's too darn bad," she said to Mugs. She got up, seeing all the animals sitting here, staring at her. "Okay, okay. I see you guys haven't been fed yet."

She puttered around the kitchen getting dinner for the three of them. It was past time for her to get some food too. But the fridge hadn't been restocked, and she desperately needed to go shopping yet again.

"How come shopping consumes so much of my time?" she asked. "It should be fast and easy." She knew those newfangled delivery services were available, where she could order online to get the groceries she wanted. She wasn't quite ready for that yet. Nor could she justify the delivery fee.

With the animals happily munching away, she made herself a simple sandwich, with raw veggies on the side, and sat at the kitchen table to eat. Her gaze kept returning to the medallion. And her mind kept revisiting where it had been found, then took her to the patch of bare ground under the original site for the bench.

Somebody could have buried the body on Penny's property, but anyone other than George and Penny digging up the yard would have been seen and considered suspicious, so that narrowed it down to Johnny's family. Penny wasn't strong enough to manhandle a body, although she might have helped George.

But then why would George keep up the pretenses of looking for his younger brother? He'd already know where his younger brother was. He could have just turned his back on the whole farce and ignored it. Although, if he'd killed his brother, he'd have tried to throw off suspicion by acting as the grieving brother.

Doreen knew in her heart that Johnny was probably dead, and she figured Penny knew it too.

When Doreen was done eating, she washed her few dirty dishes, then glanced around the house, ensuring everything was still where it belonged. After the same intruder had gotten inside her house twice—maybe that third time too?—she felt more than a little paranoid.

As she prepared to go upstairs and to start in on Nan's closet again, Mack pulled up. Mugs barked at the door but his tail wagged happily. She walked to the front door, undid the security, and held up the ziplock baggie for him.

He looked at it and frowned.

"It's a nice piece," she said. "Do you think it's real gold?"

He nodded. "Not only is it likely real gold, that could be a gem in the center. But I can't be sure."

"Which means, if somebody saw it they would have most likely stolen it."

"Yes." His frown deepened.

"Maybe take it and see if any bloodstains are on it?" she asked hopefully.

He just raised his eyebrows.

She shrugged. "You don't have anything else to go on. You might as well take a look at this. It was his possession. It was found at the place where he was last seen. Maybe he was injured there. There could be blood."

"I'll take it back to the office, but it was his, so his skin cells would have transferred to his medallion. So that's to be expected." He pocketed the bagged-up item and stepped back, looking around the living room. "I'll be glad when these expensive antiques are gone."

"Hopefully on Monday," she said with a nervous laugh. "Now it's like sleeping in a mausoleum. I'm so worried about anything getting damaged that I don't sit on it, and I don't use it. I just walk around and give each piece a wide berth."

"Sounds like the right thing to do." He turned and walked down the porch steps.

She watched him go, hating that sense of loss she often felt when he left.

He gave her a wave as he got into his vehicle, backed out of her driveway, and drove around the cul-de-sac, disappearing from sight.

With a heavy sigh she stepped back inside.

Her grandmother called just then. "How is Doreen?" Nan asked. "And how's that lovely Mack?"

"I'm sure Mack is fine," Doreen said, desperate to keep her voice neutral. "And I'm tired, but I'm good. I took the long way around, walking back from your place."

"My place?"

"Sorry, I'm more tired than I thought," she said with a heavy sigh. "I was over at Mack's mother's, doing the gardening, then ended up at Penny's."

"Oh," she said. "I was hoping to invite you for dinner."

"I just had a sandwich and veggies," Doreen said in frustration. She'd have loved to have had dinner with Nan.

"Well, how about cake then?"

"I can always go for some cake and a cup of tea. Do you have a reason for calling?"

"Do I need a reason?" Nan asked craftily.

"No. But something else seemed to be in your tone," Doreen said. "As if to say, you found out something."

"Of course I did," Nan said firmly. "Do you have any

idea how much information is tied up in all the crazy heads here?"

"Which is one of the reasons why I asked you to talk to the residents," Doreen responded in a dry tone.

"It is still fairly early," Nan said. "Why don't you come on down? Maybe, by the time you get here, you'll be hungry again."

Doreen chuckled. "I did work hard earlier today, so sure. Why not?" She gave in easily. "Hopefully you'll have some good information to give me."

With the animals fed, they all wanted to lie down and sleep. She was of two minds as to whether she should take them, but it felt odd to go to Nan's without them.

Forcing them out again, and carrying Thaddeus, she walked slowly toward her grandmother's place. When she got there, she found the remaining stepping stones were still in a row, leading from the sidewalk to Nan's patio. She crossed over them, in case the gardener came out and told her off again.

Nan was watching her. She chuckled with delight when she saw the whole crew cross the lawn.

Mugs raced toward Nan to give her a bark of welcome and a kiss. Nan didn't seem to mind the slobbery wet kisses Mugs delivered on a regular basis. Goliath, on the other hand, appeared to be jealous and hopped up into Nan's lap and completely overwhelmed the space. Thaddeus was more concerned with the cake on the table. Although he had just eaten, he was working away on a corner of the treat.

"I do love these animals," Nan said. "They truly are a delight."

"They are, indeed," Doreen said. She gave Nan a hug and sat down to see a pot of tea steeping.

"And I like having you close," Nan said with a big smile. She motioned at the teapot. "By the time I make it, you're almost here."

"Perfectly steeped," Doreen said. "It's a bit longer than that, but who's counting minutes?"

"Exactly." Nan leaned forward. "So what else have you found out?"

"You mean, what else have *you* found out? Right?" Doreen asked.

"Not a whole lot," Nan said. "But you went to see Penny, and you also talked to Mack's mom, so both of those ladies must have known something."

"Do you know anything about Alan Hornby?"

"No," Nan said, frowning. "He was another one of those young men in Johnny's friend group, right?"

"Yes, he was," Doreen said. "More of a fringe member though."

"*Hmm.*"

"Also found out that George helped identify the two boys killed in the car accident."

"Well, that's interesting," Nan said. "I wonder why he did that."

"I think to make sure it wasn't Johnny," Doreen said. "It was Johnny's car the boys were driving when they died."

"Is there any reason why George would misidentify the victims?" Nan pursed her lips and stared across the green lawn.

To Doreen it looked like Nan stared across the years. "I wondered that myself," Doreen said. "But there wouldn't be any reason to do so. He'd have to be hiding his own actions or trying to protect somebody else."

"Most of us would do a lot to protect those we love,"

Nan said with a beaming smile.

"True enough," Doreen said. "But that still doesn't explain why George would in this case. The boys were friends of his brother's. I don't imagine there was any great loyalty or attachment on George's part."

"But, if George wanted his brother out of his life, then that's a good way to do it," Nan said with surprising insight.

Doreen chuckled. "Sure. At least then George would know Johnny was gone, but nobody else would. However, according to Penny, George spent his life and a lot of money trying to track down his brother. So I can't imagine George would have put that much effort into keeping up the pretense. Not after the first few years."

"No," Nan said. "But then you never know."

A tiny birdlike voice called out to Nan from the inside of her apartment. "Nan. Nan."

Nan's face turned thunderous. She lowered her voice and said, "Don't answer."

Doreen raised an eyebrow and studied her grandmother's face. "Why not?" she asked in a whisper.

"She's always bugging me," Nan said. "Maisie is a pest."

"Maybe Maisie is lonely," Doreen corrected.

"*Humph.*" Nan snorted as she settled back.

"Oh, there you are." A tiny woman with a shock of lavender hair stepped through Nan's living room onto the patio. She turned her bright face toward Doreen. "You must be the granddaughter."

"Yes," Doreen said with a smile. "I'm Doreen."

Maisie caught sight of Thaddeus eating the bread. "Oh my." Her smile fell away. "Isn't that dirty?"

"Isn't what dirty?" Nan snapped. She stroked Thaddeus's back and shoulders defensively. "Thaddeus is hungry.

Why should you care?"

Doreen was quite perturbed at her grandmother's manner. She'd never seen her like this.

"That may be," Maisie said with a sniff, "but that bird is walking all over your table."

"Well, honestly, Goliath would too," Doreen said with a laugh. "If we let him, that is."

Maisie looked horrified at the idea.

"I guess you don't have any pets?"

Maisie shook her head. "No. I could never handle the hair or the dirtiness. Animals carry disease, you know," she said in a conversational tone, as if thinking—and heaven only knew where she got that thought from—that the two women listening to her would share her point of view. "Animals are terrible that way."

Nan rolled her eyes toward Doreen, who was hard-pressed to keep the smile off her face. "Maisie, what did you want?"

For a moment Maisie looked confused.

Nan pointed back at her living room. "There's a reason I didn't answer the door, dear. I have company."

Maisie gave her a finger pointing. "Hardly. Doreen is family. That's not the same thing at all."

Watching the play between the two women was fascinating. It gave Doreen a different insight into her grandmother's life here. Doreen didn't understand the relationship between the two women, but it looked obvious it wasn't all that easy or smooth.

"I'm pretty sure Joe is looking for you," Nan said.

"Oh, that's all right," Maisie said blithely. "He's in my room, resting." She batted her eyes at Nan. "He does need his rest afterward, doesn't he?" And then, with a sweet smile and a chuckle, she disappeared.

Doreen gave a horrified gasp. "Did she mean what I think she meant?"

Nan nodded. "The two of them are carrying on like they're eighteen," she said. "I don't mind in the least, but it would be nice if they kept it to themselves. But Maisie is one of those shrieking partners."

"Oh, dear," Doreen said, struggling to stifle the laughter threatening to pour outward. "Most people like that are attention-getters."

Nan nodded. "I couldn't have said it better."

"So is it just Maisie who pisses you off?"

Nan gave an irritable shrug of her shoulders. "Not really," she said, "but Joe used to be my friend." The emphasis was on the last word.

Fascinated, Doreen studied Nan's face. "Did Joe ditch you for Maisie?" she asked gently.

Nan shrugged. "No, I ditched him first. But he sure didn't take long to pick up with Maisie."

"I rather imagine it has a lot to do with the perception of time," Doreen said. "When you're here, I think mortality is a little more evident. Maybe you guys don't wait the usual length of time that goes along with a breakup."

"Some men never wait," Nan said with a sniff. "And Joe is one of them."

"That's good to know," Doreen said. "At least now you won't make the mistake of going out with him again."

"Not too many men in here are any good anymore," Nan said. "I do keep the blue pills in my drawer. But it's kind of depressing when you have to give them to the men yourself."

Doreen sat back, choking on the words threatening to

come out.

"Don't look so shocked, my dear," Nan said drily. "You'd be a lot better off if you and Mack would get over the courtship part of your relationship too. A good old romp in bed would suit you two just fine."

Doreen laughed out loud. "Thanks for the advice, Nan," she said cheerfully. "Not that I'm looking for any."

"Of course you aren't," Nan said. "Which is why it's so much easier to give it to you. If you were to ask my advice, that'd be a pain in the arse. But the fact that you're not means I get to comment as I see fit." Then she broke into bright laughter.

There wasn't a lot Doreen could say to that. At least Nan was laughing again. "Did Joe or Maisie know any of the kids in the gang back then?"

"I don't know why they would," she said with a curl of her lip. "They're both newcomers."

"What does *that* mean?" Doreen asked with a laugh. "Have they only been here twenty years?"

Nan straightened her back and looked at her granddaughter. "I hear the laughter in your voice, but, until you've lived in Kelowna as long as I have, you don't understand how the newcomers are so very different from all of us oldies."

"Well, if they are newcomers after twenty years," Doreen said, "I must be in the toddler category."

"You're my family," Nan said. "And that changes things entirely."

"I'm sure Joe and Maisie have family too," she said gently.

"Whatever," Nan said. Then she giggled. "But I did take fifty bucks off Maisie earlier."

"You what?" Doreen was afraid to ask.

"I bet her about Joe and a blue pill."

"Oh, dear. Nan, I really don't want to hear about this."

"It's all right, but that's why Maisie came over. She was trying to tell me, in her way, that he didn't need the blue pill."

"So how did you earn fifty bucks off her?"

"I bet he wouldn't need it," Nan said, "because I had given him the blue pill earlier."

"You gave him a blue pill so he could have sex with Maisie?" Doreen asked in shock. "And then you bet Maisie he wouldn't need one when she went to bed with him?"

"Now you got it," Nan said.

"I think that's cheating, Nan." But a part of her wanted to giggle out loud.

"All is fair in love and war," Nan said complacently.

Chapter 15

Friday Later Afternoon …

"OKAY, DEFINITELY TIME for a change of conversation. Do you know anybody here who is an oldie?" Doreen asked with a smile. "If so, maybe you could ask them about Johnny."

"I have," Nan said. "But nobody appears to know anything."

"Well, it was a faint hope. But you did call me for something, didn't you?"

Nan looked at her in surprise, and then her face lit up. "Oh my, I completely forgot." She hopped up, walked into her living quarters, and came back out. "I asked Richie because I know he's been here since Kelowna was basically established," she said. "Lovely man."

Doreen desperately wanted to ask if he needed blue pills but needed to keep the conversation straight and not let her grandmother go sideways.

"He did say not all was well within the group."

"How does he know?"

"The girl in question who died a year ago was his niece. His great-niece. And he said she had a lot of trouble with the gang."

"Gang, meaning all of them?"

"Yes. Apparently she was a little too free and easy with her affections," Nan said. "And her great-uncle didn't like that one bit. But, when he questioned her about it, she said she stopped going out with Johnny because she found someone else."

"Any idea who that was?" Doreen asked, sinking back into her chair. "I don't know that it matters at this stage, but it would be interesting to know who."

"I'm not sure," Nan said. "But, if anybody could figure it out, it would be you."

"What's Richie's last name?"

"Smithson," Nan said. "He is a lovely chap."

"How old is he?"

"I think he's eighty-two, maybe eighty-three," Nan said. "It doesn't really matter though. His mind is as sharp as anything."

"Good," Doreen said. "Maybe you could ask him some questions about the accident."

Nan reached across the little bistro table, pulled up her phone, and sent a text.

"Did you just text him?"

Nan lifted her face to study her granddaughter. "Are you having some memory problems, dear? You just asked me to question him about the accident."

Oh, dear. Another rabbit-hole moment. Doreen shook her head. "No, I was wondering if you were though because—just moments ago—you told me nobody here knew anything."

"Sure, but that's not Richie. Richie is different," she said with a wave of her hand. "He's not anybody. He's special."

And again the questions were itching to flow from her lips, but she dared not. Then she couldn't help herself. "Special in what way?" she asked.

"Not that way," Nan said shortly. "No better way to ruin a friendship than having sex, my dear." She lifted her head again from her phone, holding it, as if waiting for Richie to get back to her immediately. "You should remember that with Mack."

Doreen stopped and stared. "You're the one who just told me that Mack and I would do well for having a romp together." She snorted. "How does it figure that now you are telling me not to?"

"Oh, my dear, I'm not telling you *not* to," she said. "Absolutely go and do it. But, if it's not for the right reasons, you'll find you're not friends at the end of it."

"Right," Doreen said, shaking her head. "Did you hear back from Richie yet?"

"No, not yet," Nan said, waving her phone. "You'd have heard a ring, dear. Maybe you should go home and rest. You do seem to be a little off today."

Doreen snapped her lips closed. *Somebody* was off, all right. But she didn't know if Nan was taking her down that weird and wonderful rabbit hole again or if she was just playing with her. Sometimes Doreen couldn't really tell.

Just then Nan's phone warbled in her hand. "Richie says the two men who died were in Johnny's car."

"But we know that," Doreen said patiently.

"So then why did you ask?" Nan asked in irritation.

"Nan …"

Her grandmother sighed and settled back. "I do appear to be a little irritable today."

"I'm so sorry," Doreen said. "Maybe I'll go home now."

"No, no, no, no," Nan said with a smile, patting Doreen's hand. "I'm the one who's sorry. I guess Maisie upset me more than I expected."

"I'm sorry for that too." Obviously her grandmother felt jilted that her lover had quickly found someone else. "Maybe Richie will have some other information tomorrow." Doreen pushed back her chair and stood.

Nan's phone warbled again. "Ritchie says the accident was caused by another vehicle."

Doreen's butt thumped back down on the chair.

"Like a hit-and-run?"

Nan was still reading. "Something like that. Car went over a cliff, and the cops never found the other vehicle."

"Then how would they know somebody ran them off the road?"

"There was a witness," Nan said, looking at her in surprise. "Didn't I tell you that?"

Doreen pinched the bridge of her nose. "No, you didn't tell me that. Who was the witness?"

"The girlfriend of course."

"So she wasn't in the boys' car, but she saw another car run them off the road?"

Nan nodded. "That's what Richie says. She was adamant another vehicle was involved."

"Why would she be so adamant about it?"

Nan shrugged. "Who knows? It happened at that really bad corner on the outskirts of town. Big hairpin turn up in the Black Mountain area."

"Well then, maybe a vehicle didn't run them off the road," Doreen said, "if it's such a bad corner."

"Which is also why the police didn't necessarily believe her."

"Of course they didn't," Doreen said. "Because it sounds like she was making it up. And what was she doing there at that time? Because that makes even less sense."

"Apparently she was driving behind the guys," Nan said. "And she'd tried to get help for them, but the vehicle was already on fire."

"So she called the police and told them that another vehicle had run them off the road, correct?" Doreen wanted to make sure she understood what supposedly went on.

"Yes, exactly. And now she's dead, so we can't ask her anything."

Doreen felt like she was going in circles. Sometimes Nan's mind seemed to be even more circuitous than usual. "Unless ..." She leaned in and studied Nan's face. "Unless the girlfriend wasn't alone in the car."

Nan immediately picked up her phone and sent another text. They waited for a long moment; then Richie sent back an answer. "No, she wasn't alone."

Doreen groaned; getting information was like pulling teeth here. "Who was in the car with her?"

"According to Richie, Alan Hornby."

Chapter 16

Friday Evening …

As Doreen and her animals strolled home, she pondered through the muddle of information from Nan. Doreen didn't know if Nan had been really tired today or just upset because of Maisie. But, either way, Nan's mind had been definitely irrational. Was Nan getting Alzheimer's? How she could possibly ask her grandmother to go to the doctor to get some testing done she didn't know, because she would be more than a little horrified and insulted to hear about Doreen's train of thought.

But really, with all this muddling of conversations, it was harder to sort out what was true and what was false. Maisie had obviously hurt Nan with the affair with Joe. At least that was Doreen's take on it. Still, her grandmother would get over it, like she'd gotten over many other breakups in her life. Maybe Nan was more upset that Joe had chosen Maisie as Nan's replacement and not somebody else. It was amazing how many times people were okay with a lover going off and dallying with somebody else, as long as the previous lover approved of the someone else.

Doreen wandered home, contemplating this Hornby

character. When she got to her house, she found an unfamiliar vehicle parked out front. She walked around the back of the vehicle and took a quick photo of the license plate. As she walked up to the front door to see where he might be sitting or waiting for her, she found nobody there. She walked around to the backyard with Mugs sniffing heavily at her feet and found a late-middle-aged man sitting on her back steps.

As she approached, he hopped up and gave her a big wide smile. "Hi," he said.

"Hi," she cautiously said in response. "What can I do for you?"

"For one, you can stop poking into things that don't have anything to do with you."

"Such as?" Her head tilted as she studied him. He had to be about fifty years old, maybe a little older.

"I'm Hornby, Alan Hornby," he said, "and you keep asking questions about me."

"Who would have told you that?"

"You gotta understand the old folks' home," he said. "Richie told my aunt Velma that you were asking questions."

"I am," she said, "because nobody has seen Johnny since he disappeared."

"What does that got to do with me?" he asked. "And Johnny disappeared decades ago."

"Maybe nothing," Doreen said. "I was trying to cross the *T*s and dot the *I*s. Apparently you were in the car with Susan when you saw another vehicle swipe the two guys driving Johnny's car. Is that correct?"

He frowned, his head also tilting to the side as he studied her. "What business is it of yours? Where did you hear that?"

"I heard it," she said, "while I was visiting Nan. I think it came from Richie because that was his great-niece who was in the vehicle with you."

Hornby glared. "Man, I tell you. Those old folks, if they don't have something to gossip about, they make up something to gossip about," he said.

"Isn't that the truth?" she said. "But, so far, you haven't answered the question."

"You're right there," he said, "because, to be truthful, I can't remember anymore." He tapped his head. "It was a long time ago."

"You don't remember whether you saw two good friends die in a fiery crash of a stolen vehicle right in front of you? Talk about suspicious." Not that she had proof the vehicle had been stolen, but there was also no proof Johnny had sold it either.

She studied Hornby, looking for any signs of deceit. The trouble was, he had that big beaming smile that said he knew she had no proof and that, with the girl dead, nobody knew anything, so he could say whatever the hell he wanted.

"Nope, my memory is not very good anymore," he said. "Too much booze and drugs."

That was just possible enough for her to consider it. "It's a little hard to believe you don't remember *any* of it," she said.

"I remember Johnny's disappearance," Hornby said, "mostly because it was on all our minds for such a long time. We had absolutely no way of knowing what happened to him. And we all wanted to know."

"Did you though?" she asked. "Did you really?"

He glared at her. "What are you suggesting?"

"I don't know what I'm suggesting," she said honestly.

"But think about it. Johnny disappears. You have two good friends die in a fiery crash in front of you in Johnny's car. Followed by ... by what? Who was driving the vehicle that ran them off the road?"

"The police never found out," he said. "And I don't understand what difference it makes all these years later. They're still dead."

"Maybe it doesn't make any difference. Maybe it was an accident. Then again, maybe it wasn't," she said. "But it makes a difference since Penny still has no idea what happened to her brother-in-law."

The humor drained from his face. Hornby nodded. "I know George was completely cracked up about it. George and Johnny were close."

"They were close," she said, "according to Penny. But were they close according to Johnny?"

Hornby took a minute to process that; then he nodded. "Yeah, I think they were. Johnny hung on to George as the stalwart part of his world. Once their father passed away, it was just the two of them. He had a medallion he got from his father. He wore it all the time. Played with it sometimes around his neck. It was like a piece of his father that Johnny carried with him."

"We found that," Doreen said. "We found it broken in the yard where he was last seen."

Alan just stared at her.

She could see him withdrawing slightly inside. Was he looking down memory lane? "How much did he care about that medallion?" she asked.

"He'd never take it off," he said. "And I mean *never*."

She nodded. "So, considering we found the medallion— and we found his dagger too, by the way—we have to wonder what happened to Johnny."

"He was probably killed by a drug dealer," Hornby snapped. "He was always trying to score drugs for us."

"Maybe," she said. "But, in that case, there'd be a body."

"Not if the drug dealer was scared of what he'd done and decided to take the body and deep-six it somewhere."

"*Deep-six it*," she said conversationally. "That sounds more like dropping it into the ocean."

"Considering we live by a lake," he said in a dry tone, "I hardly think the ocean would come into play."

"Point taken," she said with a big smile. "However, I think, after all this time, the body probably would have shown up again."

But then she remembered the vehicle she had just found with a little boy and the older man. "Unless he drowned in the lake inside a vehicle."

"In which case," Hornby said, "it should have been his own vehicle because then he'd have made a clean getaway, and nobody would ever know what happened to him."

"True." Stumped, she just stood here.

"If you're trying to find a killer," he said gently, "you're barking up the wrong tree. We were all messed up back then. Johnny was messed up back then. George was the mainstay in his life, but they fought all the time. Just like all brothers fight."

"Understood. Thanks for answering the questions."

He chuckled. "No problem. How about a cup of coffee?" He motioned his arm toward her kitchen.

She hesitated, not really sure why.

He saw the hesitation and chuckled. "I guess you're Mack's property then, huh?" He hopped up, gave her a mock salute, and walked away.

Chapter 17

Saturday Morning …

THE NEXT MORNING Hornby's words still burned a hole in Doreen's head. *She belonged to Mack.* It wasn't that it was right or wrong, just that such a complete connotation of ownership was too much like her marriage. She didn't want any more of that in her life.

To think somebody was making those kinds of insinuations, making a mockery of her friendship with Mack … well, it was just wrong.

She stared gloomily out the window, wondering why the clouds always seemed to match her moods. "Too bad I don't have the power to create sunshine everywhere," she muttered, feeling off since her conversation with Hornby last night.

She almost chuckled because plenty of self-help gurus out there would tell her, if she switched her mood, then everything around her would appear bright and sunny too.

"Too bad I'm not of that ilk." She poured her first cup of coffee and stepped out on the veranda. While she had outdoor furniture on both the veranda and the front porch—courtesy of Nan—Doreen wandered down the steps and across the backyard so she could look at the creek. Thaddeus wandered behind her, pecking away at various things on the ground. Goliath had raced ahead, dashing around like a crazy cat. Still, he was happy, so she could hardly begrudge him that moment. Mugs uncharacteristically moped alongside her.

"What's the matter, buddy? Didn't you get enough sleep last night?"

He didn't bark or even woof. He didn't pick up his pace. He just dragged his feet beside her.

"Yeah, I kind of feel the same way today."

If anybody else heard her talking to all the animals like she did, they'd think something was wrong with Doreen. *Maybe so.* But the truth was, she preferred having her animal family around more than a lot of other people. Particularly that guy, Alan Hornby, from last night. She shouldn't let his words get to her, but it was hard not to.

She was still outside at the creek when she heard her phone ring. She'd left it on the kitchen table. She shrugged and said, "Tough. Whoever it is, they'll have to call back." It was probably Mack. And, for a perverse reason based entirely on Hornby's conversation last night, she figured she would just let Mack wait. She wasn't here to jump when he said jump.

Immediately she felt terrible because it wasn't his fault. "Come on, guys. Let's go in and see what Mack wants."

She sipped her coffee as she walked back. The animals were all uncharacteristically silent now. In the kitchen, she picked up her phone. Sure enough, Mack had called. She called him back.

When he answered, she said, "I was out in the garden."

"Good," he said. "It's Saturday. You should be enjoying

yourself."

"When you don't work Monday to Friday," she said, "Saturday has as little meaning as Monday does."

"Well, that's a good thing," he said with a laugh.

"Did you do anything with that medallion?"

"I sent it to forensics," he said. "Don't forget. Just because the case has never been solved doesn't mean it's been forgotten."

"No, but you don't have man-hours to keep putting work into these cases," she said, "and that seems very sad and wrong too."

"We can't take our efforts away from current crimes either," he said.

"I know. Budget, budget, budget."

"Exactly. You're in an odd mood this morning."

She groaned. "Yeah, I had a visitor last night."

"What?" he cried out. "Are you okay?"

"Oh, sorry," she said. "It wasn't an intruder. When I came home from Nan's place, a car was in the drive, and nobody was on the front porch, so I went to the backyard to find a visitor sitting on my back steps."

"Were you expecting this person?"

"No," she said. "It was Alan Hornby. He wanted me to stop asking questions about Johnny's disappearance."

The silence lasted on the phone for all of ten seconds, then Mack exploded. "What? Did he threaten you?"

"I think he was almost flattering me. Maybe flirting a little. I'm kind of out of the game, so I'm not sure. But he did suggest we go into my house and have a cup of coffee together, which I not-so-politely declined," she said with a note of humor. "Maybe he got the better part of that deal because it is still *my* coffee."

"Your coffee is great," he said. "What else did he say?"

"He doesn't really know anything. He was in a vehicle with Susan, when a car sideswiped Johnny's car ahead of them, and their buddies were run off the road."

"They saw a vehicle run the two guys off the road?"

"That's what the girlfriend told her uncle. But she's dead, and her uncle Richie told Nan. Richie also told Velma, who is Hornby's aunt, that I was asking questions. Then Hornby came over here to tell me to stop. He also said he can't remember anything about the accident, but, if he said they were run off the road back then, then that must have been what happened. Now he's saying too much drugs and alcohol over the years have caused his memory to dim."

"Is that right?" Mack said in a dry tone. "I don't doubt the drugs and alcohol have certainly had an impact on his memory, but, when you see your two good friends burn out in front of you, I highly doubt you forget that."

"Can you check the file and see if anything was mentioned about the car being run off the road?" She sighed. "Richie just told Nan about it, but that should have been something the cops were all over back then at the time of Susan's statement."

"Sure, they would have been," he said. "I can check and see what's in the file. I don't remember offhand. I'm not sure I saw anything about it actually."

"That's what I'm afraid of," she said. "It's been a long time, and memories slip. Maybe they didn't see or say anything. Or it's just a convenient excuse."

"That's certainly possible."

"What are you doing today?" she asked.

"Not sure yet," he said. "I'm hoping to spend some time doing yard work, and I'll visit my mom for a bit. I'll drop by with the cash I owe you today."

"That would be good," she said. "I need to go shopping again."

"Right. We were supposed to do pasta, weren't we?" he asked in surprise. "Was that today?"

"Maybe," she said, "if that's okay with you."

"Sure," he said. "I'll go shopping and pick up what I need. It slipped my mind. I'm really sorry about that," he said, his tone apologetic and surprised at the same time.

She understood how he felt. Normally he was very good at remembering things like that. "It's no biggie," she said. "What time do you want to eat?" She checked the clock. "It's early, not even nine o'clock yet."

"We'll plan on pasta for dinner tonight. If you want to come with me, we can go shopping now. I could drop the stuff and you back off, then go about my day, whatever that'll be, and come back later this afternoon. We can cook then."

She brightened. "That might not be a bad idea because then I can see what you buy too."

"Right. I tend to forget shopping is something you're not used to either."

"Unless it's for one-thousand-dollar shoes," she said in a dry tone.

"Seriously?"

"Yeah, I've had a few of those." She groaned. "I wish right now I had all that money back in my pocket."

"I'm sorry," he said. "I'm sorry you've had to reassess how you live."

"I hear you, but I'm much better off where I am," she said. "Much happier."

"Good," he said. "I'll swing by in about twenty

minutes."

Just enough time for another cup of coffee. She poured herself a second cup and put on a piece of toast. "Getting a little low on peanut butter here, guys." She wandered around, making a short list of a few necessities, like toilet paper. She raised her eyebrows at the single roll left. "That ain't happening."

She could use treats for Mugs. And, after all the omelets, she needed more eggs. But thankfully Mack had bought the last ones anyway. She didn't have much in her fridge, so she could definitely use more cheese and sliced meat. Sandwiches were a standard she thankfully loved.

As soon as she was done, she grabbed her purse and walked to the front door. "Mugs, I have to leave you behind, buddy."

He woofed several times. He hated being left behind. Maybe because he thought Goliath would pick on him; she didn't know. She reset the alarm and stepped out the front door, locking it.

She walked down to the end of the driveway just as Mack pulled in. She hopped into the front of his truck and said, "Mugs is not happy."

He chuckled. "I don't think it's a bad thing for him to get used to being alone for a little while."

"Maybe not," she said, "but I worry he'll turn the fancy furniture into toothpicks."

At that, Mack laughed. "That image is a good way to start the day."

"Good for you," she said. "I woke up feeling like the world was against me, and no sunshine was left anywhere."

"Do you think it was because of Hornby's visit last night?"

"I don't know," she said. "I feel like people are lying to me, lying to everyone else. I really think Johnny is dead, and people know more than they're letting on."

"Who is it you think is lying?"

"Hornby, for one," she said. "But I'm not sure which part he's lying about."

Mack drove straight to the grocery store and hopped out. Doreen got out on her side, once again remembering Hornby's words about her being Mack's possession.

When he grabbed a cart and waited for her, she realized they were acting like any normal couple, and anybody outside their circle would assume they were dating. A part of her really liked that, but another part worried she and Mack were giving the wrong impression. Still, it wasn't her fault that others just assumed something.

As they wandered through the grocery store, she stopped in front of the fresh vegetables, looking for her salad and sandwich stuff. She picked up a head of lettuce, some radishes, green onions, cucumbers, and tomatoes. Happy with that, she turned to watch Mack in surprise as he grabbed carrots, celery, lots of tomatoes, and something dark and leafy.

"What's that?" she asked.

He looked at the big leaves in his hand. "This is kale."

She nodded. "I've heard of kale shakes and kale chips, but I didn't think it would look like that."

"This is what it looks like," he said. "This is the black kind, but it's always nice to have a bit of green veggies."

"You mean, *black* veggies," she said with a smirk.

He nodded.

She put her groceries in the top little basket, and he filled the base. She wasn't even sure what to do with half of the vegetables he put into his part of the cart. She found herself wondering if she should get her own. "Am I taking up too much of your space?" she asked hesitantly.

He looked at her in surprise. "You mean, that little bit?" He shook his head. "No, that's nothing. Surely you're getting more than that, aren't you?"

She gazed back at him blandly. "I like my veggies and dip, and I have enough here for sandwiches too."

"It's barely enough to keep a hamster alive."

She shrugged, walked to the fruit section, found a few apples on sale, and picked up two bananas to add to her pile.

He chose a big bunch of bananas and bagged a dozen apples.

She stared at him. "That means you're eating like three to four pieces of fruit a day."

He counted the fruit and shrugged. "I might not get back to the store in the next week, you know?"

As they walked down the aisle, she saw a man smirking at them. She froze, and somebody behind her stepped into her. She yelped. Mack turned, and the person behind her apologized.

Flustered, Doreen motioned with her hand. "Sorry, it was my fault." She hurried forward past Mack.

"What was that all about?"

"Hornby," she snapped. "He's up ahead."

While Mack scanned the crowd around her, she deliberately kept her head down so she didn't have to look at Hornby. As she and Mack continued their shopping, she found mushrooms, but they had a hefty price tag. She really would like a few, if only for raw munching. She bagged four small ones, putting them with her items.

Mack leaned over and said, "Are you deliberately buying

a couple items because that's all you want or because they're expensive?"

"It's a combination," she said.

He didn't say another word, but he filled a bag with mushrooms and tossed it into the cart.

She looked at it and smiled. "Can you really use that much food?"

"Absolutely," he said. "Lots of this is going into the spaghetti sauce."

She scrunched up her face. "Which ones?"

He chuckled and separated out the celery, onions, tomatoes, and mushrooms. "I've got a bottle of red wine that I'll open and use with it too."

"Interesting," she said. "Red wine in bourguignon maybe."

"Do you know how to make a beef bourguignon?" he asked with interest.

She shook her head. "No, but I like eating it." She stared at all the vegetables he'd pointed out. "It will be interesting to see how you make all of that turn into something yummy. Personally I don't like celery."

"It doesn't matter if you do or not," he said with a grin. "It goes into the spaghetti sauce. And we need garlic too."

She watched him in fascination as he picked up some weird little clove things. "Don't you bake those whole and serve them with camembert?"

"Maybe *you* did," he said. "But the rest of world chops it up and sautés it with meat."

She followed him as he added eggs, bacon, hamburger, and milk in the cart, stacking up a grocery bill that her heart would have loved to afford. But, as it was, she couldn't justify that kind of money much less know how to cook most of it.

When they got to the bakery, she picked up several loaves of bread and several tubs of peanut butter to go with her milk for her tea and more eggs for a new omelet—and she added in some cheese.

Mack looked at her purchases. "Well, it's growing slightly, but it looks like I'm a pig and you're a bird."

"Not at all," she said. "I wouldn't know what to do with most of what you have."

"Good point." He motioned toward the cashier. "Let's go."

She pulled into the first nearly empty register. As she unloaded her groceries, she looked up to see Hornby two aisles over, staring at her. He had a big grin on his face.

"Don't look now," she said in a low tone that only Mack could hear, "but Hornby is at eleven o'clock."

Mack looked up and checked out the guy who had been hassling her. "What's that smirk mean?"

"I think it has to do with one of the comments he made to me."

"What was that?"

She shook her head. "I don't want to talk about it."

Mack shot her an odd look.

She shrugged. "I think it's safe to say, Hornby is one of those troublemaking kinds of people."

"Yeah? Is that a new talent, or did he make trouble back then too?"

"I rather imagine he made a ton of trouble back then," she said. "He's probably gotten better at being subtler about it now."

"Interesting insight," he said.

She shrugged. "Not really. It's just a fact of life. People

get more experienced and become sneakier at causing pain. And they learn how to maximize the pain inflicted. It's manipulation at its best." Sensing his odd look, she refused to look at him.

After a moment Mack said, "Do you think Hornby had something to manipulate?"

"I didn't believe anything that came out of his mouth," she said, "so I assume he had an awful lot to do with either Johnny's disappearance or his buddies who died in the vehicle."

At that, Mack sucked in his breath, and his gaze turned lethal as he studied her face. "You think Hornby had something to do with their deaths?"

She tossed him a look. "It was one of the first things I thought when he said he couldn't remember anything about the accident."

"But that would also imply Susan knew all about it."

"According to her uncle, she kept telling everybody who would listen that a vehicle had run the guys off the road."

"And?" he prompted.

"Maybe a vehicle did," she said drily. "Maybe she was trying to tell the cops without implicating herself. Maybe the vehicle that ran their friends off the road was the one they were driving."

Mack nodded thoughtfully. "I didn't see anything in the files, but I haven't had a chance to get through the whole thing."

"I'm sure not much is in there," she said. "Johnny sat down on the bench, was having a beer, and the next thing his family knew, he was gone. Nobody supposedly knows anything about him. Yet the medallion he would never part with, the vehicle he adored, and his favorite dagger were all left behind."

"When you put it that way," Mack said, "it does sound like something very suspicious happened, doesn't it?"

"Absolutely," she said. "I'm pretty damn sure Hornby was a big part of it."

"We're back to that assumption thing."

"Absolutely no way to prove anything," she said. "Everybody involved is dead except him."

"Convenient, isn't it?"

"Except Susan died of breast cancer," she said. "Last year as I heard it."

"Huh," he said. "Maybe we should take a closer look at that death."

Doreen froze, slowly turned to him, and in a low voice asked, "Do you think he could have killed her?"

"I don't know," Mack said. "Depends if she got ill and had a change of heart, wanted to cleanse her soul of some wrongdoing."

"And how would we ever know that?" she asked with a chuckle.

"Maybe you should talk to Richie," he said.

"That's a great idea."

Chapter 18

Saturday Midmorning …

MACK WAS GONE; the groceries were put away, and she once again sat on the front stoop with a cup of coffee. She looked at her coffee and said, "I need a job, so I can keep drinking you at the same pace I have been. Talk about addictive."

Still, a full-time job wouldn't give her many free hours for her hobby. Something she was loving more and more every day—of course, she was still riding the wave of success, which reminded her of her current case. And right at the top of the things for her to do was talk to Richie.

She wondered how to get a hold of him. Was it fair to go through Nan? And would it bring up sad memories if she asked him questions about his great-niece? It seemed hardly fair when they'd only lost her a year ago. Would he have dealt with the loss mostly by now?

She pulled out her phone and sent Nan a text, asking about Richie's great-niece's health.

Nan called her. "What have you found out?"

"Nothing really," Doreen said feebly. "I just wondered what her state of mind was before she died."

"Richie is sitting here, playing poker with me," she said. "I'll put you on Speakerphone."

Doreen heard cards slapping on the table.

"I'm here," said a man with a rough masculine voice. "What's this about my great-niece?"

"I'm sorry to disturb you," Doreen said. "I was wondering about her state of mind before she died."

"What kind of a question is that?" he asked, snorting. "She was pretty darn sad. Knew she was dying of cancer. She was also in a lot of pain."

"Did she give any signs that she wanted to, you know, go to confession or had trauma she wanted to … ask forgiveness for?" She winced. "I know that's a really rough way to say it. I wanted to figure out if she wished she hadn't done something in her life or had done something better."

What an idiot she was. But this was better than her actual question. What she really wanted to know was did his great-niece confess to any murders before she died. And who could answer that question?

"She was very melancholy at the end," Richie said gruffly. "Sad for all the things she wouldn't get to do."

"I'm sorry for her," Doreen said. "She was young still."

"Yes," he said, "but she also knew she was paying the price for a life lived hard."

"Drugs and alcohol, you mean?"

"That too," he said. "She was also a thief for a while, due to her drug habit."

"Ah, so maybe she was sorry about that?"

"Definitely," he said. "But, if you're asking if she had anything to do with the deaths of those two boys or Johnny, you're barking up the wrong tree. She was a very gentle soul."

Doreen held back her gasp when he acknowledged what she'd been hinting at. She hadn't known the right way to say it. "Do you think there's any chance she was in the vehicle that ran those two boys off the road?" she asked quietly. "If she was a passenger, and Hornby had been the one driving?"

"I don't know," he said, his voice thickening. "I have to admit though that the thought did cross my mind a time or two. According to her, the vehicle that hit Johnny's car was patched with lots of pieces from other vehicles," he said with a chuckle. "It was a very noticeable vehicle out there."

"That's what I mean. If there had been yet another vehicle on that road, surely the cops would have found it."

"Well, you would have thought so," he said. "But the truth of the matter was, they never did. Susan said she gave them the description over and over again, but, without a license plate, they could do little. They did put out an alert, but the vehicle was never seen again."

Just like Johnny. But she kept that thought to herself. "Do you remember her description of the vehicle?"

"She said it was a small car with lots of different colored panels. But I think the real issue you should be looking at is, why would somebody run them off the road?"

"Right," she said. "We're back to lack of motive."

"Except they were all into drugs," Richie said with a hardness that surprised her. "I did everything I could to get that girl off those, but, once they got into her system, she was lost."

"I'm sorry," Doreen said. "I won't bother you any longer. If you think of anything else Susan might have said, or if she might have kept journals or notebooks or a diary or something," Doreen said hopefully, "keep me in mind."

"You're really looking into Johnny's disappearance,

huh?"

"Penny is still looking for answers," Doreen said without hesitation. "I'd like to see her get that before her time runs out."

"Like George," he said with a *harrumph.* "That was a sad day."

"Also the day that George helped ID the two boys," she said. "I'm sure, in the back of his mind, he was afraid one of those bodies was Johnny's."

"I think we all thought that," he said. "It was his car. So who else would be driving that sucker?"

"Good point," she said and hung up.

Immediately she called Mack. "Hey," she said as soon as she heard his voice. "Can you check in the cold case file if anybody did a forensic check on the vehicle the two men died in?"

"I've got the file here," he said, "but I haven't gone through it all. Obviously the forensic team went over the vehicle. What aspect is bothering you?"

She grinned, happy he wasn't asking her to butt out. "We know for sure it was Johnny's car. But do we know for sure that, A, Johnny wasn't in the trunk, dead already or dying from the vehicle crash, and, B, did any forensic evidence show something like a ton of blood to say that maybe Johnny had been there?"

"After a bad fire like that, blood wouldn't have been traceable, but a body in the trunk would have been found," he said. "Notes in here state Johnny had no reason to disappear and made no further contact with his family, but nobody could prove one way or another that he was deceased. He's still a missing person's case."

"Did Penny or George ever try to declare him legally

dead?" she asked.

"No notes are in the file about it," he said, "and it's not something necessarily that would have been followed up on here. That would be a question to ask Penny."

"Maybe," Doreen said. "I'm not sure how much tolerance Penny will have for these questions though."

"She's the one who asked you to look into it, right? So, therefore, she shouldn't have a problem with you asking for clarification."

"So far, she has been decent," Doreen said, "but you never really want to push it."

He chuckled. "I don't think you understand what that point is. You're forever pushing everything."

"I'm not that bad. I can see how *you* might feel that way," she admitted. "But I just find this case makes no sense. I mean, when you have a family who you love, why would you walk away?"

He said, "Let me ask you this. You had Nan, and you loved her very much, but still how much contact did you have with her in previous years?"

She could feel his words almost as a visceral blow. "That's not fair."

"No," he said, "it isn't, but extenuating circumstances in your life stopped you from having a closer relationship with Nan. You have to consider maybe something similar happened in this young man's life."

"Like a wife?" she asked cynically. "More likely he was protecting George and Penny."

After a moment of silence, Mack finally said, "That's one angle the police had to look at. Was the family threatened? Was Johnny made to do something to keep his family out of danger? We don't know what went on back then."

"I still think it connects to the group of kids," she said.

"Maybe it does, considering only one person is left alive from that group."

"I think another girl was involved too," Doreen said. "Somebody a little bit on the outside, kind of like Hornby was a little bit on the outside. I don't know her name yet."

"Well track her down," he said humorously. "You seem to have taken over this case completely."

"Can you tell me if any police man-hours are available for this cold case?"

"Depends what comes back from the testing on the medallion," he said seriously. "I expect it to be only Johnny's DNA. Who else's would it be?"

"No clue but it would be nice if someone else's DNA were on it. We'd at least have a suspect to look at."

"At that point the case would become very active, and it wouldn't be a case of *us* doing anything," Mack reminded her in that tone of his that said she would be butting out, whether she liked it or not.

She groaned. "So I bring you all the information to help you move things forward, and then you force me to step back?"

"Remember the 'It's dangerous' part?"

"It's not my fault I always get to the root of the matter, and, by the time I get there, people are a little pissed that I found them out."

"Just like Cecily," he said. "You got into trouble at the end."

"Okay, so *you* can get into trouble this time," she said in exasperation, getting up in a huff and returning to the kitchen for more coffee. "I don't have a death wish, you know? It's not like I'm trying to cause trouble. I'm trying to bring peace and closure for Penny."

"I get that. Penny gets that, and maybe half the world would get that, but whoever might be involved in this case won't give a crap."

"Like Hornby?"

"He really bothered you, didn't he?"

"Not only did he come to my home," she said, "but he also threatened me, and then he was flirting with me."

"Which one bothered you the most?"

She pulled her cell away to stare at it, frowning. "What kind of a question is that?"

"Just wondered how terrified you are of getting back into a relationship. You never seem uncomfortable around me," he said, "but Hornby was directly in your face, pushing the issue."

She hated the direction he was going. "Whatever," she said, dismissing it.

He chuckled. "I'll be over there in a few hours. Try to stay out of trouble."

She tossed her phone on the kitchen table, looked at her animals, and said, "Let's go outside and do some work in the garden. Maybe that'll make me feel better."

Normally gardening was a soothing activity for her, a balm to her troubled soul, not to mention giving her some exercise and helping her to wear off some pent-up energy.

With her gardening gloves, a bottle of water, and her proverbial cup of tea, she headed out to the back corner, where they had pulled up the dilapidated fence and the posts. She figured, if she did the worst part of the weeding at the far back corner first, maybe it would be easier as she got closer to the house.

Setting down her water and tea, she pulled on her gloves.

The corner was filled with what looked like huge pockets of daisies, black-eyed Susans, and maybe some echinacea. It was hard to be sure as most of the plants were just showing the early foliage.

She studied the leaves to confirm this plant was truly echinacea when she heard a soft noise. She spun around but couldn't see anything. Then she heard Mugs chuffing—this weird sound he made that wasn't a bark, wasn't a growl, but like a heavy sniff upon a sniff, with some added background noise. He chuffed his way to the corner of the fence, but it wasn't her fence; it was her neighbor's fence. Mugs stood there, intently investigating everything around him. Goliath, not to be outdone, walked along at his leisure. And then he took off like a golden orange streak.

She followed the cat as she walked closer to the creek. "Goliath! Goliath, stay here please."

Instead of answering her, Goliath remained silent. And the continuous *chuff-chuff-chuff* came from Mugs. Then, in a startling move, Thaddeus hopped on Mugs's back. At this point Mugs was so focused on the trail he was following that he didn't seem to notice the bird.

She studied the two cautiously. "Thaddeus, that might not be the best idea."

"Giddyup, Mugs. Giddyup, Mugs," Thaddeus squawked in a loud voice.

Doreen gasped as Thaddeus tried to ride her dog. Mugs took several hesitant steps forward, then stopped. Thaddeus dug his claws in and pecked at the dog's head. Mugs took off, barking like crazy, racing around in a circle, as if trying to bounce Thaddeus off—which didn't work—but finally Mugs slowed and returned to the same spot. Thaddeus, apparently happy with his ride, hopped off, and strutted at the dog's side.

She studied the area, trying to figure out what was upsetting them. The last time they'd behaved like this was when they found a license plate that led her to solve the previous cold case on Paul Shore. It had been an amazing and a very heartwarming, worthwhile exercise.

"Has this got something to do with my current case?" she asked Mugs.

Now Mugs couldn't take his eyes off whatever was bothering him on the far side of the creek. Thaddeus, however, shot her a look that said, *Boy, are you stupid.*

She glared back at the bird.

He ruffled his feathers and ignored her.

She should be used to that by now but wasn't.

Doreen walked closer to where Goliath had disappeared. Brush grew all alongside the creek. She didn't spot Goliath, but she thought she spied Goliath's tail twitching, flicking back and forth. She crept up behind him, not wanting to scare him into the water, but, at the same time, if he was hunting a bird or something equally lovely, she would tell him off right and royally.

And then suddenly Goliath exploded backward through the brush, wrapping himself through her legs, racing past Mugs.

She almost tripped and fell as she regained her balance. She stared at the streak as it veered toward the veranda. "Goliath, are you okay?" Unable to leave yet, she returned to where Goliath had been, and, holding on to the brush as an anchor, she crept down a couple feet toward the creek. Just two or so weeks ago, the water had been icy-cold. She hoped the creek water had warmed up by now, with all the sunshine and hopefully no more snowmelt. If she fell in, the water should be fairly warm at this time of year.

Standing just inches from the trickling stream, she inspected the area Goliath appeared to look at. But nothing was there. She crouched lower; then suddenly Mugs was at her side, chuffing away. Thaddeus, now at his side, hopped up onto her shoulder, and the three looked at the water.

Chapter 19

Saturday Afternoon ...

"OKAY, GUYS. YOU are really starting to freak me out," Doreen said. "We're not supposed to find any more bodies. Remember?"

Mugs shot her a look.

"The good news is, I don't see anything." She stared in the direction of Penny's house. It wasn't far from the creek either.

With a sinking feeling, Doreen wondered if Johnny had been knocked unconscious and put in the creek. "No, no, no," she said. "That's silly. No way that could have happened without finding a body in all this time."

Then again, the high floodwaters from decades past had sent a full-size truck down this very creek and even poor little Betty Miles's arm and hand, so who knew what else might have come past Doreen's house? But still, she wasn't going there. Not yet.

She reached out a hand to dip into the creek, and Mugs growled. She froze. "What's the matter with you?" she asked. "Have all the animals gone nuts right now?"

But his gaze was still on the spot in the creek in front of

her. She dug around but didn't see or feel anything. Nothing reflected the sunlight. Nothing appeared to not belong here.

She removed a few rocks in the creek, and water rushed in to fill those holes, lifting up some of the sand beneath and pulling it back. Unable to help herself, she kicked off her flip-flops and gingerly stepped into the creek. *Warm enough.* She proceeded to pull away some of the muddy creek bank, opening up a much larger area in the creek bed, allowing a bit of a run for the water to flow in and to flow out, taking a lot of the sand with it. Within minutes the area was down to just the rock layer. She loved how water worked that way.

She still couldn't see anything out of the ordinary. She worked her way farther up the creek in Penny's direction, with Mugs getting ever closer and closer. Finally she looked at him and asked, "You want to take over?"

He barked and then barked again.

She sighed and kept digging. "This better be worth it," she muttered and reached in again.

As she moved rocks around in the water, something small popped to the surface and started to float away. She snagged the small piece of wood. She was about to toss it aside when she saw *Johnny* scratched on one side. Upon closer inspection, it wasn't a single piece of wood but two pieces of wood nailed into a cross with his name filling the crosspiece. She sat down on the bank beside Mugs as he sniffed her new find.

"Okay, this is a little creepy," she said. She laid it on the path and took a picture with her phone, immediately sending it to Mack. Thaddeus waddled up and tilted his head to stare at it. For once he was quiet. Making the cross was something she could see the kids of their gang doing, as some kind of a memorial. But why here? Particularly if

Johnny's body had never been found. Meaning, his death had yet to be confirmed.

Her phone rang.

"What is that?" Mack asked.

"It looks like a little cross with Johnny's name on it," she said. "This thing is only like six inches long and maybe four inches across. Mugs found it in the creek. Actually maybe Goliath found it."

He groaned. "Seriously?"

"What do you want me to say?" she said. "I was working in the backyard, and Goliath came out here. Mugs started chuffing away ..."

"*Chuffing?*" Mack asked.

"Hey, Mugs. Could you chuff a little more again so Mack can hear you?"

But Mugs just yawned.

"Okay, so he's not doing it right now," she said. At Mack's barely smothered laugh, she snapped, "*But* he was doing it. ... And Mugs wouldn't leave this area alone either—at least once the scaredy-cat took off for home—so I dug up a section along the bank to widen the creek a bit, plus removed some rocks in the stream itself to get the water moving along better. Mugs barked the closer I got to where this was buried. Then he became completely unconcerned the minute this thing surfaced."

"Why is it you think it's a memorial thing?"

"You know how when someone dies on a trail, people put a cross there as a memorial? That's what this looks like. It's obviously old. It looks like it's been in the creek since who-knows-when, and it's got Johnny's name on it."

"So you think somebody threw it in the creek or had it standing up nearby as a memorial for him?"

"That's what this feels like," she said. "But you know what? Don't trust me. When you come by, I'll show you."

"You've already pulled it out and sent me a picture of it. How will I know where it was?"

"I'll grab a stick," she said, reaching for a broken branch, "and mark where I found it. How's that?"

"Good enough," he said. "It'll still be a few hours before I'm done at Mom's."

"Okay, I have lots to keep busy until then," she said. "Of course now …"

"*Of course now* nothing," he said. "Finding somebody's way of saying goodbye to an old friend doesn't mean anything more sinister than that."

"Nope," she said. "But I'd love to know who threw it in here. … And why they picked the creek as the memorial site." With that she hung up.

She sent the picture to Penny and then called her. "Hey, I just sent you a picture. I found something in the creek bed. I was thinking about how your place isn't far off the creek itself. Anyway, I found a little tiny cross with Johnny's name on it."

"I just looked at the picture," Penny told Doreen. "I have no idea what that is or who would have made it."

"There's not a ton of craftsmanship in it. It's pretty crude," Doreen said hesitantly, sitting nearby it and the creek. "It reminded me of how people will hang wreaths and crosses on the side of the road when there's been a fatality."

"Exactly," Penny said. "But to put that on the creek implies maybe he drowned?"

"The year he went missing was the year of the heavy flooding. Did Johnny swim?"

"Oh, absolutely he did but not well," Penny said. "That

was also the year Paul Shore went missing."

Doreen sat down with a hard *thump*. "Right. Didn't other children go missing back then?" she asked, her voice sounding a little bit the way she felt on the inside, dreading to hear her answer. "There were other missing boys, right? As I recall, two."

"There were," Penny said. "I can't remember how many. Or their names. Again you'll have to talk to Mack because that was a long time ago. But I think you're right. Two little boys went missing. It's one of the reasons I think the town turned on the handyman Henry Huberts so quickly because they suspected him in all three children's disappearances."

Doreen remained silent, considering these other unsolved cold cases, her cell phone at her ear.

Penny eventually said in a cautious tone, "But I don't know what that has to do with Johnny's disappearance."

"You said in your letter that he went missing in August of that year, right?"

"Correct."

"And now we're reminded of the horrible flooding that happened earlier that same year, and today I find a cross with Johnny's name on it in the creek bank. Maybe somebody accidentally killed him. Maybe they had a fight, and Johnny drowned, or maybe he got lost in the water, and they were afraid they would get blamed," Doreen said.

Penny was quiet, thoughtful, before she said anything. "We were always warning him about the dangers of the floods when he was younger. He wasn't big on being around water. He would never go to the lake, even though we live in one of the most gorgeous locations in the world."

"And people kayak down this creek a lot, don't they? Not yet, obviously, as there's only a little water, although," she looked around the area, "I guess it's been rising steadily."

"Oh, yes. Canoe, kayak, float on tubes all summer while there's enough water. It's quite the place." Penny smiled. "It's always low in the spring but with every month it rises until the snow melts up in the ski mountains and then …"

"Right," Doreen said, nodding, yet of course, Penny couldn't see this over the phone. "But, in high-water times of the year, it would have been dangerous."

"Yes. I think Paul Shore went missing in May that same year, when we had the really big runoff. Johnny went missing later in the summer," Penny said. "The water would have dropped back to normal levels by then."

"Okay. That's good to know," Doreen said, relaxing a bit with relief. "I guess by August we are into much lower water levels, aren't we?"

"Yes, even though the floodwaters got superhigh that year and had caused chaos earlier. But, once that heavy rush of water passed, what with the melting snow coming from the tributaries into the main creek, the water levels kept dropping. … I know Johnny did spend a fair bit of time with his buddies at the creek, but mostly drinking and hanging with his friends, not swimming or anything like that. I don't think we ever thought he might have drowned."

"That's because, if the water level was low, and he had drowned, his body would have been found already," Doreen said calmly, staring at the calm creek before her. "Which puts us back to somebody hiding the fact that Johnny had died. Any chance that one of the kids involved with him would have had something to do with those two missing little boys?"

"I have no clue," Penny said in surprise. "I don't remember any rumors to that effect. I just know the two little boys went missing that year, and I think it was early in the year, even before Paul went missing. But you found Paul. We never found the other two."

"Once Johnny went missing, that's where your focus went," Doreen said.

"Of course. George was a good boater. He was a really strong swimmer, and he was forever trying to get Johnny to practice swimming, but Johnny was very resistant to the idea."

"He could have been resisting just because his big brother was telling him that he should do it," Doreen said with a chuckle, picking up a small rock and tossing it into the creek.

"Quite possibly. But George was very insistent, because, to him, it was a safety issue. One of those life skills everybody should learn," Penny said in all seriousness. "Like learning to drive."

"I agree totally," Doreen said, nodding her head again. "Anyway I just wanted to let you know what I found." She stood, brushing off the seat of her pants.

"I can't believe everything you are finding," Penny said. "I mean, that's major progress. I found the dagger, but we just now found his medallion, and now you found that creepy cross."

Doreen had to agree with Penny on the description. After she hung up, Doreen picked up the cross and carried it past the deck to the veranda, where she laid it on the small table there. She studied it for a long moment. The small piece of wood had a fairly uniform shape, like the edges were shorter on the top of the crosspiece and wider on the bottom, as if maybe a deliberate design attempt. And the name had been carved in it with a knife, Doreen thought. Not very deep, but it wasn't burned in or etched in with some wood-burning tool. All in all, it wasn't as crudely made as she had first thought, but it was effective, especially when she considered the fact it had survived all those years in the water. Unless another Johnny had gone missing. She groaned at that idea.

"It *is* a common name," she muttered. "And it's all too possible that somebody else with that name might have died, and this referred to somebody else's Johnny."

On that note, she decided to take a look at deaths and other missing Johnnys in the area from around the same time that Johnny Jordan went missing.

Back inside, she made herself a sandwich for lunch, then sat in front of her laptop to research drownings of anybody with the name of Johnny. She found two in the last thirty years, one closer to Fintry, which was almost an hour up the lake on the opposite side. The lake currents operated in weird and wonderful ways, and bodies floated so they could have ended up all over the place.

The second Johnny was from Kelowna but had gone missing from a boat in the middle of the lake while out drinking. She winced at that thought. Apparently a large group of young men and women, nineteen in all, were on a big party boat. One of the guys had gone overboard. Nobody had noticed until he was almost underwater. Two men had jumped into the lake to rescue him but lost him in the murky depths below. His body was never found.

That sent chills down her back because of the similarities. But this particular Johnny had disappeared nineteen years ago, so it wasn't the Johnny that Doreen was looking for. But if large groups of young people were partying on the lake nineteen years ago, they definitely were twenty-nine years ago.

Then she searched for missing kids named Johnny. The only one who came up was Johnny Jordan. Then she searched for John, Johnny names with different spellings, Johan even, etc. The cross was very definitely for a Johnny with a *Y*. After that, she looked for car accident victims because, if someone had had a child who had been killed in a car accident, but his favorite place was the creek, his mother might very well have left a memorial at the creek closest to where he'd died.

Doreen was grasping at straws but didn't have a lot of other options right now.

She picked up her sandwich. Hearing a weird sound, she turned to see Thaddeus sitting on the kitchen table, watching her. His head tilted to the side and bobbed, as if willing her to understand. She pulled off a slice of cucumber from her sandwich and put it in front of him. Immediately he pecked at it.

Meow.

She glanced at Goliath, staring at a piece of ham hanging off the corner of her sandwich. She groaned but tore off that piece and put it in front of him. Mugs jumped up with his front paws on her chair, his most woebegone look on his face. She sighed and gave him a piece of cheese. "That's it, you guys. No more."

Of course they didn't listen. She shifted so she couldn't see them and quickly finished her sandwich, then put her plate in the sink. "What do you think? Back out to the garden?" But the animals had already raced ahead of her to the back door. She chuckled, grabbed a dry pair of gloves, and headed outside.

She stopped working at four. She was hot and sweaty, and what had started out as perfect working conditions had ended up getting really warm. She had maybe a six- by ten-foot stretch weeded and dug out nicely. The daisy patch looked absolutely wonderful. They needed water now that she'd disturbed their roots so much. She struggled to bring the hose all the way to the back of her property, ended up connecting several hoses to reach this bed, but finally she stood in the heat and soaked them down.

As she glanced at the next bed, the echinacea were overcrowded and heavily leafed, crying out for attention. "You guys are next." Then she sprayed Mugs with the hose. He ran around, jumping at the drops. Goliath was nowhere to be seen, likely off snooping in the bushes along the pathway. Thaddeus sat atop a rock, drinking the fresh water that had pooled on the ground. She laughed, turned the spray on above her to cool off a bit and then walked back up to the house to shut off the water.

With Mack coming over soon, it was time for a shower. She felt she had done enough work for the day. At this rate, it would take months to get her own garden back under control. And that was without planting, transplanting, or incorporating any new design elements. But it was her place, and it was her time and energy, so she would do what she wanted to do, when she wanted to do it. Depending on her finances of course.

Chapter 20

Saturday Dinnertime …

B Y THE TIME Mack arrived, she was in the kitchen, fresh coffee dripping, counters and table all cleaned up and ready for whatever magic he was prepared to show her.

He walked in, placed more groceries on the counter, and smiled at her. "Are you ready?"

She motioned toward the bag. "I thought we had everything already. Isn't that what's in my fridge?"

"We had most of it, but I didn't buy any pasta. Remember?"

She frowned, then shrugged. "Honestly, I don't."

He withdrew a bottle of red wine from his bag and placed it on the table.

She studied the label. "I've never seen this before," she said, eyeing it. "I'm not a huge fan of reds, but I do love whites and rose. Especially the sparkly stuff." She grinned.

"Welcome to how real people eat," he said. "That's a cheap bottle of wine. It's good, and it's local. Plus it's absolutely perfect to have a glass while you're making pasta sauce with some of it too."

"Interesting." She watched as he unpacked a few more

mysterious items she didn't recognize.

He shooed her away and said, "You work on the pasta. I'll work on the sauce."

"If that meant anything to me," she said with a tilt of her lips, "then I would hop to it and get started."

"Get your largest pot." He stopped, frowning at her. "I hadn't thought about that. ... Do you have pots?"

She lifted her finger in the air. "I don't, but Nan does." She went to one of the pantry cupboards and opened it. "What size pot do you want?"

He joined her, rubbing his hands. "Now this is what I'm looking for." He reached inside and pulled out a decent-size pot with two small handles on opposite sides. "This Dutch oven will do."

She looked at it curiously. She'd never heard the term before and didn't know how it could possibly apply. It wasn't an oven, and what on earth made it Dutch? Or was that what the Dutch called a pot? Not wanting to ask and to appear even more foolish, she closed the cupboard door and watched as he took it to the sink.

"Give it a quick wash and a rinse and then fill it with water up to here," he said, drawing an imaginary line on the inside of the pot.

Obediently she stood at the sink and did as he asked. Cleaned and rinsed, she waited until the pan filled up. She shut off the water and looked back at him. "And?"

"Put it on the large burner at the back of the stove," he instructed.

He busily chopped onions and garlic, and she saw he had snagged another pot while she'd been filling hers. It was on the front burner. She sniffed the aroma coming from his pot as she lifted her pot to place on the back burner. With that done, she leaned in closer to sniff the pot in front of her. Mugs stretched up his front paws to the oven door and sniffed. Then, he'd missed out on a lot of good smells now too.

"What is this? Butter and garlic?"

"Butter with a little bit of garlic, yes, and a bunch of herbs. If you use dried herbs, warming them releases the flavors."

"I can definitely agree with that," she said. "I don't remember anything quite so aromatic."

He chuckled, stirred the contents, dumped in freshly chopped onions and then added ground beef. She watched as he calmly took a wooden spatula and stirred the mix.

"When do you know it's done?"

"When the meat turns brown and the onions turn translucent," he said. "The garlic you don't really have to worry about because it cooks so fast."

The combination was really getting her appetite going. "I don't know what else goes in there, but I want to snag a forkful right now."

"That's exactly how it should smell," he said.

She watched in fascination as he proceeded to add more ingredients. When she wondered what came next, he reached across and turned her pot of water on high.

"Grab the olive oil," he said.

She looked at him sideways.

He lifted an eyebrow. "Surely you've had olive oil served with your fancy meals?"

She nodded. "So, I'm looking for one of those little glass cruets that you pull a stopper from and pour?"

His eyebrows shot up. "Maybe in your world, but, in my world, we don't pour olive oil into a crystal jar just so we can pour it back out again." He chuckled. "Nobody has time for that." He pointed at the kitchen table. Beside the wine was another bottle.

She picked it up and read the label. *Olive oil.* "Isn't it supposed to say *extra virgin*?"

"It does," he said. "Read the fine print underneath."

She squinted. "I would have thought that fine print should be bigger." She handed him the bottle.

"It probably is on *your* bottles," he said in a dry tone. He took off the lid and poured some olive oil into the Dutch oven. "I count to three and figure that's good."

She looked at the amount swimming on the top of the water. "How am I supposed to learn if you don't measure?"

"Are you taking notes?" he asked, while he now chopped tomatoes and celery.

She gasped, grabbed her phone off the counter, and started videotaping everything. "I completely forgot." She hesitated, wondering if she should ask him to start again, but he must have caught a sense of what she would say because he held up a hand.

"Don't even bother. I am *not* starting over."

She sighed. "Okay, but, on the video, could you at least tell me what you did and how much?"

"One pound of ground beef, a couple smashed cloves of garlic, chop up a whole onion, and cooked until the meat is brown and the onion translucent. As for the herbs, well, that's a little hard to remember," he said. "I'm a cook who doesn't measure. I add a bit of this and a bit of that."

"A bit of what this time?"

"In the original group," he said, "oregano and thyme and marjoram, some paprika …"

His voice trailed off as he dumped in his freshly chopped

tomatoes, celery, and she wasn't sure what the other thing was. She leaned in and asked, "What's that?"

"It's a bay leaf. Not to worry, I'll pull it out before it's served."

She'd never seen such a thing before. He'd taken a leaf, like one from her plants outside, and plunked it in his sauce. Instead of being bright green, it was dry-looking, brittle. He continued to add what looked like canned tomatoes. "Why fresh *and* canned?"

"Because it'll be too dry if I don't add some liquid," he said, "and I didn't have quite enough fresh tomatoes."

She nodded, as if that made sense, but, from her point of view, that was a ton of fresh tomatoes. Still, the aroma was kicking in beautifully.

He pointed to the pot with the water and olive oil. "Now get the salt and add it in that pot."

Obediently she walked to the table, picked up a salt shaker, and put in a couple shakes.

He looked at her and said, "More."

She shook again.

"More."

She shook again.

"More."

Finally she stared at him in exasperation. "How much salt do you want in there?"

He pulled the top off, poured some into his hand, and dumped it into the pot of water.

She gasped. "That much salt is seriously bad for you."

"It's going into the water," he said. "We're not drinking the water, and I'm not adding it to the sauce. We'll put pasta in the water. It will get just the right amount of flavor. Then we'll drain it, so we leave all that salt behind."

She frowned, not sure she believed him, muttering that too much salt was bad for their health.

He ignored her, which was probably a good thing. Then he picked up the lid and shoved it on top of the pot of water with a little more force than was necessary.

To get back at him, she picked up her cup and poured herself some coffee—but not him.

He put the spoon down, crossed his arms over his chest, and glared at her.

She shrugged. "Well, it's not like you were being nice."

"I'm making you dinner."

She wrinkled her nose. "That's not fair."

He stared at her in astonishment. "Why is that not fair? You should pour *me* a cup of coffee when I'm making *you* dinner."

"You asked to make me dinner a while ago. So now you're taking something from a few days ago and bringing it forward to today to get your way."

He stood there, confused, then shook his head. "Forget it. Nobody could work their way through that."

She decided she should probably be nice anyway. He was a guest, after all. She picked up a clean mug out of Nan's stack of mugs and poured coffee for him, placing it beside him and said, "Thank you."

Once again he looked at the cup and said, "You said *thank you*. Isn't it me who was supposed to say *thank you*?"

"You're welcome," she said, beaming a smile in his direction.

He snorted and returned to stirring his pot. "You and Nan have a lot in common."

She looked at him suspiciously. "I don't think you meant that in a nice way." She looked down at his cup and then back up at him. "Just take a sip before you say anything because I'm pretty sure that whatever comes out of your mouth won't be nice."

"Nan is a great woman," he said.

She started to feel better.

"But she's also as nutty as a hatter sometimes."

She slammed her cup down. "Are you saying I'm crazy too?"

"No," he said, "but crazy is as crazy does."

She stared at him, trying to understand.

He waved a hand. "Forget it. Now I'll let all this simmer."

She checked on the contents in his pot that had somehow turned from being a lot of different chunks of ingredients, separate and distinct, into this beautiful-looking sauce. "How did it go from one to the other so quickly?"

"Cooking," he said succinctly. "That's all it takes, leaving it alone to simmer. We'll add a bunch of peppers, and then we'll let it simmer some more while we have our coffee."

She nodded. "What about the pasta water?"

"The pot is pretty full, so it'll take another ten minutes to boil, maybe longer."

"Is this one of those dishes that's better the next day?" she asked, eyeing the pot of spaghetti sauce suspiciously. She'd never seen anything quite like it.

"In a way, yes," he said. "It's definitely something that gets better with lots of time to simmer."

"So we can't eat it today?" She stared at him in horror.

"I am," he said with a huge grin. "I'm starving."

"So am I," she admitted. "I had a sandwich earlier, but I also did a lot of work in my garden, so I'm tired too."

He looked out at the garden and pointed to the far back corner. "Right, and I almost forgot. Where's the cross?"

She walked toward the formal dining room table and pointed out the cross leaning against the little window. "There."

He stepped closer but didn't touch it for the longest moment. Then he picked it up and checked to see how the two pieces of wood stayed together. "They've used a pinner."

"And that means what?"

"It's not a nail," he said. "Anybody could have used a nail, but they've used a pinner, which means somebody had good equipment because this looks like an air-compressor pinner." He rotated it in his hand. "It's just as likely a father made it for their child to carve the name in and place where they wanted it. Help them deal with the loss of a friend.'

"Which means it could have been anyone." Doreen bent closer to see what he was talking about. "It looks like a staple."

"Almost," he said. "This isn't from a staple gun though. It's much finer. And there are two of them. That's why what you see looks to be a staple."

She didn't quite understand, but, as long as he did, she was good with it. "Does that mean anything to you?"

"No. But we see similar items at crash sites and often at crime scenes. It's human nature to want to honor a difficult death." He set it back up in the window.

"I figure it had been made specifically for this purpose," she said, "because you can see how evenly centered the crosspiece is and how the ends go down at an angle. It's not like this was just too jagged pieces of driftwood tied together."

"You're right," he said. "Plus *Johnny* is less scratched in as much as carved in."

"Exactly. But I don't understand why. I wondered about it and asked Penny if Johnny might have drowned, like Paul Shore did."

Mack turned to look at her. "Was that the same year?"

She nodded slowly. "Paul went missing in May, just as the high floodwaters hit," she added. "But Johnny didn't go missing until August, and the water should have dropped by then."

Mack looked out at the creek, as if thinking back. "High water can start anytime in May most years—there are always exceptions—depending on how much snow is up in the mountains and how quickly it comes down, which also depends on rainstorms and other types of weather. We can get heavy flash floods right through July. But you're right. By August the lake level has dropped, and the creek itself has slowed down to a narrow slow channel. By September it's completely calm."

"Also Johnny didn't swim well." Her words were quiet. "So what's the chance he drowned accidentally? Or maybe had a little help," she emphasized. "Then whoever was there didn't want to leave him to be found so moved him to a new location where nobody would ever find him."

"All plausible," he said, "but remember that part about needing evidence."

She pointed at the cross. "That seems to indicate somebody thought maybe Johnny died in the creek."

"Sure. But we found it down at your place again," he said.

"Not quite," she said. "It was up a bit. Maybe ten feet away from my place."

"Close enough," he said. "It's hardly worth arguing

over."

She shrugged. "Well, I'd argue about it," she said. "Otherwise you'd just pin that one on me too."

He groaned. "Even if Johnny did drown in August, there would be a body at that time of year. And, no, I wouldn't blame that on you."

"Unless there was another strange accident," she said. "You know? Like, did a bridge collapse? Did a truck hit a bank and crash down a bridge? I mean, all kinds of terrible things could have gone wrong. But, yes, I would say the likelihood of finding a body in the dry season would be in the 80 or 90 percent mark."

"Right," he said.

"So then we're back to maybe Johnny drowned and was moved," she said. "Or there was a fight, and maybe somebody held him underwater too long and killed him. You realize that a person can drown in just like two inches of water?"

"And again we're guessing," Mack said in a dry tone. "Have you ever considered writing novels? You have a vivid imagination."

"I know," she said. "But, once my mind gets locked on a problem, it won't let go."

"I noticed." He walked back to the stove and gave the sauce pot a stir.

Doreen joined him, watching over his shoulder, and could see these lighter-colored bubbles popping up through the center before Mack turned them under into the mixture. Then he lifted the lid on the pot of water and put it back down again.

"It's a nice little stove," he said.

She nodded. "It looks nice, fancy, modern. In a way it

almost doesn't fit the atmosphere of my kitchen for that reason alone."

"Sure, but you're learning," he said. "And you're a blend of old and new yourself."

"I certainly am while living here. I could go check up and down the creek for more evidence," she said thoughtfully. "The only thing is, it's been twenty-nine years."

"True," he said, "but you still found the cross."

"Goliath and Mugs did."

At that, Thaddeus squawked. "Thaddeus did. Thaddeus did."

She reached out her arm, and Thaddeus walked up it.

"Where have you been, big guy?" Mack asked, stroking his feathery back.

She could tell Thaddeus had just woken up. "He sleeps a lot," she said. "Is that normal?"

"No clue."

"But then we are doing lots of activities," she said thoughtfully. "So he likely needs his beauty rest when he can get it."

Thaddeus sat on her shoulder and pecked at her ear.

"He's hungry," she said in surprise. She looked around, and, sure enough, all the animals' food bowls were empty. She groaned. "I still can't seem to get in the habit of feeding them at a regular time."

"So does it mean he's hungry when he pecks you?" Mack asked, studying the bird. "Did he hurt you?"

She shook her head. "No, not at all."

Heading to the front closet, Doreen got Thaddeus's food and placed a little on the kitchen table. Immediately Thaddeus hopped off her shoulder and sat on the table, pecking away at his food. And then, out of the corner of his eye, his gaze fixed on the green piece of celery stalk, leftover from Mack's chopping tasks. Thaddeus hopped up to the countertop, walked over, and pecked at it.

Doreen glanced at Mack. "Do you mind?"

He shook his head. "It's going in the garbage anyway." He moved it over to the kitchen table, so Thaddeus could have better access. Between the bird seeds and the celery, Thaddeus appeared to be quite content.

She fed Goliath then, but he only made his appearance when she banged her spoon against his bowl and placed it on the floor. Then he was right here, winding between her legs.

"I already put it down for you, silly," she said affectionately, reaching down to rub his ears.

As soon as she did that, his nose came up high enough that the aroma of his food hit the right spot, and he launched himself forward and started to eat, crouched down on all fours.

Mack chuckled. "At least they enjoy their food."

"Yeah, they do," she said.

She fed Mugs, who seemed to be much less interested in his dog food than in the pot on the stove.

Mack noted Mugs's focus and shook his head. "Oh, no you don't, big guy."

Just then the front door bell rang. Mack looked at Doreen, his eyebrows raised.

She shrugged. "I don't have a clue." She picked up a towel, wiped her hands, and walked to the front door.

The alarms weren't set because she and Mack were inside. She opened the front door and found Hornby, grinning like a crazy man.

He pushed past her and said, "I thought I'd come by and have that cup of coffee."

"Don't bother," she snapped, pointing toward the front door. "Get out."

"Why should I?" he said. "It's obvious you live all alone and need somebody to keep you company," he said with a half leer, half sneer.

Insulted, she shook her head. "Get out, or I'll call the cops."

Mugs, who had followed her, obviously didn't like her tone of voice because he growled at Hornby.

Hornby looked down at Mugs. "God, he's ugly."

She gasped. "Don't say that." She stepped to the fireplace and picked up her poker. She marched up to him and held it out like she would hit him. "Get out of my house."

He laughed at her. "Oh my. Aren't you so cute. What's the matter? How come you're not friendly to a single guy like me? I just want some company too."

"I choose my own company, thanks, and you're not on the invitation list," Doreen snapped. "Now get out." Then she noticed his gaze roaming the living room, looking appraisingly at all the knickknacks and furniture. She took a few more steps toward him, threateningly. "Get out now."

He turned to sneer at her. "Or what?"

Chapter 21

Saturday Evening ...

"OR ELSE I'LL arrest you for trespassing and any other charges that apply," Mack said from the kitchen doorway, his arms across his chest. He looked at Doreen, the fireplace poker ready for her time at bat, and raised his eyebrows.

"He's assessing the contents of my living room," she said, "not to mention threatening me."

"I didn't threaten you," Hornby said, sauntering toward to the front door. He turned an eye on Mack. "What the hell do you want with this dried-up old prune anyway?"

She gasped and charged after him.

He laughed, stepped onto the front porch, and slammed the door in her face.

She opened the door and yelled, "I'm warning you. Get off my property and stay off." She slammed the door again as she stepped back into the living room. She watched through the window as he drove down the cul-de-sac. But something about his small car made her wonder. "Does that bumper belong on that vehicle? And, on this side, there's a panel of a different color."

Mack studied the vehicle and nodded. "Yeah, but it's not that uncommon. Particularly if people have accidents without insurance coverage, and they want to fix the damage cheap. They'll go for parts from a junkyard, and it doesn't matter what color it is."

"Do you think people's buying habits are the same everywhere?"

"What are you talking about?"

"Susan said the vehicle that ran the two boys off the road was put together with all different panels. As in, it was a mishmash of colors, like somebody had tried to build or repair a vehicle with other auto parts from, you know, destroyed vehicles."

"Yes, I do remember that."

"So could this be the same car from twenty-nine years ago?" she asked.

"Not sure, but I'd say it's newer than that. But … maybe all of Hornby's vehicles ended up looking like this. I'll have to check into that further." He withdrew a notepad and a pen from his pocket and jotted something down. "But Hornby was supposedly in the vehicle with Susan."

"Right." Doreen tried to put it together in her mind. "Do you think she gave a half-assed confession?"

"I don't know," he said. "I'd have to look into that file, see if her statement is even in there."

"*Something* should be there."

"I hope so as she's not around anymore for us to question."

"No," she said, "but her great-uncle is. Maybe other family members are still alive too."

He turned to look at her, his hands on his hips. It wasn't anger that she saw; it was worry. "Hornby is dangerous," he said bluntly. "You get that, right?"

"I do now," she said. "He forced his way into the house. Then he wouldn't leave as he was casing the joint."

"Only when he saw me standing in the kitchen doorway did he turn to leave."

"Hey," Doreen asked, "how come he didn't see your car in my driveway?"

"One of your neighbors must have visitors parking on the street, and one of them cut off part of your driveway. I didn't want to box you in, so I parked a couple doors down."

She nodded, but her frown remained.

"It's not like Hornby should recognize my personal vehicle."

"What do you think he would have done if you weren't here?" she asked slowly.

"Well, funny you're considering that now because you weren't thinking about your own personal danger earlier," he said. "You were thinking about him assessing the contents of your house. And where to hit him with that fire poker."

She winced. "Because he was staring at individual pieces, as if calculating its value. As if he already knew this house was full of valuables."

"So maybe we should check his association with your intruder," Mack said thoughtfully. "The last thing I want is yet another intruder in here, picking up what the first one missed. It would make it look like Darth McLeod was innocent, since he was locked up at the time of this proposed future break-in. That could give rise to enough reasonable doubt that his case would get thrown out."

She didn't quite follow all the legal parts, but she did understand the part about another intruder. "That is not what I want." She looked at Mugs. "And Mugs couldn't stand Hornby, which is also very indicative of him being dangerous."

"True enough," Mack said. "But I wish Mugs had barked when the intruder had initially forced his way in."

"Well, of course he didn't," she said, looking at Mack in surprise.

He frowned at her. "What are you talking about?"

She beamed up at him. "Mugs knew you were here. So, if anybody would get into the heavyweight-protector mode, Mugs would expect you to be it. If you weren't here, he would have been much more of a guard dog."

"I doubt it." He shook his head, looking at Mugs, who now lay on the floor with his ears puddling beside him. "He's not a watchdog."

"Don't insult him," she warned. "You two have a great relationship. Don't ruin that."

"Come on, let's eat," he said. "Dinner is ready."

She stared at him in surprise, her mind still trying to switch from Hornby's potential involvement in the accident that had killed the two men long ago back to tonight's dinner. "How can it be done? We didn't do anything with the pasta yet."

"I was putting it in the pot of boiling water when Hornby arrived. And that was a surprisingly longish encounter," he said. "Let's get the table set. By then it should be done."

And very quickly they sat down with two beautiful plates of spaghetti.

She sighed happily. "The only thing missing is garlic bread."

"I meant to pick up some French bread and make some," he admitted, "but I forgot. Sorry, I saw a few signs that my mother has been declining mentally. It's worrying me." He glanced over at her. "I've been distracted."

"Ugh that's tough," she said. "And I get that you're worried but I'm stuck on something else you said—you can make garlic bread?" Her eyes rounded. "I used to eat it as a snack when my husband wasn't looking," she said with a wince at the bad memories.

"Why didn't you want him to know?" he asked in an ominous tone.

She gave him that breezy smile. "Oh, you know. Back to that *I might get fat if I ate too many carbs* thing," she said.

Mack just shook his head and proceeded to twirl his fork into the spaghetti, getting a big mouthful.

She watched in amazement as the entire forkful went into his mouth. By contrast, she used a spoon and a fork. "I learned a long time ago to only take a few noodles at a time." Carefully she coiled up several noodles using her spoon, and then, with a nice tiny little bite, she popped it into her mouth and swooned. "Oh, my. That's absolutely fantastic."

Mack appeared mollified as he watched her thoroughly enjoy her dinner. "The thing about a sauce like this is," he said in a conversational tone, "we can make a large pot of it. Then you can eat it for several days, and you can freeze some."

She looked back at the pot. "So there are leftovers?"

He nodded. "Absolutely. And it's no trouble to put it in the fridge. We cooked too many noodles today, so you can warm up both them and the sauce in the microwave."

She stared at him in delight. And then she shook her head. "So that's what people do? They make enough meals for several days at a time?" As far as she was concerned, that was genius.

He smiled. "That's what I do. I'll make a stew and eat it

for two or three days. I'll make a chili and have it for two or three days."

She sighed rapturously. "Just the thought of having food for two or three days sounds wonderful." She dug into her pasta again. When she could feel his hard stare, she refused to look up. "I'm eating. I'm eating."

"Not enough," he said. "Just in the few weeks you've been here, you've lost at least ten pounds."

She considered that and shrugged. "I've been active," she said, "but it is what it is."

"That isn't something you can just brush off," he growled. "You have to take better care of yourself."

"With your help I'm doing that. But I'm a long way off from learning how to make that sauce."

"True. It was probably not a good one to start with." He pondered that a moment. "We could do something a lot simpler tomorrow," he said thoughtfully. "There's still leftover pasta. I can show you how to make a carbonara pasta. That's super, super simple. Or even just a scramble."

She listened to the terms roll off his tongue, like she was supposed to understand what language he spoke. But she was determined to learn, especially if it meant she would get food like this again. She stared at her plate. "Honestly, I've seen videos on YouTube where they have these fabulous dishes at the end, but I'm always suspicious a chef has arrived with a meal just before they're ready to sit down, so it looks like they actually made it."

He laughed. "You know what? Probably a lot of people out there do pull stunts like that, but I wouldn't count on it. It's not hard to cook. A few more dishes and you'll be fine."

"One dish," she said, "the chef used to make for me that I loved so much. It had feta cheese, fresh tomatoes, basil, and pasta. With some vinaigrette, served like a salad."

He nodded. "Pasta salad is good."

"It had artichokes in it." Suddenly her mouth watered at the remembered taste of pickled artichokes. "I have no clue what made me think of that right now. But I loved that dish."

"I'd have to pick up some artichokes, pickled of course. I presume that is what you want. But it would be easy enough to toss together. I could show you how to spin plain pasta into four or five different meals."

She wanted to cry, yet, at the same time, her laughter bubbled out. "You are a godsend," she said. "But I'll stop talking now, so I can focus on eating."

And that was what she did. With every bite, she closed her eyes and moaned in joy. When she was done, she looked up to see Mack watching her, leaning back in his chair, resting against the nearby wall, his arms across his chest, his plate empty too.

"What?" she asked suspiciously.

"I don't think I've ever seen anybody enjoy their food more," he said quietly. "It makes me think all kinds of things."

She narrowed her gaze at him. "Like what?" Was he flirting with her? It seemed to be a trend lately. She wasn't sure she liked it. She really liked Mack, but, at the moment, she liked his cooking more than the thought of getting into a troubled relationship.

He brushed a hand in the air as if washing away the conversation. "So probably two meals' worth are left in the pot of just spaghetti. What would you like to make tomorrow?"

"Something simple," she said.

"Well, there's probably nothing simpler than the salad

you were just talking about. So, when I come tomorrow at dinnertime," he said, "you can make that for me."

She frowned. "But I don't know how."

He chuckled. "Was there anything else in it, like black olives or chickpeas?"

She nodded slowly. "Both of those sometimes. But usually just black olives."

"Then I'll pick up a can and show you how easy it is."

"Perfect," she said.

He got to his feet. "Now let's get the dishes done." But then his phone rang. He pulled it out. "Damn. I have to leave. There's been an accident."

"Whereabouts?" she asked.

He frowned. "A few blocks from here."

"Oh, dear," she said. "Go. Duty calls. I'll do the dishes."

He hesitated and looked around the kitchen. "I don't usually leave the kitchen this dirty."

"It's not dirty," she said. "Go."

"If you don't mind," he said, still hesitating.

She patted him on the arm. "I mean it. Go. I had an absolutely fabulous dinner. I'll put it all away, and tomorrow we'll pick up the pieces and make something new."

He chuckled and snagged her into a big hug. "Thank you." As he stepped out the front door, he turned and came back into the kitchen. "Set the alarms. I don't want Hornby coming back inside."

She winced, followed him, closed the front door, and set the alarm. She didn't bother with the kitchen one yet because she was still working in there. Plus she might take a cup of tea out to the backyard shortly.

Clean up took longer than she'd expected, but finally she was done. With all the counters cleaned off, she made herself a cup of tea and sat outside to watch the sunset. When her phone rang, she was surprised to see Mack's number.

"Hey," he said.

"Hey," she said. "Dishes are done. I'm sitting out in the back, having a cup of tea."

"Sounds good to me. It was a car accident," he said. "It was Hornby."

"What?" she asked in surprise. "Was he the one hurt?"

"Yes," he said. "The trouble was, he had the accident because he'd been shot. He'll be okay, but I wanted you to know he's not a danger to you. At least not tonight."

"What?" her heart sank. "Will people think it was me?"

Mack went silent for too long.

"You're making me nervous. Say something."

"Why would they think it was you?" he asked curiously.

"Because he was at my house, and we had an ugly confrontation," she said slowly.

"I was there with you," he said. "I was a witness to that. And he left healthy and very unhappy."

"True," she said thoughtfully. "But this doesn't feel right."

"It doesn't feel wrong either," he corrected. "People like Hornby make enemies. A lot of enemies. So don't go thinking it was connected to your cold case."

She hesitated, her mind busily considering how it all fit together. "I get what you're saying," she said, "but you know it'll be hard not to."

"He's alive. He's in the hospital, likely heading for surgery. I can't speak with him until at least tomorrow."

"Check his vehicle over very carefully," she said. "Look for anything connected to Johnny's death."

"What would that be? It's not even the same vehicle

most likely," he said. "You think a confessional letter will be in his glove box?"

"For all you know, he's got something of Johnny's tucked away that he's been carrying around with him all this time. Too bad he didn't see the cross in my dining room," she said. "We might have learned something by seeing his reaction to it."

"You weren't too worried about what kind of reaction he might give you at that time," he said. "You were a crazy Amazonian woman with a poker in your hand."

"He was after my priceless antiques that I need to get packed up and shipped out of here as soon as possible," she cried. "I still have to wait until Monday."

"So two more nights," he said. "Anyway, you probably don't have to worry about Hornby tonight."

"And, for that, thank you," she said warmly. "I'll sleep much better now."

Chapter 22

Sunday Morning …

WHEN SHE GOT up the next morning, Doreen couldn't resist pouring fresh coffee into a travel mug, and—with all the animals in tow, and the alarms set—she walked up the creek. It was her favorite place to stroll. Although she'd slept well last night, still something about Hornby made her uncomfortable. Also, she couldn't help but wonder who had shot him and why.

As she passed the turnoff to Penny's house, Doreen wondered if it was too early to call and to ask a question. Deciding there would never be a better time, she hopped across the creek on the rocks with Thaddeus on her shoulder. Mugs traipsed through the creek behind her, now dripping little dribbles of creek water. However, Goliath howled on the far side, where he'd been left behind. He wasn't into getting his paws wet at all.

She walked back over and scooped him up against her chest. Only Thaddeus didn't like that and tried to peck the top of his head. Finally she plunked Goliath down on the other side. "Sorry, buddy. Not quite enough dry rocks here for you, are there?"

She kept walking until she came to Penny's door. She knocked several times. No answer. Frowning, she wondered if Penny was still asleep. How rude Doreen was, knocking early enough to wake up Penny.

Doreen waited a little longer, then stepped out of the yard.

One of the neighbors came out of his house, looked at her, and said, "Penny isn't here."

She turned to face him. "Really?"

He nodded. "She left last night with a suitcase in her hand."

"Oh," she said. "I'm sorry to hear that." She wasn't sure what to do about it. "Any idea how long she'll be gone?"

The neighbor shook his head. "Not a clue."

"I don't see a For Sale sign," she said out loud.

He looked at her in surprise. "I don't think she's selling, is she?"

Doreen thought back to their earlier conversation and had to wonder if Penny had said she was selling or if she was *planning* on selling. "I thought it was her intention, but I can't remember if she said it was already for sale or not."

"Maybe," he said. "She didn't have a lot of savings after George's death so might need to sell the house. That way she can buy a condo and have money in the bank. But then again, maybe she wants to get away from the memories."

"I imagine," she said, "it could go either way."

She was a little perturbed as she headed back toward the creek. She pulled out her phone and called Penny's number. When there was no answer, she left a voicemail.

The foursome tripped their way back down the creek bed to her little bridge and walked across, having come full circle from home. "It's still early, guys. Do we want to do some garden work?"

They all looked at her like she was crazy. She had to admit that she probably was. Not to mention she was also hungry.

When she got back in her house, she gave them breakfast and made toast and cheese for herself before she sat down at her laptop. How much did she really know about Penny? Not a lot and still that niggling question remained as to why she might have left. She could have gone to a friend's house in town, staying overnight because they wanted a couple drinks, and she didn't want to drive home. Really no way to know. Besides, no need to be suspicious of Penny because she had asked Doreen to look into Johnny's death. If Penny had had something to do with his death, then she wouldn't expose herself to an investigation like that. Besides, Penny was pretty small. She couldn't have killed Johnny. Or rather, she could have killed him but not moved him afterward. At least not alone …

It was also an interesting coincidence that Hornby arrived at Doreen's house, got shot shortly thereafter, and Penny disappeared, just like that.

Doreen's mind was trying to fit the pieces together. The trouble was, she didn't have enough pieces. What if Penny had shot Hornby? What if Penny thought Hornby had killed Johnny, and she'd shot Hornby, hoping he'd crash and kill himself?

"Guys, once again Mack would be shaking his head at me." In her mind she could hear him clearly. For fun she tried to imitate his voice in a comical way. "Doreen, we can't go around making assumptions or wild guesses. We need proof."

Mugs woofed several times.

She chuckled, got up from her laptop, and poured herself another cup of coffee. She sat back down and researched Hornby and then Penny. She was younger than her husband, younger than Hornby too. Penny might have been closer in age to Susan or that other girl in Johnny's group. Yet Penny said she didn't know about any girl but Susan. As Doreen's searches failed to give her any leads, one question she had been trying to answer resurfaced once more: who was that second girl in Johnny's group?

She called Nan. "Would you mind asking your friend Richie who his great-niece's girlfriend was during the time of Johnny's disappearance," she said. "I understand the three guys hung out with Susan, but I thought another girl did too."

"Good morning to you," Nan said in a delighted twitter. "I'll call you back in a few minutes." And, like Nan was prone to do, which was great, she hung up without needing any further explanation.

Doreen sipped her coffee and continued to research Penny but found nothing out of the ordinary. Penny and George had been married for a long time. And, outside of some volunteer work she was involved in at a church's Christmas bazaar or some fund-raiser, Penny's name didn't show up very often. Doreen thought about who else she could contact from back then, but there wasn't anyone. She sent Mack a text and asked if there was any reason for Penny to have up and left.

When the phone rang, she assumed it was Mack. But instead it was Nan.

"Her name was Julie," she said. "But we're not sure what her last name was. Her parents lived across from the Hornbys in the same cul-de-sac."

"That makes sense. The kids lived next door to each other," Doreen said. "But how am I supposed to find out what her last name is?"

"You can probably check the land title records," Nan said. "Or you could ask Mack." On that note, she went off on a peal of laughter and hung up.

"*Ask Mack*," Doreen repeated. "Well, that's not helpful."

She brought up a map of Kelowna, zoomed in on the cul-de-sac where Penny and Hornby had lived and came up with an address for the house across from Hornby's childhood home. Because they were both on the corner of the cul-de-sac, it was pretty easy to tell which house it was. At least she hoped.

Just then Goliath laid across her keyboard. She groaned and dragged him off to cuddle him. Finally she picked up her cell phone.

How would I find out who lived at this address 29 years ago? She typed into a text, adding the address, and fired it off to Mack.

After she sent it, she wondered if he would get fed up with her questions. She went to the internet and typed in that address to see who was on the current registry. But it wasn't online. That database was unavailable. She thought it should be available. Now if anybody wanted to check all of Doreen's private information, she might have something different to say. But it was frustrating to be close to answers but not able to get the real ones.

Whoever this Julie was, she was important to the case. If for no other reason that she might be the last one of the girls alive—or the last one alive period. With Hornby shot and in hospital, as much as Doreen didn't like the man, she didn't want to hear he had died from his wounds. This Julie person was the only other one with possibly any answers as to what had happened so long ago. If Julie was even still alive.

Mack's answer came back. **Willoughby.**

She grinned and typed in the name Julie Willoughby on her search window. And up popped all kinds of articles. Poor Julie had had a rough life. She was arrested in one article, apparently for breaking and entering when she turned eighteen. A group of kids had had a wild party, drank too much, and then somehow thought it was a good idea to break into one of the neighbors' homes. But no mention was made of the other kids in the group.

A few other articles mentioned Julie, but they didn't yield anything new. And, in the last few years, nothing was said about her.

Doreen sighed, then wondered if the Willoughbys were still living here. She sent Mack a question. **Is the same family still living there?**

She had to wait for more answers. Goliath slid to the floor, bored.

She got up and checked the fridge because, by now, she was starving again. She pulled out some cheese and crackers, knowing they would have pasta for dinner again. She figured she'd survive on this quite nicely.

He sent back a simple text. **Yes.**

She crowed. "Okay, guys. Road trip again."

She finished her cheese and crackers and grabbed Mugs's leash. Goliath joined them at the door. Thaddeus wanted a ride. She led the way out the backyard again and up the creek to the cul-de-sac. Penny's house was still dark. Hornby's house was dark also, but the house across from it, the Willoughbys' house, had lights on.

Doreen walked up to the front door, Thaddeus on her

shoulder, Goliath strolling behind her at his pace, and Mugs sat at her heels. When the door opened, a woman answered.

Doreen looked at her and smiled. "Don't suppose you're Julie Willoughby, are you?"

The woman looked at her in surprise. "Yes, I am. Who are you?"

"I'm Doreen. Nan is my grandmother," she said by way of explanation. It seemed to her all the townsfolk knew who Nan was.

Julie's face brightened. "How is Nan?" she asked affectionately.

"She's doing just fine," she said. "I have a few questions, if you've got a moment."

The woman opened the door. "Sure, come on in."

Doreen hesitated at the doorway. "What about my animals?"

Julie's gaze widened as she took in Thaddeus. Then she saw the cat and the dog, and she laughed. "Now I know who you are," she said. "You're the bone lady." She waved all the animals inside. "Come on in. I was just sitting down to a muffin. Would you like one?"

"Yes, I would," Doreen said. "Thank you." Seated at the kitchen table, she said, "I wanted to ask you a few questions about Johnny's death."

The woman looked at her in surprise. "Johnny?"

"Johnny," Doreen said. "Johnny Jordan. Your neighbor's younger brother."

Julie sat back, as if the shock was more than she expected. "Oh, that's definitely not a period of my life I talk about very much."

"Understood," Doreen said. "Do you know Penny very well?"

Julie nodded. "Well, not only are we neighbors but Johnny and I used to be good friends."

"Of course. Penny asked me to look into Johnny's disappearance. I came over here this morning to ask her a few questions again, but she's not home."

"I just saw her yesterday morning," Julie said.

"One of your neighbors said she took a suitcase and left last night," Doreen said. "I presume she's gone on an overnight trip somewhere."

Julie stared out the window at the house across the street. "I always wondered what went on in that house. George and Penny seemed to be so happy that it was almost sickening, but that was to hide the truth."

"What truth?" Doreen asked in confusion.

"Nobody is *that* happily married. I used to ask Johnny about it. He'd laugh and say that's who they were."

"A sickening-sweet, happy, loving couple?" Doreen asked. That had been her impression from what Penny had said.

"No. A fighting, backstabbing, very unhappily married couple," Julie corrected. "One of the reasons I spent as much time as I did with Johnny was so he could get away from the place."

That took Doreen a moment to digest. She didn't want to think Penny's marriage had been so bad that Johnny had just wanted to get away from it all …

"You have no idea where he disappeared to?" Doreen asked slowly, tilting her head to study the woman across from her. She was older than Doreen, younger than Nan, caught somewhere in a time loop. Her hair was in a bun at the back, but it oddly suited her. "Are you an artist?"

The woman laughed and nodded. "I am. How did I give

myself away?"

"You have a very creative look to you," Doreen said with a smile. "I don't suppose you have any paintings of Johnny from back then, do you?"

Julie shook her head. "No. I didn't start painting until later."

"What caused you to go in that direction?"

"Losing Johnny," Julie admitted. "I loved him dearly. But I wasn't part of the in crowd. Like Hornby, I was more or less in the outside circle."

"Hornby was in an accident last night." She watched Julie's reaction carefully. The color drained from her skin.

"He was what?" She switched her gaze to Hornby's house across the road from her.

"I gather you know him well too?"

"Of course," she said. "We're all tied to the events of so long ago. But we're hardly friends."

"And you have no idea what happened to Johnny?"

Julie shook her head. "No, of course not. If I had any idea, I'd have spoken up. For a long time I wondered if it was Hornby."

"You mean that Hornby might have killed him?"

"Well, no doubt Johnny is dead," she said, "because I know for a fact that he would have contacted me."

"Why is that?" Doreen asked.

"Because he loved me," she said simply. "We were going to run away together and start a whole new life, but he disappeared."

"Do you think he might have run away without you?" Doreen asked, hesitating to put the thought into words.

"Lots of people asked me that," she said with a sweet smile. "But, no, that's not what happened. I knew him too well. Besides, he could have just told me that he would go and come back for me. We were supposed to meet that evening and make plans, but he never showed up."

"How long was it from when you last talked to him and then when you were to meet him? What kind of time frame was that?"

"An hour," Julie said quietly. "An hour tops. If I had just walked across this yard and spoken to him at the back of Penny's place, there's a good chance nothing would have happened to him. But we were going to meet at the park in an hour. I got there a little early. But saw no sign of Johnny. I walked around to Penny's backyard and looked over the fence and called for him. But there was no sign of him. I never saw him again."

Chapter 23

Sunday Late Morning ...

DOREEN STOOD OUTSIDE Julie's house, studying the Hornby place, thinking about the triangle between Hornby, Johnny, and Julie. Definitely something had been going on here. Julie thought maybe Hornby was part of it.

As Doreen walked down the steps, the door opened again behind her. Julie leaned against the doorjamb and frowned at her. "Do you think Hornby had something to do with Johnny's disappearance?"

"I don't know," Doreen said. "I have my suspicions. But without a body ..." She shrugged. "I don't know that there's anything we can do about it. What would be the motive?"

"Me," she said bleakly. "Hornby wanted me, and I had made it very clear I wasn't interested. Johnny was the perfect person for me. We had a fantastic future all mapped out." She glared at Hornby's house. "I always wondered. But I never could figure out how or why."

"I had guessed somebody arranged to meet him in the park," Doreen said, "like you mentioned."

"I did arrange to meet him," Julie said. "But he wasn't there, and he never showed up."

Doreen knew she had no reason to believe Julie, but there was just something—that note of desperation to Julie's need to look for answers—that Doreen trusted. "So far the only suspicious character in all of this is Hornby, but he's just been shot and in a car accident. So if somebody really hated him …"

"Not just somebody," Julie said. "Everybody."

"Tell me more," Doreen said invitingly. They still stood on the front steps. "Did George and Penny know about your relationship with Johnny?"

"No," Julie said. "We kept it private. Johnny didn't think they'd approve, since he'd recently broken up with Susan. But we'd liked each other before that. He didn't want to hurt Susan, so their relationship limped along longer than it should have. As soon as they split, we hooked up."

"Thank you for sharing that. I'm looking for something important, and I can't quite figure out what it is." Mugs wandered into the garden beside her. Doreen immediately shoved her hand into her pocket and pulled out a poopie bag. "I hope you don't mind." She motioned at Mugs.

Julie looked into her garden bed and chuckled. "No. A dog has gotta do what a dog has gotta do."

Grateful for that attitude, Doreen walked behind Mugs, waited until he did his business, then carefully scooped it all up, making sure she got the pieces of bark mulch that had a little bit of the droppings with it. She turned to walk to the garbage cans. "May I put the bag in one of your cans?"

Julie waved her hand at them. "Go ahead."

"Thank you so much. I don't know when your garbage is picked up, but I'm hoping this won't stink too badly." She walked toward the cans.

"For the longest time, we didn't have to worry about

garbage collection. The garbage truck driver for this area lived across from me," she said with a laugh, pointing at the house across the cul-de-sac. "Sometimes he'd even make special trips just for us."

Doreen stared over at Hornby's house and then back at her. "Hornby?"

"No, not Alan," she said. "His dad. That's what I meant about *for the longest time* but not anymore as his dad is retired now."

"Wow though. That would have been helpful. I have all kinds of stuff I'll be getting rid of. How convenient to have a garbage truck accessible."

"Absolutely," Julie said. "My mother was forever putting out pieces of junk furniture, and he'd take them away for her. The rules have all changed now, and the city is stricter about that stuff."

"Did he ever take the garbage truck home?"

Julie chuckled. "He wasn't supposed to, but sure he did. Sometimes I think he did that to help out the neighborhood, so the residents could throw extra garbage in. He was very, very conscientious. Although the city wanted forty hours a week from him, I swear he gave them forty-eight every week." She smiled.

"Is he still around?"

"Oh, sure," she said. "He's down at one of the old folks' homes. He's getting on now. Not sure how old he is, but he's gotta be close to ninety. He's heading toward a hospice, last I heard." She frowned. "Honestly, he might have already passed away. I don't know. And that would be a sad day. He was a good man."

"Did you guys ever get to ride around with him?" Doreen asked.

"Well, his son often did," she said with a big grin. "And Mr. Hornby did take us around one Halloween. We were pretending to be garbage men." She chuckled. "I think we were only about ten or so. Then we thought our buddy Alan had the best dad in the world."

"I bet," Doreen said, chuckling. "I guess you don't remember if he ever brought the truck home the summer Johnny went missing, huh?"

"Johnny wouldn't have taken off in it, if that's what you're thinking. Johnny couldn't drive it. It was big and cranky. Alan used to operate the levers for his dad sometimes. But it was never a smooth, sleek model. In fact, Mr. Hornby protested getting one of the *newfangled* trucks," she said, grinning at the memories. "He much preferred the old ones. Said all that new computerized wizardry would break down."

"Right. Still how convenient for you," Doreen said with envy, thinking of her crowded house. "Did you guys ever run over and put extra garbage in?"

She nodded. "My mum did. You could fill the bin in the back, and then it would get mushed up the next time he'd put stuff in. Back then the trucks weren't very sophisticated."

"Right. Back then you had a different landfill system than we do now." Doreen had yet to go to the Glenmore Landfill that serviced all the Kelowna area, but she'd heard it had gotten much more high-tech in the last few years. The new landfill was at a totally different location too. The old landfill had been reclaimed, with a new subdivision built atop it. The new location was bigger and had space for recycling.

"Yes," Julie said. "Back then we barely had anything like we do now, which is probably really too bad because a lot of the stuff we tossed could have been recycled."

"So he'd drive the truck, collect garbage, take it to the dump, and drop it all in?"

"Usually," Julie said. "There was always heavy equipment to move the garbage around, and then some of garbage would get burned."

"That makes sense," Doreen said slowly. Then a horrible idea filled her mind. She gave a final wave. "Thanks very much. If you see Penny return, could you tell her to give me a ring please?"

Julie gave a wave and walked back into her house, closing the door.

Doreen wondered how Julie would feel about Doreen's current theory.

She headed to Hornby's house and knocked on the door. No answer. She brought out her phone and called Mack as she headed toward the creek.

"I have a working theory on what happened to Johnny," she said. "The trouble is, twenty-nine years later, it'll be damn-near impossible to confirm it."

"Oh?" he said in a lazy voice. "Can't wait to hear this one."

She snorted. "Well, I'm not telling you then. Can you tell me who is living in the Hornby house now?"

"Your grandmother can answer a part of that question or at least get the answer," he said. "Old Man Hornby was our local garbage collector forever, since eons ago, and he's a resident at Rosemoor now."

"Right. I just heard that, but also that he's headed to a hospice or might have passed on recently," Doreen said. "Was he married? Did he raise his son alone? Do you know?"

Mack gave a long-suffering sigh.

She could hear the *click* of his keyboard. "Oh, can you access your cop stuff from home?" Excitement lit up her voice.

"No," he snapped. "*Hornby, Alan* is the only son. Mother died when he was sixteen. Old Man Hornby never remarried."

"No other siblings?"

"No," he said. "Just Alan."

"Thanks." She picked up the pace as she headed toward the creek. "I'm coming home again."

"Where have you been?"

"Trying to talk to Penny," she said, "but there's no sign of her, and one of the neighbors said he saw her take off with a suitcase."

"If you think about it, that doesn't seem very sinister," he said, snickering. "She's probably had enough of all your questions."

She frowned into her phone. "That's not very nice."

"True," he said.

"I imagine she's still looking for answers, particularly for George."

"Maybe," he said. "But what if they weren't that happily married couple, as you initially thought? Or maybe George killed his younger brother in a fit of rage."

"I did consider the idea," she said, "but then tossed it. George spent way too many of the ensuing years trying to find the truth. ... I did consider Penny," she said after a moment. "But I don't think she could've done it alone. She could have killed him, you know, by hitting him over the head when he was sitting there, unsuspecting. But she certainly wasn't strong enough to move the body on her own."

"So what now? You have an imaginary lover helping her out? A man no one has seen or heard of? What motive could there possibly be?"

"I don't know," she said. "That's one of the reasons why I tossed away that idea."

"Huh. Well, I agree with that. It also doesn't make any sense for Penny to contact you after all these years, asking you to look into it if she's the guilty party."

"I know," Doreen said. "That just added to it."

"I'm glad to hear it," he said.

She skirted around the outside of the cul-de-sac and headed for the creek, all three animals in a single line behind her. "I do have another theory though. I'll hang up now and call Nan. Bye." She clicked off and dialed Nan's number as she headed down the creek toward her home. Nan didn't answer. "Come on, Nan. Pick up. Please pick up."

But there was no answer. She tucked away her phone and marched as fast as she could back home. Thankfully the critters approved of her pace.

As soon as she saw the creek again, she felt a huge sense of relief. She could barely contain a sudden nervousness. She dialed Mack as she realized part of her unease. "I know you said he was shot and in a car accident, but just how badly injured is Hornby?"

"I don't know," he said. "Do I need to check for you?"

"Yeah," she said, "you do." She hung up on him. Inside her heart warmed that he took her concerns seriously.

When she reached the back of her house, she was happy to see she had truly set the alarm. She disabled it, stepped inside, then checked the front door, also relieved to see its alarm was set. With all the animals inside, she shut the door and turned on the alarm system again.

She couldn't explain it, but, all of a sudden, she had this horrible sense of urgency. She looked around her house, wondering how safe it was. Just because the alarms were set, that didn't mean her house was impenetrable. But it was better than what she'd had before.

Taking off her shoes, she did a quick check of the lower level. Everything appeared to be normal. Mugs wasn't upset in any way.

She glanced at her watch. It was later than she'd expected. Still, her mind buzzed uneasily. She crept upstairs, trying to miss the squeaky stairs, still hoping it was safe up here. She slipped into the spare bedroom and listened. No way she could hide the animals' presence, and that was a problem. She waited a long moment, checking the spare room, finding nothing here. A bathroom was across the hallway, but Mugs had gone in there and came back out again, his tail wagging.

She eyed him suspiciously. The only person he'd wag his tail for would be Mack. Still Mugs headed toward her, so that was good too. She probably was going crazy, but the last thing she wanted to do was go into her damn bedroom.

Goliath, however, had no such qualms. With his tail twitching, he sauntered into the bedroom and disappeared from her sight. Mugs followed him. When she didn't hear anything, she sighed with relief. She stepped into the bedroom with all its chaos and found nobody there.

Just to be sure, she checked the en suite bathroom and then, with a deep breath, plunged into the big closet to make sure nobody was hiding in there. There wasn't anyone. Feeling foolish, she came out with her phone ringing. It was Mack.

"Why did you hang up on me?"

"Because I had this terrible feeling once I got inside the house," she said. "I just finished checking under the beds and in the closets, and nobody's here."

His voice turned grim. "I'm on my way over. Back your way out of that house for the moment."

She froze. "Why?"

"Because Hornby is no longer in the hospital."

Chapter 24

Sunday Late Afternoon ...

SHE HADN'T KNOWN her legs could carry her that far or that fast. But spurred by her, the animals flew behind her. She quickly unlocked the front door and stepped outside, racing down the front porch steps to the end of the driveway. There she danced around, waiting for Mack to show up. She hated that Hornby was loose.

Why would Mack even assume that Hornby would come after her again? Well, maybe because he'd already come here twice, and the last time he'd threatened her. So what were the chances he would come a third time?

Probably pretty damn good.

She turned to stare out into the street, looking for Mack's vehicle. When she still didn't see it, she walked into her front yard and then around to the back of the house. Surely if somebody were here, Mugs would have picked up on it.

As she walked past the side door to the garage, it burst open, startling her. A man jumped out, snatched her in his arms, one going around her neck to choke her. She couldn't even cry out. She gargled, scratched him hard with her nails, tried to stomp on his toes, then kicked up backward, trying to hit him in the groin.

When Mugs realized she was in trouble, he jumped on her attacker. Thaddeus came squawking down, landing on her attacker too, digging in his claws and pecking at his forehead. The man roared behind her, his grip loosening, cursing. And, dammit, she recognized Hornby's voice.

She spun around, her fist out, and clocked him one in the jaw. He stumbled backward, took one look at her, his eyes full of hate. "You're all nuts," he roared, brushing Thaddeus off his head. He disappeared, running as fast as he could through the backyard.

Doreen snatched Thaddeus up, crooning to him, even as she tried to control Mugs.

Just then Mack's truck came flying up the driveway. Mack must have caught sight of them from the entrance to the cul-de-sac. He was out of the truck, racing toward her in a heartbeat. He wrapped her in his arms. "Are you hurt?"

She shook her head. "Go after him. It was Hornby."

Mack had his phone in his hand. He ran behind her house. She grabbed Mugs again, fighting to keep him at her side. There was no sign of Goliath.

"Go left," she yelled to Mack. "Go left."

He changed direction and headed to the creek.

She stood, looking at the outside garage door she couldn't open fully before. She slid a hand around the wall, checking for a light switch. When she found it, she flipped it on, groaning because the garage was completely full of old furniture and boxes. But, from what she could see, nobody else was in here. Nor was there any room for someone to maneuver through the mess.

The door had been forced open and appeared to be

planed off on the edge to make it easier to open and close. So he'd been hiding, right inside the door, waiting for her. Either waiting for her to go to sleep and would trigger the alarm or hoping to catch her outside, like he had. Because of Mack's warning, she'd gone straight outside and had fallen victim to the maniac waiting for her.

Shaking, she walked back inside the house and put on the teakettle. She couldn't see Mack and had no idea if he'd called for backup or not. Just the thought of him out there with that crazy man made her quake in her boots.

"What if Hornby has a gun?" she asked Mugs. "He could turn around and shoot Mack dead."

What she also had to consider was maybe the asshole was coming around again, back to her place. She made herself a cup of tea, and, as she turned, she heard a hiss. She spun around to see Hornby standing in the kitchen doorway. And, sure enough, he had a gun in his hand.

She looked at him, knowing, when she'd come into the house, she hadn't reset the alarm. "Damn it, Mack will be really pissed at me for this one," she said with a bad attempt at humor.

Hornby's gaze just glinted.

"What did I ever do to you?" she asked.

"Asked too many questions," he said. "I wondered how much trouble you would be. But when I saw you continuously talking to Penny, I realized you would be a bigger problem than I thought. Once I saw you coming out of Julie's house, I knew you would be a huge pain in the arse. One I had to get rid of."

"Interesting," she said, leaning against the counter behind her, her hot cup of tea in her hand. She judged the distance between them. Boiling water was a poor weapon against a gun, but it was what she had. "So what did you do? Break Johnny's neck?"

He just shrugged, not saying anything.

"Are you sure you don't want to tell somebody after all this time?" she asked. "Or do we have to bug your father for the real answers?"

"You leave my dad alone," Hornby snapped. "He's a good man."

"Yep, he sure is," she said. "Does he know what you did? Did he help you out with that?"

He glared at her. "You don't know anything."

"If that was the truth," she said, "if I really didn't know anything, then why would you be worried about me?"

He took two steps forward, and she switched her hold on the hot tea in her hand, readying herself.

And then she heard footsteps. Mugs woofed several times at her feet. "*You* could attack him," she said to Mugs.

Mugs woofed several more times. This time his neck bristled, as did the hair along his back.

She studied it in interest. "He really doesn't like you, does he?"

"That's okay," Hornby said. "After I shoot you dead, I'll make sure I kill all three of these friggin' animals." He put a hand to his head. When he pulled away his fingers, she could see blood on them.

"*Ooh*, yeah. That's Thaddeus. His beak is hard. And, when he's pissed off, you really don't want to get in his way," she said, chuckling.

"What the hell are you laughing about?" he roared. "You should be pleading for your life. You're one crazy-ass lady."

At that, Mugs raced toward him.

He lowered the gun to shoot the dog.

She stepped forward, crying out, "Don't!"

He raised the gun toward her, but it was too late. The hot tea flew in his face. She bent over and tackled him as his arm went up to wipe at his face. She hit him in the belly and down he went, his gun going off and firing into the ceiling.

She heard a roar behind her and saw Mack had arrived. But it was too chaotic to keep an eye on him. Mugs busily chewed on Hornby's arm. Hornby screamed for help, and Mack stomped on Hornby's gun arm, kicking away the weapon.

She, on the other hand, sat on Hornby's chest and plowed her fist into his face. "You were going to shoot my dog." Then the pain hit, and she cried out, staring at her throbbing hand.

Goliath, sitting on the fifth stair up, came through the railings and jumped on Hornby's face. Then he jumped off, leaving huge claw marks across it.

Hornby screamed as the claws ripped open his skin. And then he started to sob. "She's crazy. Somebody needs to lock her up, and somebody *needs* to shoot these animals."

She couldn't help herself. She smacked him across the face with her injured hand. "I am not crazy, and nobody is hurting my animals."

Mack reached down, grabbing her by the shoulder. "Easy," he said. "He's not going anywhere. I've got him. Can you please get off him and let me flip him over to put cuffs on him?"

She stared up at Mack, loving that worried expression on his face as he stared down at her. She smiled. "I'm okay, you know?"

He nodded. "I know you are, but you might want to take another look at yourself."

Frowning, she saw she was now covered in Hornby's blood from Goliath's claws. She reached up to pat her cheeks and sighed. "Now I'm really upset. The last thing I want is to get covered in this crazy man's blood."

"Who are you calling a crazy?" Hornby roared. "You're the crazy one."

"Really?" she snapped. "You're the one who broke your friend's neck and stuffed him in your dad's garbage truck and then used the truck to smash his body in with the trash, so nobody would see him. When your dad went out the next day to collect garbage, not knowing Johnny's body went along for the trip, Johnny was then taken to the landfill at the end of the day. That's how crazy you are. Why would you do that?"

"Because he was taking off with my girl," Hornby snapped back. "He had no right. Julie was mine."

"Julie and Johnny," Doreen said with heavy emphasis, "were an item. Julie didn't want anything to do with you. Even back then she saw what a crazy coot you were." Her fists balled up on their own, and she went to punch him again.

Mack grabbed her arm and stopped it just inches away from Hornby's face.

She glared at Mack. "Somebody needs to knock this guy out."

"Nobody will punch him, at least not again," Mack said with a sigh. He tugged her forward and off his captive. "Besides, you hurt your hand."

She glared at Hornby, her throbbing fist still held back by Mack. "What about those friends of yours who died in the car accident? Did you kill them too?"

"I had to kill them," he said simply. "They saw me."

She gasped. "So, not only did you kill Johnny but you did it in front of others?" She shook her head in disbelief. "How stupid are you?"

"You crazy bat," he roared. "I am not stupid. I didn't mean for them to see. I was in the back yard and knocked him out. He must have lost the medallion then. I got Johnny home by dragging him through the park. I decided to put him in the garbage truck right away, so nobody would know. And they happened to be coming by."

"What was the price of their silence?" she asked. And then she knew. "Johnny's car, wasn't it?"

He nodded glumly. "Yeah, it was. But I knew that wouldn't be enough, so, when I saw them on the road, I ran them off. At the time I knew it would look like an accident, or at least Susan would believe it was an accident because she'd been sleeping. She'd been out partying hard the previous night and was still stoned and drunk. She was the passenger in my car and had passed out. Only she woke up in the aftermath, and I gave her the explanation she ended up telling the cops. So she didn't know anything firsthand."

"What about her identifying the multicolor vehicle?"

He shrugged. "She glommed onto the image of a multi-colored vehicle because that's the one she was in. She was so stoned and still drunk that she didn't have a clue. As for the rest, well, she just mimicked what I said to try to hide her mental state. Afterward she didn't remember much at all. We were *witnesses* to our friends' death," he said sarcastically. "And no blood or scrapes were on my vehicle, not obvious ones, so the police couldn't do anything."

"Did you kill her," she asked abruptly.

"No." He chuckled. "I thought about it but she was useless all her life. The only good thing she did was die early."

Mack hauled Hornby to his feet, snapped his arms behind him, and cuffed him.

"Wait," she cried out. "Did you break into my house trying to steal antiques? Were you working with Darth?"

"No way would I work with him. I was getting in on the goldmine before he could." He snorted. "Or would have if you hadn't interrupted me."

Doreen looked toward the doorway to see two uniformed cops. She recognized both and shrugged. "Hi, guys."

Chester, the younger one, reached up and scratched his head. "Hi. So do you have access to our cold cases or something?"

"Or does Mack just give you access," Arnold said with a wide grin.

She pointed her finger at him, grimaced from the pain, then just frowned. "Neither. Penny Jordan, Johnny's sister-in-law, asked me to look into the case. What was I supposed to do, say no?" And then she understood another little piece. She turned to look at Alan Hornby. "You threatened her, didn't you?"

He glared at her. "Who the hell are you talking about now?"

"Penny. You threatened her. That's why she took off. My questioning her scared you. You realized it all came from her, so you threatened her."

"Hell, she was putting the property on the market anyway," he said. "I just made a hard suggestion that she should do it sooner rather than later, before she didn't have a chance to do it at all." He sported a big grin. "Besides, you know how everybody talks about their *great* marriage? They fought *all* the time."

"Did it ever occur to you," Doreen said quietly, "that

sometimes fighting is people's way of airing grievances. But afterward, things are good again."

"Whatever," he said. "Personally I think she probably had a hand in George's death."

"Why the hell would you say that?" Doreen asked.

The two cops stared at Hornby in avid fascination.

He shrugged. "Because the guy just upped and died. Everybody said he had a heart condition. But I saw him at the time, and white foam came from his mouth." He snorted then. "Besides why haven't you figured out who shot me? Like you give a damn about that."

"Maybe no one cares about you. But I'm sure somebody did an autopsy on George," Doreen said. "And foam doesn't necessarily mean he was murdered."

"No, but Penny having a lover at the time George died could." He sneered. "So your nice and perfect Penny was not so nice and perfect."

Doreen gave him a bland little smile. "People like you can't stand to see anyone happy. There's rot in your core. You can't resist spreading it all around you. Well, now you'll be with your own kind. The rotten kind. You should finally feel right at home."

With that, Mack marched Hornby out the front door to hand him off to the two cops following them.

They just shook their heads. "Man, oh, man," Chester said. "Since she arrived in town, all we do is work overtime."

"You're welcome," Doreen called out. "I've also made the streets much safer. And, when you get overtime, you get extra pay, and I don't get paid at all for my help. So quit your complaining."

The two men probably didn't even hear what she'd said though. They were down the steps and walking toward the cop car. She held her uninjured hand over her eyes for a long moment, her mind running endlessly as she thought about poor Johnny's end.

When she felt Mack's arms come around her and hold her close, she burrowed in deeper. He held her for several long moments. Finally she let out a heavy sigh and felt some of the tension rolling off her back. She looked up at him. "Thanks for the warning," she said. "I got out as soon as I could."

He nodded grimly. "You did and right into Hornby's arms."

"Yeah. That wasn't your fault," she said. "I'm the one who said nobody could get in or out of the garage via the outside door, and I was so wrong because he was hiding in there."

He tilted her head up. "You mean, there's room in there to hide?"

She wrinkled her nose. "Barely. But it looks like I need to get one of those big garbage bins and put ninety percent of what's in the garage in the bin. It's pretty bad. And I think Hornby must have done something to the door because it opens and closes now. Before, when I tried, it was all I could do to open it a little. And then it squeaked terribly too."

"Which means this was premeditated, his attack on you," Mack said. "Good to know." He gave her a slight shake. "Did you throw your tea at him?"

She leaned back, looked down at her tea-covered, blood-stained blouse. "Yes. And now I need another one." She stepped out of his arms, walked back into the kitchen, and put on the teakettle. She stared out at the garden, collecting her thoughts. But her mind was just such a mess. She turned to look at Mack. "You know what? If I had the money, I think I would sign up for one of those self-defense courses."

He crossed his arms and looked at her grimly. "It would be nice if you would stop getting into situations where you need self-defense."

She nodded. "But I don't try to get into trouble. Once I figured this out, I was going to tell you. But I wanted to check the maps on the old Kelowna landfill to see if there was any hope of finding Johnny's body."

Mack shook his head. "I highly doubt it. We can see if there are any records, but it's been twenty-nine years, and the old landfill has been completely covered over and reclaimed. No, there won't be much chance of finding his bones, especially with the new subdivision built on top of the old landfill."

She nodded. "So, in a way, it was the perfect crime."

"It was," he said. "Except for you."

She gave him a wide smile. "I didn't do anything really," she said. "I just asked a bunch of questions, poked a bunch of people, waited to see what would pop up. Secrets like that are really great big zits. When you poke hard enough, they explode with all kinds of nastiness coming out."

He shook his head. "That's one hell of an analogy. I'm not mentioning that one to the cops at the station."

The teakettle squealed. Doreen turned it off and made herself another cup of tea. "Do you want a cup?"

"Hell, I want something a whole lot stronger." He went to the front closet, reached up to the very top shelf, and pulled out a bottle of whiskey.

She stared at it. "I didn't know that was up there." Disgruntled, she added, "I'd have had half a dozen drinks myself over the last few weeks."

He poured two glasses with a shot in each.

She noted they were freehand shots and rather hefty.

He handed her one and said, "Drink up."

"I'm not in shock," she said.

"No, I am," he said in a hard tone. "And I don't drink alone. So drink up." He lifted his glass, clicked it with hers, and then tossed his back.

She shrugged, did the same, and coughed as the liquid fire poured down her throat. She choked and gasped, finding it hard to catch her breath. "Are you trying to kill me?" she croaked.

He gave her a glass of water, which helped.

Finally she sat at the table and relaxed. "Will this day ever be over?"

"It will," he said. "It definitely is now."

She looked up at him and smiled. "So how about spending a few hours at the end of this very long day with a friend? We'll take a cup of tea, sit in the garden, and forget about murders and murderers."

He smiled, made himself a cup of tea, and reached out a hand. "Come on. Let's go outside for a few minutes and relax. Then we'll create something from the leftover pasta and enjoy a meal. Afterward we can call it a day."

"Agreed," she said as together they walked out to her garden.

Epilogue

In the Mission, Kelowna, BC
Sunday afternoon …

MACK GOT A hold of Penny over the phone to give her the official account, and she returned home from visiting a friend in Vernon. As soon as she hit town, she walked to Doreen's place. When Doreen opened her front door, Penny threw her arms around her.

"Thank you so much," she cried out and hugged her again. After a moment, she stepped back and said, "I'm so sorry. I didn't mean to run out on you. But I didn't know what that horrible man meant to do. I couldn't stick around long enough to find out."

"It's okay," Doreen said. "He can't hurt you again."

Needing to walk and talk, both of them still too keyed up to just sit inside, they walked along Doreen's backyard as Doreen gave Penny all the details. When their questions and answers ran out, Penny noticed the large garden beds along the side fence. "This is going to be lovely," she said, motioning to a long stretch of Doreen's overgrown garden.

"I've got a long way to go to get it back to what it was," Doreen said. "It's a lot of work."

"Understood. It's the same at my place," Penny said. "And not sure I want to now. Before Johnny disappeared, I loved gardening. Then it became a way to wear off the worry and tension over the years, but after George's death …"

"I'd leave it as is," Doreen said. "You're selling, and your yard doesn't look too bad."

"And yet, selling the house feels like a betrayal to George."

Doreen looked at Penny. "Were you happy with George?"

Penny beamed. "Very happy with him. He was a good provider, a good man."

Doreen didn't know if she should ask about George's death. It was an uncomfortable topic. Just because Hornby had made some accusations, that didn't mean it wasn't true but also didn't mean Hornby wasn't just causing trouble. "How did George die again?"

"A heart attack," Penny said, her face stilling. She put a hand to her heart. "He went very quickly."

Penny walked toward the rear of the property, where a large bunch of echinacea stood tall. The blooms hadn't opened yet, but it looked to explode with flowers soon.

"I'm sorry for your loss," Doreen said. "That must have been very difficult."

"Oh, it was," she said. "It was, indeed."

Doreen looked at the low patch of echinacea in her garden and smiled. "I remember how your plants are much bigger than mine." She motioned at her poor echinacea, adding, "I have all kinds of other plants crowding mine, as well as more plants I need to move like foxglove, belladonna, nightshade…" She slid her glance sideways, checking Penny's reaction to her list of poisonous plants, but saw absolutely nothing. Satisfied, Doreen linked her arm with Penny's and faced her new gardening friend. "I wanted to give you more of the news personally, before you heard it elsewhere."

"Thank you for that," Penny said. "I should get home now." She looked back at Doreen's gardens as they walked toward the creek. "You know what? Considering we found the dagger in the dahlias at my place and then that medallion out in my front yard too, I won't ever look at a big clump of plants like that without wondering if more evidence is hiding in it."

Doreen's mind kicked in, repeating *evidence in the echinacea, evidence in the echinacea.* But that was not today's story. That would have to wait for another day. With a smile she said, "Forget all about that for now," she said. "We can garden another day."

Penny chuckled. "Sounds good to me. At least we have something in common."

Doreen nodded. "We do, indeed. We plant things, all kinds of seeds, even ideas we weren't aware we were planting …" Her tone was cryptic.

Penny looked at her sideways, but Doreen just smiled and suggested, "Maybe you should set up a memorial garden for Johnny now." At Penny's startled look, Doreen explained further. "I know that came out of the blue. But I was thinking, you know, as I looked at that echinacea, how you have lost both Johnny and George, and both of them loved your home."

"But I'm selling it," Penny said. "Remember that?"

Doreen nodded. "Maybe that's a nice way to leave it then, as the home you all shared together," she said. "Creating a memorial garden before you move out would be a very nice thing to do for them. If the new owners rip it out, well, all fair and good. You wouldn't have to do much. Just set up two rings of rocks and a little marker stone in the center of each ring and say some kind words over it. You'll get Johnny's medallion and his knife back at some point in time from the police. There is that little cross as well."

Penny looked thoughtful as she stared at the creek. "You're thinking about me getting closure, aren't you?"

"I am," Doreen said, but she was also thinking of something else that just wouldn't leave her alone. "For your own sake. Plus you don't know how long it'll take to sell your house." she said. "But, if you think about it, it could be a few months or even a year. You haven't put it on the market yet, have you?"

Penny shook her head. "I couldn't while you were investigating," she said starkly. "It seemed wrong to. Now that you're done, and we know what happened ..." She shook her head. "George spent most of his adult life searching for his brother, and to think that he never found out, ... but, in just a few days, look what you accomplished?"

"I'm really sorry about the long passage of time without answers," Doreen said, her voice compassionate. "I think one of the hardest things for people is to never find out the truth."

"And you did it so fast," Penny said in amazement. "That's what really blows me away. I only talked to you like, what, last Tuesday, Wednesday? And then, all of a sudden, it's Sunday, and here you are already, with it solved."

Doreen didn't know what to say. While she formulated an answer, Penny burst out, "Why couldn't the police have done that years ago?"

"Because years ago, people stayed mum for a lot of different reasons. Things were different back then. People kept secrets, likely out of fear," Doreen said slowly, thinking about what it had taken for the answers to come to the surface. "And I think Hornby stayed low and out of trouble, until he left town as soon as he could. Now so much time has passed, he thought he was safe."

Penny said, "It makes no sense. He killed all three of those boys, for nothing."

"Yes," Doreen said, speaking slowly. "It also helped Hornby keep his secret when Susan couldn't remember anything from the car accident. She was under the influence of the drugs and still hungover, so it's no wonder the cops didn't take her seriously. Yet she's the one who kept saying a multicolored vehicle was involved, whereas Alan said it happened so fast that he couldn't remember anything, other than a small car. Black, he thought, but he wasn't even sure of that. Could have been dark green or dark blue. Apparently he'd been fighting with Susan."

"And, of course, it was all make believe anyway," Penny whispered. "It's just too incredible."

"It is," Doreen said, "but, honestly, often the truth is the simplest answer of all."

"They had found no DNA back then that led to any suspects. They had no digital anything back then," Penny said, "like to see if Johnny showed up in another county or whatever."

Doreen nodded. "And, of course, Alan's father stuck up for him and gave him an alibi. Mr. Hornby believed his son was at home and didn't see the body in the trash truck's compactor. Julie's family wasn't any better. Nobody wanted to point the finger at Alan Hornby, even though nobody liked him. Even Julie had no way of knowing that an argument or picking one man over another would cause this kind of a reaction."

"But to think it was love triangle gone wrong," Penny said in bewilderment. "And for all of it to stay a secret over all these years ... We didn't even know about Julie."

"But Mother Earth gives up her secrets eventually," Doreen said. "Think about the dagger. Think about the medallion. Think about the cross."

"There's no chance of Johnny's body being found, is there?"

"No, I doubt it," Doreen said softly but firmly. "I'm afraid that idea has to be set aside. He was placed in the old landfill. Everything there was all mulched together and reclaimed, as the city does its job, and now a whole new subdivision has been built up there. I think the community of Wilden is there now."

Penny looked at her. "All those new fancy big houses in Glenmore?"

"I think so," Doreen said. "If not that area, another one nearby." She watched her friend, still trying to take it all in, to make peace with it. "Come on. You're a bit shaken up. I need a walk anyway. Let's get you home."

"It'll be dark soon. Are you sure?" Penny asked, but she looked grateful nonetheless. "I have to admit that I'm feeling pretty shaky. Knowing that it's over, that all this which haunted us—which haunted almost my entire marriage—is over. Now if only you had moved to Kelowna years ago," she joked, "then George would have known what happened before he died."

"The thing is, back then, I probably wouldn't have been doing what I'm doing now anyway."

"Why is that?"

"Because I'm a different person from who I was even a few years ago," Doreen said with half a smile. She called for Mugs. "Mugs, you want to go for a walk?"

Immediately her basset hound, who'd long lost his pedigree and his good manners, appeared, jumped up, and twirled around on his back legs. She giggled. "Now if only we could make money with a circus act," she said. She bent down, gave him a quick hug, then pulled his leash from her back pocket to hook it on.

"You don't normally put him on the leash, do you?" Penny asked.

"No," she said. "Not since I moved here, but he is leash trained. I just figured that, every once in a while, I should do it to keep him in the habit."

At that, they stepped out on the creek pathway, and a streak of orange bolted toward them. "Goliath, want to go for a walk?"

From the veranda at the back of her house, Doreen could hear Thaddeus calling out, "Wait for me, wait for me."

Doreen chuckled. "I guess Thaddeus wants to come too."

Penny was fascinated as Doreen squatted down, waiting for the bird to waddle to them. She stretched out her arm, and Thaddeus hopped onto the back of her hand and sidestepped all the way up to her shoulder. Once there, he brushed his beak against her cheek. She reached out and gently stroked his back. "I wouldn't go without you, big guy."

As if he understood, he nudged her a couple more times and then settled in. Just as she was about to take a step, he said, "Giddyup, giddyup."

Instantly she froze, turned her head to look at him, and

said, "No way am I following your commands."

He twisted his head, looked at her, batted those huge eyes of his, and said, "Thaddeus, go."

"Yes," she said in exasperation. "You can tell that you'll be going somewhere," she said. "You're already on my shoulder, and we're already out of the house."

And then he seemed to settle without more arguments. As she glanced at Penny, her new friend tried to hold back her chuckles. She rolled her eyes at Penny. "It's pretty bad when the bird treats me like some sort of an old gray mare," she snapped. "Oh, wait." She returned to her house, reset the alarms on the front and back doors, and then rejoined her animals and Penny. "Now let's go for a walk."

"I heard the beeps." Penny glanced back at the house. "Do you always set an alarm when you go for a walk? You don't look like the type to me."

"Normally I wouldn't be," Doreen said cheerfully. "But I have an antiques dealer coming tomorrow to look at a few pieces," she said, carefully fudging the truth. "I would hate for anybody to go inside and help themselves."

Penny nodded. "Oh, my, no," she said. "When I think of all the hours George and Nan spent arguing about her antiques …"

"Why arguing?" Doreen asked.

"Because George thought she should sell them, and Nan said she had another plan in mind."

Doreen's heart warmed when she thought about Nan's *other* plan. "Yes, Nan was holding on to them for me," Doreen said with a wistful smile. "My grandmother is pretty special."

"Oh, she's special all right," Penny said, chuckling. "George used to come home from one of his visits, and, although he'd be brighter and full of laughter, he'd say that Nan was especially crazy."

"A lot of people have told me that she fell somewhere in that realm," Doreen said. "I am afraid she's losing some of her memory now though."

"She's probably not taking all those supplements George told her to take. They worked like a charm for her."

"What kind of supplements?"

Penny shrugged. "I'll have to take a look," she said. "I have the notes at home somewhere. George always had a fascination for natural remedies. Nan was having trouble even back then."

"And they helped her?"

Penny nodded emphatically. "Oh, yes. George used to comment on it all the time."

"Well, if you could get me that list, that would be awesome," Doreen said. "I have absolutely no idea about supplements. And I really don't like doctors."

"No, once you deal with something like George's heart condition," Penny said, "you have to consider how much the medical profession actually knows. Obviously they're helpful a lot of the time, but some of the time it makes you wonder if they aren't just pushing drugs."

"Exactly," Doreen said. "But if you had supplements that worked instead, that would be huge."

"I think it's the same list he gave me, so I can certainly find out when I get a moment," Penny said. "Do you think Nan would take them?"

Doreen nodded. "Particularly if I say it was the same stuff that George used to give her."

"That might work too," Penny said. "Those two really did get along like a house on fire. Nan was pretty upset at

George's funeral."

"I'm sure she was," Doreen said. "I think one of the hardest things about getting old is watching all your friends die before you."

"Very true," Penny said. As they walked up to Penny's house a good half hour later, Penny motioned and said, "If you want to come in for a few minutes, I can look for that list."

Doreen brightened. She'd been looking for an excuse as it was to go inside and see how Penny lived. So far she'd only been invited into a few houses, Nan's, Julie's and Doreen's murderous neighbor, Ella. Doreen nodded and said, "Sure. Thank you very much." Together, the five of them trooped into Penny's home.

Inside Penny's house, Doreen looked around. It was stuffed with pretty floral-patterned couches, large floral paintings, and, yes, … floral carpets. It was also pristine. "You haven't started packing, have you?"

"Well, it's not like I've sold my house yet," Penny said in a dry tone.

As Doreen looked at Penny's big living room, it wasn't really cluttered, but it was overstuffed with mementos. "If you got a staging crew or a Realtor in here," she said, "I'm pretty sure they'll insist on all the pictures coming off the walls, all the stuff being moved off the countertops, hauling out the big hutches you've got. Realtors can be quite brutal."

Penny's jaw dropped. "You know what? I was thinking about bringing in a stager to see what they'd charge me. But it sounds like you know a lot about it."

"Not necessarily," she said, "but I've watched lots of shows on TV. And my husband did a lot of buying and selling."

"Right," Penny said.

Doreen could almost see that, in Penny's mind, those disqualifiers just raised Doreen's status several notches. Doreen didn't understand how that worked because, of course, people should be doing their own investigation and research on this type of thing before deciding. Besides, in Doreen's mind, she should be demoted not promoted for her husband's activities. "Have you picked out a Realtor?"

"Absolutely. I was going to ask Simi Jeron," she said. "I've known that family for thirty years or more."

"Oh, good," she said, "that should make it easier. Ask her about staging and decluttering when she's here."

"Well, she's already been here once, but we haven't signed any paperwork yet."

"That's when the boom will get lowered," Doreen said, chuckling.

"I hope not," Penny said, walking into her kitchen, approaching a large cupboard, opened it up. She took out a small notebook sitting on top of the box of vitamin bottles and brought it to the kitchen table and sat down, flipping through the pages. "Ah, here it is," she said, "a page just for Nan." She held it up and then read from it. "Vitamin D, ginkgo, B12, and I'm not sure what this other one says."

"Do you mind if I take a look?" Doreen asked, holding out her hand. Penny handed it over. As Doreen looked at it, she said, "I'm not sure what that is either. May I get a copy of this?"

"We'll photocopy both sides."

Passing the book back, Penny made copies of both sides and then gave Doreen the two sheets.

"Thanks."

Penny nodded with a smile, and both women returned

to the kitchen, where Penny tucked the book back into the vitamin corner.

"Must've been nice that George was so interested in health," she said.

"A lot of good it did him," Penny said bitterly, and she winced. "I'm sorry. I shouldn't have said that."

"I guess you're angry he died, huh?"

"Isn't that the stupidest thing?" Penny asked. "Even after a year, I still look around our house, and I get mad at him. We had all these plans for retirement, all these things we would do now that he wasn't working anymore, and here he ups and dies on me."

"Well, can't you do those things on your own?"

"I could," Penny said, "but I don't really want to. They were things we would do *together*. They were *our* plans."

"Versus *your* plans?"

Penny froze for a moment and slowly nodded. "Very insightful." She glanced at her watch and said, "Oh, my goodness. I have to run. I have to meet someone."

"Oh, absolutely no problem," Doreen said. "We'll go and let you get on then." She and her animals were ushered to the front door. Goliath had taken up a seat in the middle of George's big recliner. Doreen scooped him into her arms, with Thaddeus still on her shoulder, and Mugs trotted behind them. "It was a nice visit," she said, "and I'm glad I had good news for you."

As she stepped down the front steps, Penny said, "And once again, thank you," she said sincerely. "I will definitely sleep better now."

With a half wave, Doreen watched as Penny got into her vehicle and reversed out of her driveway and headed down the street. But Doreen had stopped on Penny's driveway.

Doreen *really* shouldn't do what she was thinking of doing. But it was pretty damn hard to talk herself out of it. With a shrug, she decided it would worry away at her, so she might as well put her mind to rest.

She put Goliath down, Thaddeus taking the opportunity to get down as well, and quickly headed into Penny's backyard, where Johnny had his favorite place to sit. Doreen didn't even know why Penny's echinacea bed was bugging her, but she thought she'd read somewhere how echinacea was used in all kinds of medicine. It certainly wasn't—as far as she knew—a killer, but anything was a killer if you took too much of it.

Doreen made a quick trip through Penny's backyard, mentally jotting down what was here: marigolds, lilies, calla lilies, black-eyed Susans. None were flowering yet. Daisies were about to explode with blooms. ... This would be a lively garden when summer hit. She really appreciated the wide variety, even a few straggling tulips. She stopped and stared at them and shook her head. "What are you guys doing drooping over like that?"

She stopped to study stalks reaching for the sky. They wouldn't bloom for another month or two, and this bed was far too crowded for them to do well. Then there was the belladonna and foxglove mingling in the patch too. *Drat.* So was their presence that bad? She couldn't tell. But as the same poisonous plants lived in Nan's garden... Possibly Nan and George had shared a love of poisonous plants as well as antiques?

Glancing around, Doreen noted how little shade the echinacea plants would probably get during the daylight hours, backed up against the fence as they were, which wouldn't help their growth. As she dropped down in front of the massive green patch—at least three feet across, with dozens of plants in there—she frowned, realizing their roots would be completely twisted together. Echinacea plants loved company, particularly its own family, but, at one point in time, they would fight and hate each other—just like every other family.

Too-close confines caused too-much strife.

She checked the ground around the roots, unable to help herself, and realized that they were also very dry. The ground was poor here, with many rocks noticeable in the soil. Echinacea could survive in crappy soil. A lot of plants could survive. But the intention of a garden was not to have them survive; it was to have the flowers thrive. And again, as she glanced around the backyard, what had once been Penny's pride and joy at this point in time was probably just a constant source of work and bad memories. As Doreen walked past the echinacea, she thought she saw something else burrowed in the center of one of the plants. But just then, a man asked from the park side of the fence, "Hey, what are you doing back there?"

She popped out of Penny's backyard gate guiltily, leaving the gate open for her animals, and plastered a bright smile on her face. "I walked home with Penny," she said, "but she had to take off. I just wanted to take a quick look at her garden. She has done so well here," she said, injecting a bright warmth to her voice.

The man looked at her suspiciously.

She looked him over, from the top of his six-foot frame to his dirty sneakers and held out a hand. "I'm Doreen Montgomery, and who are you?"

Reluctantly he shook her hand. "I'm Dave."

"Dave?"

His frown deepened. "Just Dave."

She nodded and smiled and said, "Well, if you see Penny, and you want to tell her how I was in her backyard, that's fine," she said. "She knows that I'm a crazy gardener too. I was checking out her echinacea."

"Echinacea?" he asked doubtfully, looking at the green splotch against the fence.

"Echinacea," she said firmly. "We were talking about mine at my house earlier."

At that, his face seemed to settle, and his shoulders sagged, as if with relief.

"Not to worry," she said. "I'm not a thief. I'm the one who helped solved Johnny's disappearance."

At that, awareness came into Dave's eyes. Of course Mugs's slow approach, his head lowered and moving from side to side like a pissed-off bull drew more attention to Doreen. So did the orange streak that raced between Dave's legs, and he grinned. "Now I know who you are."

Thaddeus, not to be outdone, squawked, "No you don't. No you don't."

"Yeah, sorry about them," she said. She gave Dave a quick finger wave. "And now I'll head home before my critters decide that they like Penny's garden better than mine," she said in a joking manner.

Dave watched as she and her animals ambled toward the creek. "Why are you walking along the creek?" he asked, calling behind her.

"Because I love it," she said. "It's my favorite place to walk."

He shrugged and said, "Nothing but dirty water down there. It's full of ducks and all kinds of waterfowl."

"Hopefully I'll see some today."

"You won't catch me walking through the water, that's their toilet." And with that, he headed off.

She walked a few more steps and turned to look back. He strode away, not having explained his presence at Penny's property. Doreen frowned and thought about that, then sent Penny a quick text. **Stopped to take a quick look at your echinacea plants. A stranger named Dave came up and didn't seem terribly friendly. Wasn't sure what he was doing in the park behind your place. Just a heads-up.** And she left it at that.

"Come on, Goliath, Mugs ..." Thaddeus squawked as he waddled toward her, but then Mugs came racing forward with Goliath on his heels, and, in a surprisingly quick move, Thaddeus jumped on Mugs, screaming at the top of his lungs, "Giddyup, Mugs. Giddyup, Mugs."

By the time Doreen had crossed the bridge and headed up her backyard, Thaddeus had long giving up riding Mugs, subsequently walking. Now he was tucked into the crook of her neck, swaying with her every step. She crossed the bridge as her phone beeped with a return text. **He's a lovely neighbor, but he doesn't like strangers. That echinacea is doing terrible. As are some of my more specialized plants. Suggestions?**

Doreen grinned. Perfect entrance to find out more. **Absolutely. Maybe we'll have tea another day and check it out.**

Perfect.

This concludes Book 4 of Lovely Lethal Gardens:
Daggers in the Dahlias.
Read about Evidence in the Echinacea:
Lovely Lethal Gardens, Book 5

Lovely Lethal Gardens: Evidence in the Echinacea (Book #5)

A new cozy mystery series from *USA Today* best-selling author Dale Mayer. Follow gardener and amateur sleuth Doreen Montgomery—and her amusing and mostly lovable cat, dog, and parrot—as they catch murderers and solve crimes in lovely Kelowna, British Columbia.

Riches to rags. … Controlling to chaos. … But murder … well maybe …

Doreen's success at solving murders has hit the news-wires across the country, but all Doreen wants is to be left alone. She has antiques to get to the auction house and a relationship with Corporal Mack Moreau to work out, not to mention a new friendship to nurture with Penny, Doreen's first friend in Kelowna, and Doreen doesn't want to ruin things.

But when a surprise accusation won't leave Doreen alone—about Penny's late husband George's death and made by one of the men Doreen helped put away—she thinks that maybe it can't hurt to just take a quick look into her new friend's past.

Before Doreen knows it, she's juggling a cold case, a closed case, and a possible mercy killing … along with cultivating her relationships with Penny, Mack, and Doreen's pets: Mugs, the basset hound; Goliath, the Maine coon cat, and Thaddeus, the far-too-talkative African gray parrot. And while Mack should be used to Doreen's antics by now, when she dives into yet another of his cases it's becoming increasingly hard to take …

Book 5 is available now!
To find out more visit Dale Mayer's website.
http://smarturl.it/EvidenceDMUniversal

Get Your Free Book Now!

Have you met Charmin Marvin?

If you're ready for a new world to explore, and love ill-mannered cats, I have a series that might be your next binge read. It's called Broken Protocols, and it's a series that takes you through time-travel, mysteries, romance... and a talking cat named Charmin Marvin.

Go here and tell me where to send it!
http://smarturl.it/ArsenicBofB

Author's Note

Thank you for reading Daggers in the Dahlias: Lovely Lethal Gardens, Book 4! If you enjoyed the book, please take a moment and leave a short review.

Dear reader,

I love to hear from readers, and you can contact me at my website: www.dalemayer.com or at my Facebook author page. To be informed of new releases and special offers, sign up for my newsletter or follow me on BookBub. And if you are interested in joining Dale Mayer's Reader Group, here is the Facebook sign up page.
facebook.com/groups/402384989872660

Cheers,
Dale Mayer

About the Author

Dale Mayer is a USA Today bestselling author best known for her Psychic Visions and Family Blood Ties series. Her contemporary romances are raw and full of passion and emotion (Second Chances, SKIN), her thrillers will keep you guessing (By Death series), and her romantic comedies will keep you giggling (It's a Dog's Life and Charmin Marvin Romantic Comedy series).

She honors the stories that come to her – and some of them are crazy and break all the rules and cross multiple genres!

To go with her fiction, she also writes nonfiction in many different fields with books available on resume writing, companion gardening and the US mortgage system. She has recently published her Career Essentials Series. All her books are available in print and ebook format.

Connect with Dale Mayer Online

Dale's Website – www.dalemayer.com
Twitter – @DaleMayer
Facebook – dalemayer.com/fb
BookBub – bookbub.com/authors/dale-mayer

Also by Dale Mayer

Published Adult Books:

The K9 Files
Ethan, Book 1
Pierce, Book 2

Lovely Lethal Gardens
Arsenic in the Azaleas, Book 1
Bones in the Begonias, Book 2
Corpse in the Carnations, Book 3
Daggers in the Dahlias, Book 4
Evidence in the Echinacea, Book 5
Footprints in the Ferns, Book 6

Psychic Vision Series
Tuesday's Child
Hide 'n Go Seek
Maddy's Floor
Garden of Sorrow
Knock Knock…
Rare Find
Eyes to the Soul
Now You See Her
Shattered
Into the Abyss
Seeds of Malice

Eye of the Falcon
Itsy-Bitsy Spider
Unmasked
Deep Beneath
Psychic Visions Books 1–3
Psychic Visions Books 4–6
Psychic Visions Books 7–9

By Death Series
Touched by Death
Haunted by Death
Chilled by Death
By Death Books 1–3

Broken Protocols – Romantic Comedy Series
Cat's Meow
Cat's Pajamas
Cat's Cradle
Cat's Claus
Broken Protocols 1-4

Broken and... Mending
Skin
Scars
Scales (of Justice)
Broken but… Mending 1-3

Glory
Genesis
Tori
Celeste
Glory Trilogy

Biker Blues

Morgan: Biker Blues, Volume 1
Cash: Biker Blues, Volume 2

SEALs of Honor

Mason: SEALs of Honor, Book 1
Hawk: SEALs of Honor, Book 2
Dane: SEALs of Honor, Book 3
Swede: SEALs of Honor, Book 4
Shadow: SEALs of Honor, Book 5
Cooper: SEALs of Honor, Book 6
Markus: SEALs of Honor, Book 7
Evan: SEALs of Honor, Book 8
Mason's Wish: SEALs of Honor, Book 9
Chase: SEALs of Honor, Book 10
Brett: SEALs of Honor, Book 11
Devlin: SEALs of Honor, Book 12
Easton: SEALs of Honor, Book 13
Ryder: SEALs of Honor, Book 14
Macklin: SEALs of Honor, Book 15
Corey: SEALs of Honor, Book 16
Warrick: SEALs of Honor, Book 17
Tanner: SEALs of Honor, Book 18
Jackson: SEALs of Honor, Book 19
Kanen: SEALs of Honor, Book 20
Nelson: SEALs of Honor, Book 21
SEALs of Honor, Books 1–3
SEALs of Honor, Books 4–6
SEALs of Honor, Books 7–10
SEALs of Honor, Books 11–13
SEALs of Honor, Books 14–16
SEALs of Honor, Books 17–19

Heroes for Hire

Levi's Legend: Heroes for Hire, Book 1

Stone's Surrender: Heroes for Hire, Book 2

Merk's Mistake: Heroes for Hire, Book 3

Rhodes's Reward: Heroes for Hire, Book 4

Flynn's Firecracker: Heroes for Hire, Book 5

Logan's Light: Heroes for Hire, Book 6

Harrison's Heart: Heroes for Hire, Book 7

Saul's Sweetheart: Heroes for Hire, Book 8

Dakota's Delight: Heroes for Hire, Book 9

Michael's Mercy (Part of Sleeper SEAL Series)

Tyson's Treasure: Heroes for Hire, Book 10

Jace's Jewel: Heroes for Hire, Book 11

Rory's Rose: Heroes for Hire, Book 12

Brandon's Bliss: Heroes for Hire, Book 13

Liam's Lily: Heroes for Hire, Book 14

North's Nikki: Heroes for Hire, Book 15

Anders's Angel: Heroes for Hire, Book 16

Reyes's Raina: Heroes for Hire, Book 17

Dezi's Diamond: Heroes for Hire, Book 18

Vince's Vixen: Heroes for Hire, Book 19

Heroes for Hire, Books 1–3

Heroes for Hire, Books 4–6

Heroes for Hire, Books 7–9

Heroes for Hire, Books 10–12

Heroes for Hire, Books 13–15

SEALs of Steel

Badger: SEALs of Steel, Book 1

Erick: SEALs of Steel, Book 2

Cade: SEALs of Steel, Book 3

Talon: SEALs of Steel, Book 4

Laszlo: SEALs of Steel, Book 5
Geir: SEALs of Steel, Book 6
Jager: SEALs of Steel, Book 7
The Final Reveal: SEALs of Steel, Book 8
SEALs of Steel, Books 1–4
SEALs of Steel, Books 5–8
SEALs of Steel, Books 1–8

Collections
Dare to Be You…
Dare to Love…
Dare to be Strong…
RomanceX3

Standalone Novellas
It's a Dog's Life
Riana's Revenge
Second Chances

Published Young Adult Books:

Family Blood Ties Series
Vampire in Denial
Vampire in Distress
Vampire in Design
Vampire in Deceit
Vampire in Defiance
Vampire in Conflict
Vampire in Chaos
Vampire in Crisis
Vampire in Control
Vampire in Charge

Family Blood Ties Set 1–3
Family Blood Ties Set 1–5
Family Blood Ties Set 4–6
Family Blood Ties Set 7–9
Sian's Solution, A Family Blood Ties Series Prequel
    Novelette

Design series
Dangerous Designs
Deadly Designs
Darkest Designs
Design Series Trilogy

Standalone
In Cassie's Corner
Gem Stone (a Gemma Stone Mystery)
Time Thieves

Published Non-Fiction Books:

Career Essentials
Career Essentials: The Résumé
Career Essentials: The Cover Letter
Career Essentials: The Interview
Career Essentials: 3 in 1

CPSIA information can be obtained
at www.ICGtesting.com
Printed in the USA
LVHW080249300819
629407LV00012BA/615/P